WATCHING THE WATER

Book 1 in the Heart Tides series

Donna Gentry Morton

Donna Gentry Morton

BQB

Virginia

This is a work of fiction. All of the characters, names, incidents, organizations, and dialogue in this novel are either the products of the author's imagination or are used fictitiously.

Published in the United States by BQB Publishing
(Boutique of Quality Books Publishing Company)
www.bqbpublishing.com

Printed in the United States of America

978-1-937084-48-6 (p)
978-1-937084-49-3 (e)

Library of Congress Control Number: 2016948915

Book design by Robin Krauss, www.bookformatters.com
Cover design by Maura Petrosino, www.bluefla.me

Other Books by Donna Gentry Morton

Seeking the Shore, Book 2 in the Heart Tides series

To my big sister,
Rebecca Ann Williams
If you hadn't given me that lighthouse figurine to place on my desk as inspiration, this story might not have ever been finished. You cleaned my house so I would have time to write. You were the first to read every page and told me to keep going.
Thank you, Becky.
Baby Sis loves you.

And

To the memory of my late husband, my soulmate, my It Guy, my "Hon,"
John Ward Morton
When it came to reading, you were more of a Clancy guy, but you read this manuscript and encouraged me to take it as far as I could. I'm trying to do that now and wish you were here to share the journey.
I know you know, though.
Someday we'll talk about it.
Time and tide, Hon.

I'll love you forever.

1934

The heart has reasons that reason cannot know.
Blaise Pascal

CHAPTER
ONE

The Downtown Panache was a fashionable lady among the traditional white-columned hotels gracing the South. Its sleek and streamlined beauty captured Art Deco, its bright colors and exotic woods making it a favorite among the young, most of whom flocked to the rooftop where jazz beckoned them to dance beneath the stars.

From near and far, people frequented the Downtown Panache, and from somewhere came the man with the dark eyes. Eyes like fine chocolates that, once sampled, were impossible to resist.

They were what Julianna Sheffield first noticed about the man when she caught his appreciative stare from across the dining room. Startled, she looked away. His boldness filled her with an unnerving intrigue, so she tried focusing on the dessert menu before her. *Baked Alaska, Lemon Meringue Pie,* and *Tapioca Pudding* swam before her eyes like quick-finned fish. She placed the menu on the table and ran a slightly trembling hand through her shoulder-length hair, a maple cascade of waves, thanks to eight hours in the permanent wave machine.

His attention didn't waver. Feeling its persistence, Julianna couldn't keep her eyes averted and began to take him in through glances. He was older, she guessed, having at least ten years on her twenty-two. His hair matched his eyes, and his tanned face was clean-shaven and perfectly chiseled. Though seated, he appeared tall with the lean and muscular, broad-shouldered build of a disciplined athlete. He wore a navy, double-breasted suit with a whimsical tie depicting Popeye the Sailor, and he had a snap brim hat stylishly turned down in the front and up in the back, which rested on the table.

A playful smile formed on his lips, and it seemed to Julianna that he was amused by her glances. Perhaps he considered them a flirtatious catch-me-if-you-can dance of the eyes, an engaging game of cat and mouse.

Finally, he pounced, grabbing her eyes before she could look away and locking them into a gaze so intense, she was certain their souls had collided.

She was suddenly consumed. Her heart beat like a wild drum, and her thoughts roared like storm-driven waves hitting her in rapid succession. She couldn't grasp one thought for being struck by another. Amid the internal chaos, though, she heard it—a prophetic voice whispering from her core. This man could touch her life, like no other man would ever have the power to do.

She might have stayed immersed in his eyes had the waiter not intruded. "Dessert, Miss?"

When she didn't answer, he tapped her shoulder. "Miss?"

Julianna broke free of the man's gaze and turned to the waiter. "Oh, I'm sorry," she said, her voice shaking slightly. "No, no dessert, thank you."

He smiled and made a quick gesture about the table. "Your friends abandoned you?" He spoke of the four sorority sisters Julianna had dined with earlier, in town to be fitted for bridesmaid dresses for a friend's wedding.

Julianna sipped her sweet tea, wishing she could toss it on herself instead. She needed to snap from the surreal fog surrounding her, to regain her bearings. "They left me for Clark Gable," she answered, still flustered. The words sounded distant even to her ears. "His new movie, I mean."

"It's a shame you couldn't join them."

Out of habit, she glanced at her watch. "I'm expected home soon."

"Ah" was all he said before nodding politely and swooping toward the kitchen.

Julianna felt only slightly composed when she looked across the dining room to where the man had been seated. Would they be able to reclaim their connection or had the interruption broken the momentum?

Her heart sank when she saw that he had vanished, leaving nothing behind except a cloth napkin crumpled across a dinner plate.

It didn't mean a thing, Julianna told herself as she walked through the hotel lobby moments later. *It was just one of those strange moments in time. I'll forget about it in a week.*

But her heart lurched at the thought. Ha! It knew better and so did Julianna. She had been drawn to other men before, but this was so different. There was the fleeting schoolgirl crush she'd developed for a cute teenage boy who'd stolen a kiss from her at a summer picnic. She thought of the attraction she had felt for a handsome young man she met once on a blind date. Compared to tonight's encounter, her heart had merely skipped like a butterfly at such times; this was more like the flight of a soaring eagle. Every other memory felt suddenly lighthearted and sure to fade. But she knew the moment shared with this man would be tucked away for safekeeping, tenderly retrieved on dreamy, rain-soaked nights. It would find its way into quiet thoughts when she watched the sun rise above the sea. And sometimes, while walking down the street, she would search the faces of strangers, hoping his would be among them. It had only been a moment, yes. But one to be forgotten? Never.

She paused before reaching the valet, dreading the idea of getting her car and going home. Another glance at her watch warned her that her parents would soon start to wonder of her whereabouts.

No daughter of Richard and Audrey Sheffield should be wandering unaccompanied past reasonable hours, and Julianna could easily imagine the lecture awaiting her if she didn't return home soon. "But darling," her mother would say, "it's just not *proper* for a young woman to be out at all hours. Besides that, it's very *dangerous* unless you have a suitable escort."

True, there was her safety to think of, but also the family reputation to uphold, as her parents' names were well inked on the town's list of Who's Who. And it wasn't just their good name. Her father would say there was the business to think of too. Yes, she had the People's Standard National Bank to thank for their family's good fortune. But her father had the makings of a maestro, given his need to orchestrate every facet of Julianna's life. And her mother—she may be bubbly and efficient on the outside, but Julianna knew all too well that she was a dying spirit on the inside, a slave to the strict propriety of high society life.

Her parents kept a tight leash on Julianna, their only child, though there had never been any need to. She had always been compliant, partly because it had been ingrained in her by privileged society that she was a very fortunate girl who should want to please her parents for making sure that she never wanted for anything. Appreciation was a feeling she understood and agreed with, but she also believed her parents really did have her best interests at heart. For those reasons, Julianna Isabella Sheffield had never done anything unexpected in her life.

Until right now.

Because despite the desire to please her parents, she was starting to realize that it demanded sacrifice. She had never danced with that thought until recently, perhaps because their expectations now included something that was too much, something she feared would secure their happiness while squashing her own.

Right now, though, she wasn't going to think about that

something. Right now, she turned from the valet desk and faced a bank of elevators, preparing to take the one that carried passengers to the rooftop.

Somehow, she knew he was up there. Whether it was the nudge from an unseen guardian angel, intuition that whispered to her heart, or a great hope that could not be deterred, she felt certain that she was about to see *him* again. As her eyes focused only on the elevator that ascended to the roof, it chimed and its doors opened, almost as though on cue, almost as though it was beckoning her with "now or never."

She crossed to the elevator and stepped inside, adjusting her emerald silk-print dress, smoothing it about her tall figure that was neither too thin nor too voluptuous, but somewhere nicely in between. As the elevator began its ascent, Julianna looked at her reflection in the mirrored wall and was struck by the expression in her eyes.

People often told her that she had the greenest eyes they had ever seen, a compliment that Julianna modestly brushed off. Tonight, though, she had to admit that they were spectacular, so green that even the rich color in her dress dared not compete.

Tonight her eyes were gems, each facet reflecting emotions that made her feel more alive than ever before. There she saw fear of knowing that she had ceased to play it safe and anticipation that life might never be the same again.

The rooftop was set with small round tables topped with smoldering hurricane lamps that made the space glow amber beneath the early June sky. The crowd was sparse, so she had no trouble spotting the man with the dark eyes at a table against the security wall.

His face showed no surprise at seeing her. He wore only a slight and knowing smile, as if to say he'd been expecting her.

Stomach churning, she walked toward him, recognizing none of the people she passed. This wasn't the night her crowd frequented the rooftop, and she was glad. She wouldn't have to explain anything to anyone, which would be a challenge considering that she couldn't even explain it to herself. She felt surreal, as though she were dreaming or acting the part in a movie.

He stood when she reached him, confirming what she had intimated downstairs—he was tall, at least six feet and a few inches. All she could think of was that she would need to reach up to put her arms around his neck if they decided to dance. This pleased her, as she stood five feet nine and had known the awkwardness of dance partners who would have preferred she remove her heels.

His smile widened, welcoming her with a friendly warmth that put her as much at ease as she could possibly be in this most unusual situation. His eyes, dark and mysterious downstairs, reacted to the smile by taking on their own warmth, reflecting light as though caramel had blended with the chocolate. If they truly were the window to his soul, then his soul appeared happy to see her.

"I'm sorry for staring at you downstairs," he said, "but your beauty is distracting."

"Thank you," she murmured, her cheeks warming at the flattery.

She looked at the table and saw a carafe of red wine and two empty glasses. "How did you know I would come?"

"I didn't," he said, pulling out a chair for her. "I was just hoping that you would."

She started to sit, saying, "I'm Juli—"

"Shhhhh," he said kindly, pressing a finger to her lips. "No names."

Her ease was knocked aside, jolted by his intimate touch. And his words implied that he wanted to remain strangers. What was she to say? Fumbling for a response, she thought of her best friend, Virginia Fleming, who had far more experience and knowledge about men than she did. She made a quick recall of past conversations with Virginia and drew from her wisdom.

"That makes me suspect that you're married," she said, hearing the accusation in her voice. She couldn't help the images that flashed through her mind—a faceless wife staring out of a houseless window and wondering where he was.

He sat across from her and raised his left hand. "Never been close to that."

She knew that neither the missing ring nor his words guaranteed his status. His voice and steady eye contact convinced her, and she relaxed a bit. She tried to lighten her tone. "Then what? You're an international spy? Your work is so dangerous that you have to remain anonymous?"

He leaned back in his chair and laughed.

Julianna beamed, hoping he really did find her funny. Virginia always insisted that men loved women who made them laugh, so she would take his reaction as a good sign, especially when he laughed again and said, "I like that story, I really do." Interest sparked his eye and he suddenly sat forward, scooted his chair closer to her, and rested one elbow on the table, looking like a man about to engage in lively conversation. "You must be a writer."

"Only of pathetically boring essays on people like Chaucer, Milton, and Melville," she said, then went on to explain. "I was an English major in college. I just finished a few weeks ago."

"Well, congratulations. And now we have a reason to toast," he said as he poured their wine, his movements smooth and without pause, as though they had been sharing the red warmth together for years. "But Melville wasn't boring. All that stuff about chasing whales and fighting the sea? The man wrote what he lived."

"I know, but after you've written a hundred papers on a hundred writers—" Her voice trailed as she noticed that he was leaning in very close, as if not to miss a single word she said. She struggled to speak with his lips so close to hers. She wanted to feel them against hers in a long kiss. Blushing, she glanced away and spoke to the back of a woman standing near their table. "Well, I guess they all start to seem mundane."

"But at least you were writing something," he said as he took her hand and drew her attention back to the two of them. He placed her palm against her wineglass, then one by one, closed her fingers around it. "Writing is a privilege."

"I'd never looked at it like that," she said, swallowing hard and praying he didn't hear what sounded to her like a loud gulp. As she watched him guide her fingers, she wondered if he might notice how her pulse was racing through her wrist.

How was it that he touched her with such confidence and ease, as though it was the most natural thing in the world for him to do? He did it while speaking of ordinary things, turning them into intimate conversations that made her long for more of him. She tossed back her hair in an attempt to corral her thoughts and return them to the actual discussion they were having. "You—you seem interested in the craft. Are you a writer?"

Quiet settled for a minute, followed by his firm, "No." The spell of another moment broken, he released her hand and sat upright. "I'm an international spy."

"Of course you are," she said. "That's why you can't reveal your name."

"Well, truth be told, names have a way of haunting sweet memories," he said. "Names make it hard for me to move on after the night ends."

Julianna sipped her wine. Now she understood—it was just as she'd feared. He was seeking an intimate stranger, and when the sun rose, they would part ways forever. No regrets, no expectations. Well, he certainly didn't keep a girl guessing about his intentions. Had her actions implied that she sought anything more? Pensive, she played with her wineglass, tilting it back and forth and watching the liquid roll about. She *had* come to the rooftop unaccompanied, and after only seeing him from across a room.

She frowned, annoyed at her own naiveté, knowing she could never meet his expectations, and thinking she should have fought the sudden urge to get on the elevator.

When she looked up from her wineglass, he was studying her carefully. His expression seemed intuitive, as though he had read her concerns. "I didn't mean to imply anything improper," he said. "You have to know up front, though, that I can't form attachments right now." He took a drink of wine and smiled. "But a night of good conversation is always appreciated."

Her eyes widened. "You're only looking for conversation?"

"No, *good* conversation." The smile hadn't left his face, and she liked that, liked the way he smiled as he talked. "One night stands are for the miserable. And besides, you're not the type."

Relaxed again, she returned his smile. "You think you know what type I am?"

"Hmmm," he answered, staring into her eyes. "You want to know who I think you are?"

"I'd be most interested," she said, her heart beating wildly at his intensity.

"You're a thoroughbred—I can see that by the way you carry yourself, the clothes you're wearing." His eyes swept over her dress and down to her matching shoes and the handbag sitting by her feet. "You're not feeling too many pains from the Depression—that dress is beautiful, cost a lot, and looks new."

She nodded at his assessment. Her mother had given the dress to her last week as a birthday present.

He leaned close and took a strand of her hair. Twirling it about his finger, he went on. "But your soul is sweet and unspoiled." He let the hair drop but didn't put any distance between them. "When I mentioned your beauty, you were uncomfortable with the compliment. That says a lot about the good in you."

"I'm uncomfortable now," she said, fanning her face. "Tell me about my bad side before I die of embarrassment."

"I doubt there is one," he said. "Maybe just a part of you that isn't happy with your life."

Her hands stopped fanning, hovering in midair. "Why do you say that?" Her tone held a touch of defense.

His eyes went to her watch. "Don't know if you realize it, but you've glanced at that watch a half dozen times since coming up here."

"I have?" She winced, dropping her hands to her lap. The watch was like a whip, a reminder that time, it seemed, was her master. Always, always, she was expected somewhere by someone. Now she was checking the time without realizing it.

"Are you supposed to be somewhere else?" he asked. "I get the feeling that you are, but I'm hoping you're here," he smiled, glanced away, then came back to her eyes, "because you'd rather be here than where you're supposed to be."

She lowered her head and said quietly, "Well, you certainly know how to read, Mr. Man-of-Mystery. Read people, I mean."

"Who's expecting you?"

"My parents." She looked up and half smiled. "Add dutiful daughter to my traits."

"Dutiful daughter with a rebellious streak."

Now she laughed. "Nobody has ever called me rebellious. You've misread me there."

"I don't think so," he said evenly, exploring her face. "Would your parents expect to find you here with a strange man who won't even give you the courtesy of his name?"

She relented with a shrug. "If my mother knew, she'd be calling for the smelling salts."

"But here you are." He gestured about the rooftop. "With me."

He had revealed something in her, and it left her contemplative and speechless. Who was she, really? She came from a world where sons followed their fathers into the family source of wealth, and where daughters became replicas of their mothers and busied themselves with overseeing household staff, finding the best schools and camps for their children, and immersing themselves in all things covered by the newspaper's society editor. Of course, there were exceptions, and children sometimes struck off in unexpected directions—black sheep, Julianna's mother called them—and surely they were heartbreaking disappointments to the parents who had invested the best of everything into them. How could she, the only child her parents had, be anything less than they expected? It was no secret that her father resented that he'd been denied a son. All the more reason for her to be as perfect as humanly possible. She would marry well, then make a poised and polished transition into the same roles her mother had so efficiently played over the years. It was her destiny, was it not?

She had believed and accepted that once. But recent events had changed that. She was coming too close to the subject again, and she pushed the thought away into a corner of her mind where she would keep it until she was ready to face the reality of it.

In silence, she watched as her mystery man picked up her handbag and unfastened her watch, causing her heart to somersault as his fingertips brushed the tender skin under her wrist. "This watch might say otherwise," he said as he dropped it into the bag, "but the night really is young."

Without the watch cuffing her wrist, Julianna lost track of time as they talked. The wine was long gone before they even realized that their glasses were empty. She was drunk—not from the wine, but from the man and the conversation that was as flavorful and full bodied as the rich spirit itself. He wanted her opinion on everything, it seemed, from Faye Wray's performance in *King Kong* to President Roosevelt's New Deal. They talked of current events—of Lindbergh's kidnapped baby, of Mussolini and foreign wars, of Benny Goodman's swing music and the deaths of Bonnie and Clyde, ambushed just days ago by the Texas Rangers. He asked her about all her favorites— music, car, radio show, and color—until she finally exclaimed, "I'm only talking about myself! Tell me about you. What do you like?"

"I like a certain song," he answered as he stood and removed a black leather wallet from his inside jacket pocket. "Will you dance with me if the orchestra plays it?"

She nodded and watched as he took some bills from the wallet, then moved to slip it back inside his jacket. When he stepped away from the table, he didn't see that the wallet missed the pocket and fell to the floor, landing wide open at Julianna's feet.

How easy it would be to find out his name, she thought, eyeing the wallet as though it were a diary she ached to read but knew she had no right to.

No names, he had said.

She picked up the wallet, intending to honor his one request, until she saw the edges of several receipts peeking out from one of the wallet's compartments.

He had said that no names made things easier. *Easier for whom?* Julianna now wondered. For him, perhaps, but not for her. Suddenly, she had to know his name, had to unmask the identity of the man who was giving her the most wonderful night of her life.

Heart banging, she pulled out the receipts and quickly thumbed through them, noting the same name written on each one.

Jace McAllister.

She glanced up and saw with a start that he—this Jace McAllister— was making his way back. Her fingers fumbled, like someone just learning piano, but she managed to return the receipts, then drop the wallet back to the floor.

"The next dance is ours," he said when he got back to the table. Towering above her, he extended his hand and helped her rise.

"Your wallet," she said, nodding toward the floor.

He grabbed it and then led her toward the dance floor. When they reached it, the orchestra began playing "I Only Have Eyes for You."

As Jace McAllister took Julianna in his arms, she felt her inexperience emerge in all its glory. She felt insecure as a schoolgirl. A stolen kiss on the cheek and a goodnight peck at the front door had not prepared her for this, for the real touch of a man holding her in his arms. She didn't know what to say or what to do.

Fortunately, he did.

He drew her to him, as close as possible, and cradled her safely, his hands caressing her back, then his fingers playfully entwining themselves in her hair. He guided her toward the privacy of shadows, taking her on a slow and swaying journey that she knew would lead to a kiss. Fear of disappointing him made her want to break and run, but she knew she was going to travel on to the destination. There was no place else in the world she wanted to be, and nothing more she wanted than the kiss that was coming. She conquered her fear by surrendering to the desire, closing her eyes and letting her head fall back, as though extending an invitation for him to lean down and bring their lips together for the first time.

She gasped as every nerve in her body glowed to life at his touch, like a thousand torches suddenly illuminating the night, so intense that she went rigid in his arms, paralyzed by the sheer power of their first kiss.

He pulled back and smiled down at her. "Relax," he whispered. "Let me do this."

He brought his lips back to hers and drew her into a kiss that was slow at first but grew in ardor. As she surrendered her self-doubt, a longing rose around her like steam after a summer rain. She marveled that his touch could fill her with such life.

Only the need for air parted them. Wrapped in each other's arms, they stood quiet in the ebony shadows. His chin rested on the crown of her head as she lay against his chest.

Finally, he broke the silence, sadness hovering about his words. "I have to leave you."

"Now?" she asked, unable to hide her disappointment. "After a kiss like that?"

A smile played on his lips. "That kiss is why I'm going."

She lifted her head and looked at him, perplexed. "I'm not sure what to say to that," she said, laughing nervously.

He smoothed her hair and explained. "If I stay any longer, I'll kiss you again. And if I kiss you again, I'll want to know your name."

With that, he gently broke their embrace and hurried away, leaving her speechless in the shadows. Music and laughter surrounded her, but it sounded muffled and distant, as though it belonged to a groggy dream.

She shook her head to clear the haze. Wondering if she looked as shaken as she felt, she went back to the table to get her purse.

A waiter approached her tentatively, as though uncertain of her demeanor. "Miss? Uh, the gentleman you were dancing with—he asked that I see you to your car."

Her hands shook and she dropped her purse. As the waiter dove to retrieve it, she said, "Thank you, but I've got valet parking."

"I'll escort you to valet," he said, handing her the purse.

"No, I'll be fine," she said, wishing to be alone with her confusion.

"But, the gentleman said—"

Julianna didn't hear the rest of the sentence. She thought only of the man named Jace McAllister, who insisted on remaining a stranger but kissed her like anything but and then left her stranded in the shadows of a dance floor.

"He was no gentleman," she said, the words sounding strangely appealing. She brushed past the waiter, tears stinging her eyes, and hurried to the elevator that took her to the lobby.

Waiting for the valet attendant to bring her car, Julianna wondered about the time and glanced at her wrist, its nakedness reminding her that Jace had put her watch inside her purse. Oh, what did the time matter? She was well beyond what her parents' deemed proper. She'd pour out apologies and say she had lost track of time talking to friends.

She wasn't even thinking about her parents anyway, but only about Jace and how much time had passed since he'd walked out of her life. It hadn't been long—less than ten minutes—but long enough for her to realize that she was a fool. She should have gone after him, kissed him, told him her name . . .

Maybe then it wouldn't have been so easy for him to pull away from her arms. Maybe then she could have told him why she had ventured to the rooftop in the first place. Maybe then he would know that she had loved him since their eyes first met in the dining room. Maybe . . . but now it was too late for any of that.

Julianna sat behind the wheel of her car, tears running in a river down her face. For Julianna Sheffield, the night had been more than the unexpected. It had been the unbelievable and the absolutely unheard of.

Passing the darkened movie theater, she thought of her sorority sisters and their lavender dresses for a friend's wedding.

The friend was Julianna.

CHAPTER

TWO

Two weeks after meeting Jace McAllister, Julianna attended the first of several parties honoring her upcoming nuptials.

She descended the turned staircase leading to the first floor of her family's Victorian mansion, Dreamland, thinking how appropriate it was that she was going to a garden party. The rose print on her pale-yellow gown was too big for her taste, making her feel like first prize in a flower show. Her mother, though, had loved the Georgette-style gown, deeming it delightful for a formal afternoon affair. When it came to proper clothes and such, Julianna knew it was best to choose her battles carefully when her mother was the general.

This was especially true if they were hosting or attending an event that would be splashed all over the society section of the newspaper. Mother cared about appearances, Mother feared being the subject of country club gossip, Mother believed everyone read the society section, and Mother actually had good fashion sense—most of the time. Some days, like today, she missed the mark, but Julianna knew Mother's strongest ammunition for winning battles was the perfect pout and sensitive sigh. She genuinely got her feelings hurt when Julianna disagreed with her clothing choices. It was simply easier to just wear it and get it over with.

Waiting at the bottom of the staircase was Julianna's fiancé, Leyton Drakeworth. Twelve years older than Julianna, he was the portrait of masculine elegance in a dark morning suit, his top hat and white gloves in hand. His short, side-parted hair was wheat blonde, and his eyes the grayish-green of a tornadic sky. He smiled as she approached, then took her left hand when she reached him.

"Ah, your ring is back from the jewelers, love," he said. "Just in time for our engagement party."

She looked at the ring, three carats of round brilliance. It had been taken to the jewelry shop weeks ago, sent away to repair a broken prong. That was why it hadn't been on Julianna's hand the night she met Jace McAllister. Thinking of Jace now, Julianna felt a small lump lodge in her throat, but she managed to speak through it. "The jeweler promised it would be."

Leyton took her arm, and they walked down the oak hallway, toward double doors with stained glass panels boasting diamond motifs. They opened to sprawling backgrounds with a white gazebo, its lattice hugged by orange blossoms and purple wisteria. Oak trees shaded the lawn, and a rainbow array of flowers clustered around concrete benches and cherub statues. It was in this garden that two hundred guests awaited.

"I peeked out earlier, and there's quite the A-list in attendance," Leyton said happily. "By the way, your gown is most pretty." He gave her a quick glance and a smile. "I think solid colors are more slimming, but that dress flatters your hair color."

She stared ahead, quietly seething at the backhanded compliment. Leyton was good at that, good at going from sweet to sour in the twinkle of an eye.

It was just one of the reasons why Julianna had to force a smile when the double doors were flung open and the orchestra filled the summer air with "Stardust" as two hundred guests clapped.

What a lie I'm telling, she thought minutes later, mingling among the crowd and feeling guiltier with each hug, kiss, and well-wish she accepted. Leyton was by her side, a hand resting protectively against her waist. They looked like love's perfect picture—young, beautiful, wealthy.

But Julianna knew there was something terribly wrong with the picture. If anyone could look at her heart and see the truth, they'd know that she would rather walk barefoot through glass than down the aisle to Leyton. He was the something she had refused to think about in Jace McAllister's presence two weeks ago.

Yet here she was, going through the motions of celebrating their engagement, waltzing with Leyton on the immaculate grounds and giving the newspaper photographer the expected response when he yelled, "Smile, you two!"

"Well, love, we're sure to grace the cover of the society section," Leyton said. "Your mother will be thrilled, and our wedding will be the social event of summer."

Julianna looked over Leyton's shoulder, taking in the lavish affair. Food that rivaled a cruise ship's buffet. Crystal and silver to spare. And with Prohibition six months dead, there was enough champagne and liquor flowing to fill a riverbed.

"It seems a little obnoxious, don't you think?" she asked. "A lot of people are getting blisters from standing in bread lines, yet here we are—spending more on shrimp than some people earn in a month."

There was a time when this would not have bothered her, back when she didn't understand just how real the suffering of this decade was. Oh, she had seen the newsreels played at the movie theaters and had heard President Roosevelt's Fireside Chats on the radio. She had seen classmates on her college campus have to drop out of school because their parents could no longer afford tuition. She had heard members of the Dreamland household staff swap stories of friends hit by hard times. There was plenty she had seen and heard, but all from the safe and filtered distance of the protected castle of privilege that had been built around her.

A journalism class her senior year of college had taken her away from the castle and into the streets. It was only supposed to be an elective, a writing course to meet the requirements for graduation. But the professor was passionately angry over the plight of those affected by unemployment. He sent his students out to gather information, to cover the stories of those suffering in their own community. That was how Julianna found herself in some of the most downtrodden sections of town, where young children slept in cardboard boxes while older ones rummaged through trash cans as their parents wandered the streets looking for "help wanted" signs. It was how she ended up beyond the city limits, out in the rural countryside where the despair from farm losses cast a gray pallor over the neglected fields, and where the only sound was the lonely whistle of trains passing through a land that once teemed with life.

"Yes, times have been much harder for some than others," Leyton agreed, bringing Julianna out of her thoughts and back into their world of excess. "You know, since coming to work for your father, I've seen many a widow lose her home to foreclosure, seen many a farmer watch his land be auctioned off." He shook his head, tsk-tsking the situation. "It pains the bank when we're forced to take such drastic measures."

Julianna tensed and irritation burned her words. "But you and Father manage to take those measures, sending poor widows and starving farmers to live in tarpaper Hoovervilles—"

"It's business, love, just business," Leyton interrupted. He tilted his head and implored her, "You're not going to turn sullen on me, are you?"

"I just hate the way our bank treats customers who have fallen on hard times."

"You needn't concern yourself with bank business." Leyton wagged a playful finger in her face. "You shouldn't eavesdrop on conversations between your father and me."

"Then you shouldn't discuss business at the dinner table."

He laughed and nodded. "Touché, love, touché. You're so right." His expression turned pouty. "I hate seeing you distressed, especially at our engagement party." His protective hand suddenly grabbed her waist, then twisted the flesh in a hard pinch. "Smile!"

She gasped and jerked away from him. "That hurt, Leyton!"

Passing dancers slowed their steps and looked at the couple.

"I'm afraid I'm forever stepping on her feet," Leyton said, throwing his hands in the air. "Perhaps a few dance lessons would do me good."

The dancers smiled and continued on. Leyton pulled Julianna back into his arms and said softly, "I'm sorry I hurt you. I only wanted you to snap from your gloom." He waved about the grounds. "You deserve to enjoy all of this."

One hand massaging her waist, Julianna searched Leyton's face, wishing it was possible to see the more compassionate man her father had introduced her to nine months ago. That man had never equated taking a widow's home to being business, just business, but had instead delighted in telling Julianna about his ideas for helping people keep their property. "Foreclosures and auctions are such an ugly side of banking," he had confided to her. "Your father is rather old school and traditional, which is completely understandable for his generation's way of conducting business, but I'm determined to show him there's a better way to work with customers who fall on hard times."

She had admired and encouraged his goals, often teasing him that he was certain to succeed if his professional ambitions were anything like his ardent pursuit of her. He was like something out of a fairytale, writing her love sonnets, bringing her flowers spilling from vases and candy nestled in heart-shaped boxes, paying her compliments, making promises, and giving her his undivided attention when they were together. He was immensely respectful, too, only kissing her on the cheek or gallantly lifting her hand to his lips, though he jokingly threatened her with unbridled passion if she ever became his wife.

There was only one promise Leyton hadn't kept. The bank continued to take homes, shutter businesses, and auction farms. Julianna knew her father could be stern and set in his long-held ways of operating the family banks, but it didn't appear as though Leyton was making any difference in the way they worked with struggling customers. His talk of such plans had gradually faded. At first, she was sympathetic. She thought he was discouraged, torn between his altruistic desires and his ambition to succeed under the grooming of her father. After they were engaged, five months after they'd begun dating, he ceased to speak of his earlier plans entirely and would lash out whenever she broached the subject.

He's not angry at me, Julianna would try to assure herself. He's angry that Father won't agree with his ideas. He's angry over his inner struggle to push for the right thing versus his chance to be mentored to one day take over the banks. She had worked hard to convince herself of it, and perhaps she would have succeeded had Leyton not begun to change in other ways. Things like the backhanded compliment and the abrupt and painful pinch. Sparse at first, they had become more frequent and were easily triggered the closer they got to the wedding. He was proving to be a man who could switch from hot to cold and light to dark in the span of a second. One thing that did remain steady was his lack of physical affection, expressing no more after they were engaged than he did on their very first date. Was he really that respectful or was he honestly not attracted to her at all?

A couple of Julianna's friends had always regarded Leyton with suspicion, warning her that any man who seemed too good to be true probably was. She had continued seeing him anyway, and now she wished she'd taken their warnings to heart. Even when Leyton was at his best, she had never been able to love him. Lord knows, she had tried, tried to feel more than fondness and goodwill for a man who seemed ready to cater to her every need and whim. Despite her willingness to love him, the feeling just would not come.

"So why did you get engaged?" her friends had asked, aghast at the diamond on Julianna's ring finger. "Why?"

Julianna saw the answers now, walking toward her and Leyton. Her parents, working their way through guests, stopped every few feet to shake a hand, kiss a cheek, or slap a back. Her father, his chest puffed like a Thanksgiving turkey, was intimidating in size and manner, his voice usually holding the severity of a cracking whip; today, though, he was gregarious. Today, he was the master host, laughing and shaking hands with the same zest he might use to pump a well.

Her mother, too, was looking festive, dressed in a peach gown, peach picture hat, and dyed-to-match satin peach shoes. When she reached Julianna and Leyton, she was breathless from all the hugging and kissing but still managed a happy little clap. She gushed, "The party is splendid!" She gave Julianna a peck on the cheek and sighed. "Your dress looks wonderful, darling. Didn't I say it was perfect?"

"Leyton says it flatters my hair," Julianna said tersely.

"Well, it does," her mother said, smiling at Leyton. "In two short months, Leyton, you'll be an official member of the family. Can you believe how quickly the wedding is coming up?"

Leyton planted a kiss on the hand of his future mother-in-law. "I wish it were tomorrow, Audrey."

Though she stood in the midst of this joyful exchange, Julianna suddenly felt as though she had floated outside of her body. She felt separate and disengaged, like a spirit observing from another realm, seeing truth in its purest form. And the truth was, she had succeeded. She had met her parents' expectations. Actually, she had more than succeeded. She had succeeded greatly, bringing them more happiness than she had imagined she ever could.

Yet where was the satisfaction she always expected to feel from this accomplishment? The sad truth of it struck her—she had misunderstood what showing appreciation meant, had failed to see that she had instead been fighting for her father's approval and bearing the burden of her mother's happiness. Had she completely ignored herself in the process? What didn't she know about who she was and what mattered to her own soul? That was the sacrifice she had begun to grasp the night she first saw and loved Jace McAllister, the one she was afraid to acknowledge. And knowing that Leyton— the something—was the expectation she could never meet was what gave her the courage to step onto the elevator.

A passing waiter bumped into Julianna, knocking her from her trance, one that seemed to have gone unnoticed by those around her. Their laughter and chatter continued, and her father took two glasses of champagne from the waiter's tray. He handed a glass to Leyton, saying, "My boy, we should toast the impending change in our relationship—soon we'll be business partners and family."

As Julianna watched the men clink their glasses together, she saw the pride on her father's face, a painful reminder that her first mistake in life was being born a girl. To her father, anyway, who had spent Julianna's childhood watching enviously as other men romped with their sons. To the gentle daughter who carried his own blood, he had been more of a statue that stood back, with no interest in tea parties and no time to pause and admire drawings carefully rendered by tiny hands.

The tides changed when she reached high school and he began to check her on everything, from manners to schoolwork to ballroom dance skills to the way she wore her hair. He was always challenging her to take things up a notch. For the longest time, she had basked in the attention, feeling like the protégé beneath his spotlight, thankful that he wanted her to be the best she could be. It was only after she and Leyton were officially engaged that she began to question her father's real motives for wanting her to shine above others. Was it because she was his only bait for reeling in a son-in-law? Though she waged a fierce battle against the thought, it came back to fight her almost every time she heard her father and Leyton speak about soon becoming family. Resentment edged its way into her heart, where it struggled for power over the affection she felt for her father.

He landed a friendly slap on Leyton's back. "When you joined my bank, did you think it would lead to this?" He gestured about the grounds, where the town's crème de la crème milled about.

"No, sir, I didn't," Leyton answered as he draped an arm around Julianna's waist and kissed the top of her head. "But I'm certainly glad it did."

Julianna's father smiled at the couple, and for a second Julianna basked under the warmth of her father's approval. Until she remembered that her father's smile was part of what had drawn her into this mess to begin with.

Before Julianna had even met Leyton, her father talked a lot about him—this brilliant, young stockbroker who had joined the bank shortly after the market crashed in twenty-nine. Over time, their association became more than business, as meetings stretched into dinners, and sunny afternoons found the men abandoning work, golf bags in tow. The older man's voice took on a fatherly tone, and he began to say that Leyton felt like family. Like a son.

Her mother, too, liked Leyton, but seemed more grateful to him than anything. When nightmares about their banks failing had started bursting into her dreams, Julianna's father had calmed her, saying their banks—their money—were solvent, and that young Drakeworth had been instrumental in protecting their family's interests during hard times.

Julianna glanced away from her father's smile, knowing how quickly it would vanish if he could read her heart.

Her father had a beautiful smile, though. And while she had been its recipient in the past, never before had she earned it as often and as brightly as she had since the day she began keeping company with Leyton Drakeworth.

Her father's approval, her mother's fears. That's why Julianna was engaged to a man she didn't love, a man who was slowly proving that all that glittered wasn't gold.

Leyton stood among several men, all officers of the bank, puffing a fat cigar and laughing the hearty laugh of someone whose life was good. When the conversation turned to something that didn't interest him, his eyes scanned the party until he found Julianna, talking to some friends. Catching her attention, he sent a wink.

Ah, she was a sweet girl, but sadly, she wasn't his type. He liked his women fair-haired and rail thin, but appearance wasn't everything. Julianna had other qualities that pleased him.

He looked around her parents' estate, admiring its emerald beauty and the prestigious guests who mingled about. Respected businessmen, surgeons, socialites, even politicians.

The world I should have always belonged to, Leyton thought as his finger tapped the cigar and knocked its ashes to the ground. He then took a sip of bourbon, his preferred poison.

His father had drunk bourbon. Actually, his father had been a slave to anything, even rubbing alcohol if that was all his trembling hands could find and grasp. The memories always saddened Leyton. Those same hands had once been gifted in working with wood, taking an ordinary block and crafting it into detailed animal figurines that might have fetched a decent price. The descent into alcoholism destroyed that path, though, and replaced it with a desperate road that only had one destination—the next drink. What Leyton found to be even more tragic was that his mother had joined her husband on the very same road.

Remembering his mother, Leyton could only shake his head. What a shame. He'd always thought she'd have been a loving woman, had she ever been able to stay awake or stay home instead of either sleeping off or seeking out the nectar that she lived for.

Like a sudden spring storm, Leyton's face darkened. Yes, she might have been loving, had she ever been sober enough to mend his clothes and spare him the jeers from other boys. Had she ever seen that he was clean and spared him the pinched noses of snooty girls. Had she ever cooked a real meal and spared him the cramps of hunger.

His parents were dead now. Maybe not literally, but as far as he was concerned. They had been ever since he left them in the Midwest over a decade ago. Some would call him cruel, but he had escaped them in a desperate act of self-preservation. Everyone in their small town predicted that he would become just like them. "The apple doesn't fall far from the tree," they said. Well, this apple would be different. This apple would break from the tree and put miles and miles of ground between itself and the poisonous tree.

And that I have done, Leyton thought as he studied the back of Dreamland. Rising three stories, the mansion looked like a massive wedding cake with its white paint, steeply pitched roof, and ornate gable with frosting-like suspensions. It was houses like these that had helped inspire Leyton to overcome the cards he had been dealt.

He looked at his hands, nails groomed and fingers that gripped nothing beyond a golf club or the steering wheel of his expensive Duesenberg. Calluses had once covered his palms, made from shoveling coal, dirt, snow, and manure—whatever it took to put himself through college. Because the need to work only allowed him to attend part-time, it had taken him nearly twice as long to finish, but he had been successful, earning a degree in finance and graduating with honors.

Back then, he had been Leyton Wilson Jr. but he wanted nothing that linked him to Leyton Sr. Leyton shed his father's name with regret; he felt bad for the older man. What could be more of a disgraceful testament to man's character than his own son not wanting to share his name? Still, he needed to make a complete break if a fresh start was really possible. Sitting in the train station, waiting to board a southern-bound express, Leyton had picked up a newspaper and seen the obituary of a Matilda Drakeworth, the widow of a tobacco king. The only survivors listed were "several nieces and nephews." From that moment on, Leyton called himself a nephew of Matilda Drakeworth. Now he could have the good name to go with the good life he intended to find.

He was surrounded by that life now and was so close to having more. He always needed more, and knowing he could get it was the motivation that directed his days and the comfort that let him sleep at night. He had never forgotten what it was like to be hungry, but now his pangs were for the security of more, and his ambition was a voracious appetite that had to stay full and satisfied.

He took pride in his ambition and credited it as the drive that afforded him his success. He felt certain that he had always had it, that it was what got him out of bed on snowy Midwestern mornings and pushed him to trudge on to school, even though there wasn't a hot breakfast or proper coat to make the walk more tolerable. It was what kept him studying into the night so that he could get accepted into college, where he would have to ignore women, sports, and frat life in exchange for dirty jobs to pay his tuition and room and board. It was what made him vow to any future unborn sons that he would establish a life that made them proud to call him their father, that he would be someone they could count on to provide and guide. Ambition, he believed, could change the world. It could overcome despair because it was fueled by hope and determination. It took vapory dreams and shaped them into solid realities. It kept people going when the chips were down. It was the part of any equation that could make a positive difference. Ambition was good and could serve a person well.

Most people would say that Leyton had done well after coming south during the 1920s, joining Southern Gold Brokerage Firm and, later, the People's Standard National Bank. His earnings were quite good, but one potential problem initially loomed in the back of his mind. His salary could never have stood on its own if he had been forced to explain his ridiculously expensive home, car, and all-round lifestyle. Thankfully, questions were never asked-—not of him, a man from tobacco riches. What he didn't have in inheritance, he found when he dipped into the billion-dollar world of bootlegging.

Finishing his bourbon, Leyton felt a bit sad that Prohibition had ended, taking with it his ill-gotten prosperity.

Not too sad, though.

Fortunately for him, there was Julianna Sheffield. Her family was wealthy and she had no siblings with whom to split the joy. She had a trust fund, too.

Leyton waved at her from across the grounds. She really was a sweet girl. Not menacing like the ones who used to say "Souie, Souie" when he walked past them in school. He liked her heart, tender for the less fortunate, and was sure she would have been nice to him if they'd known each other as children and teens. She probably would have helped him—maybe brought him lunch or offered to be his lab partner when no one else was willing to. He also respected her reliability and trusted that she would always be where she needed to be and do what she needed to do. A healing ointment for the wounds inflicted by his absent and unavailable mother, she would always come home.

Yes, she was a good woman for him to marry. He only hoped that, in time, he would develop at least some physical attraction to her. That he would be able to love her as husband and deliver on the unbridled passion he had promised her. She just wasn't the kind of woman who physically appealed to him, and he was very, very particular.

One of the bank's officers tapped Leyton's shoulder then drew him back into their conversation. How he enjoyed the company of such men! They were intelligent, articulate, and socially equipped to be at his engagement party.

Board members, directors, officers, and vice presidents were the only people from the bank whose names had been on the guest list. Everyone else—the Nobodies, Leyton secretly called them—had been left out.

At the downtown headquarters of the People's Standard National Bank, the Nobodies who worked in the lobby weren't thinking about the festivities at Dreamland. They were having plenty of excitement at work, thanks to the well-dressed, masked man who marched into the bank at exactly three o'clock and greeted them with the silver glare of a .38 revolver.

"Good afternoon, ladies and gentlemen," he said, voice smooth and friendly, like a politician campaigning from behind a banner-draped podium. "I'm the People's Bandit, and this is," he paused and looked around at the shock-ridden faces, "a holdup."

A teller screamed, prompting the Bandit to say, "I'm not going to hurt anyone, so stay calm, keep your hands off the phones, and I'll soon be out of your way." Again, he surveyed the faces. "Who's willing to be my assistant?"

The silence surprised the Bandit, for he had assumed the security guard would volunteer for duty. That had been the case every other time he had robbed the People's Standard National Bank, or rather, its branch offices. The headquarters—the big one—he had saved for last, and he'd expected a tougher security guard than the one he was looking at now—the one cowering in the corner, his Adam's apple pulsating like first pick in a bobbing contest.

A chair scraped the floor, and a thin man rose from his seat. He cleared his voice then croaked, "I'll do it."

"And your name, sir?" The Bandit asked.

"Millege." He coughed. "Walter Millege."

The Bandit motioned with his gun, silently instructing Millege to come forward. Never, though, did the Bandit's eyes stop to focus on Millege alone, but stayed in constant motion, darting from the tellers to the loan officer to the shrinking violet of a guard.

Swiftly, the Bandit tossed a black briefcase at Millege, hitting the skinny man in the chest and causing him to stumble back a step. "Sorry, Walt," he apologized. "Now visit each teller and have her empty her drawer."

Knuckles white, Millege gripped the briefcase and hurried to the counter of tellers, the gun keeping his back in perfect range. The Bandit felt sorry for the guy, even though he had nothing to worry about. Unlike Dillinger, Baby Face Nelson, and others who shared his profession, the Bandit had never pulled the trigger on anyone. All the newspapers and radio stations swore it to be the truth. The Bandit knew that, right now, Millege was counting on the accuracy of those news reports.

Waiting for the money to be collected, the Bandit maintained surveillance of the room, not letting anyone out of his sight for more than a split second. There was little to be concerned about, he predicted, because these people were frozen, barely daring to breathe, and it looked like he would again pull off another holdup, a lone gunman with no gang or accomplice to back him up.

"He's just one man," the radio announcers always said in the days following a robbery. "So how does he walk into the People's Standard and manage to clean their clocks?"

Were the Bandit on the other side of the microphone, he could tell the audience that it wasn't hard. One man with a pointed gun, whether he planned to use it or not, could keep a hundred people at bay.

It was actually a couple of radio guys who first called him the People's Bandit, picking the name because he only robbed the People's Standard National Banks. The name stuck, and now everyone called him that, even Mr. J. Edgar Hoover and his posse of blue-suited G-men of the FBI.

Even though the Feds kept their eyes peeled for the Bandit, he knew he wasn't on their Most Wanted list. No, he'd probably have to kill someone to make it that far, but he figured he was definitely on the national Wouldn't Mind Having Him list. Locally, though, it was a different story. There, he was nestled in at number five on the list of Most Wanted. And he was certain to be number one on Richard Sheffield and Leyton Drakeworth's list.

Sheffield and Drakeworth. The Bandit chuckled behind his mask. They had to be taking these robberies pretty personally by now.

That was good. That was exactly how the Bandit wanted them to take things.

Millege was making his way back across the lobby, his high forehead glistening with perspiration, and his bony frame leaning like the Tower of Pisa as he lugged the briefcase, now heavy with bills.

"Here's your withdrawal," he said, setting the briefcase on the floor at the Bandit's feet.

The Bandit laughed. "A sense of humor—even under extreme tension. I like that in a man." He took the briefcase and hoisted it under one arm, then made a sweep of the room with his eyes. "Everyone, you've been a great audience. Thanks for the cooperation."

He left then, but not through the front door as expected. Predictability, he firmly believed, could be a deadly downfall, so he surprised everyone when he headed for the men's washroom instead.

A Convenience for Our Customers a sign on the door read.

And how so, the Bandit thought as he pushed through the door. He raised a window and dropped into a weedy back lot where his getaway car was waiting. It was a black Chrysler Straight Eight, hot-wired and purring, ready to carry him along an escape route that was mapped out to a tee.

Everything he did was to a tee. The banks he robbed were as familiar as his own home, as he spent weeks casing them inside and out. Take the headquarters of the People's Standard. He knew every window, every door on the main floor, and had figured out that his back was best covered when he stood at the wall displaying an oil painting of Richard Sheffield himself.

The Bandit loved that—loved that Richard Sheffield was, in a way, watching the back of the man robbing his bank.

He loved, too, that people were creatures of habit—that there were high tides of customer activity, followed by ebbs when all was quiet. Delivery people were chained to routine schedules. The redheaded teller always left for lunch at 12:15, paused on the steps, whipped out a compact, and dusted powder across her freckles.

It was this kind of consistency that made the Bandit's job easier, helping him avoid as many distractions and interruptions as possible. His escape route was always uncomplicated, too, but sometimes—despite the best-laid plans—things could go crazy.

Barreling around a corner on two wheels, the Bandit almost lost control of the Chrysler when he saw the jaywalking mule, ambling blithely across the street, dragging his broken cart harness behind him.

As the animal froze and bellowed, the Bandit hit the brakes so hard he thought his foot would ram through the floorboard. Sparing the mule, the Chrysler made a complete spin before coming to an idling rest.

Onlookers poured into the street and gathered around the car, eyes fixed on the masked man trying to regain his senses from behind the wheel.

"Hey, it's the Person's Bandit!" some kid crowed. He leaned in the window and peered. His hair was a jagged mop of gold, his overalls more patched than a quilt.

The Bandit fought the wooziness in his head. "People's Bandit," he corrected.

"Yeah, and there's a drawing of you in the post office!" Sirens wailed in the background and the kid grinned. "I'm gonna get me some reward money for your tail!" He pulled his head from the window, stood on tiptoe, and craned his neck in the direction of the sirens.

Spectators blocked the Chrysler but screamed when the Bandit grabbed two fistfuls of money from the briefcase and flung the bills out the window. Scrambling after the money like pigeons chasing peanuts, they opened up an escape hatch for the Bandit. He floored the Chrysler and shot away.

The mule had been a huge interruption, though, a time-killer that now had three cop cars gaining on the Bandit. His only hope for staying ahead waited in an upcoming intersection, where a slow, open-topped furniture truck was crossing.

With a sharp swerve, the Bandit cut the truck off, causing it to halt with such a jolt that two ottomans went belly-up on the pavement and a chaise lounge skidded across the street, head-on into the grill of a car.

Traffic snarled, barricading the police cars, as the Bandit continued on, soon leaving the paved roads and brick buildings of the city behind. Sighing deep relief, he ripped off the sweaty mask and tossed it on the passenger's seat. He was in the country now, heading for a holler where his own car was hidden and he could ditch the getaway car. He was guided to the hiding place by landmarks—a general store, a duck pond, a red barn, and a mansion.

A white one called Dreamland.

CHAPTER

THREE

Julianna's face ached from smiling, and she wondered if it would be rude to take a break from entertaining guests. From inside the gazebo, she looked about the grounds, seeing that everyone was busy talking and eating. She shouldn't be missed.

She hurried into the house and down the hallway, toward the front veranda. Out front, sounds of the party would be low and muffled, barricaded some by the high brick wall that surrounded the backgrounds. She could have some quiet time.

Her best friend, Virginia, was quick on her heels, though, catching up with Julianna as she opened the front door.

"I never thought I'd get you to myself," Virginia said as they stepped outside. "You've been mobbed all afternoon."

"Well, Mother does things up big," Julianna said. She and Virginia sat in the porch swing and slipped off their shoes.

"Your mother, by the way, looks peachy keen in her party ensemble," Virginia noted as she took her silver monogrammed cigarette case from her small handbag. "Light and festive, like a bowl of summer fruit."

Julianna smiled softly and rested her head on Virginia's shoulder. They had been lifelong friends, and everything between them felt comfortable. Virginia was as bold and irrepressible as Julianna was quiet and abiding—they proved that opposites attract. Deep down, Julianna knew her parents didn't approve of Virginia's flamboyant

ways, but they were careful not to offend, careful not to get their
names removed from the party list of Virginia's popular family.

Virginia lit a Lucky Strike then began wildly waving away the
cloud of white smoke that rose around her face. It was ivory and
flawless, like the face of a beautiful porcelain doll. Her eyes were
bright blue, magnificent against her short finger-waved auburn hair.

"One . . . two . . ." Virginia counted as she blew wavering smoke
rings. She puffed Luckies because of their advertising slogan—Reach
for a Lucky Instead of a Sweet—and often said they kept her tall
figure as willowy as some of the film stars she'd seen in pictures.

"I'm up to six smoke rings now," Virginia announced. "Daddy
says I'm shameless, that any girl who has time to build up her smoke
ring count is a girl with too much time on her hands." She exhaled
another ring.

Julianna laughed, prompting Virginia to say, "Well, that's the first
sincere laugh I've heard from you all day. Sweets, I thought your face
was going to crack under the tension."

"My misery hasn't been too obvious, has it?"

"Probably just to me because I know you better than anyone
else." She took a long draw on her Lucky then spoke while exhaling.
"As your best friend and maid of honor, it's my duty to say that you
simply cannot—cannot—marry Satan Drakeworth."

Now Julianna really laughed and sat forward in the porch swing.
She turned to Virginia and implored her. "Do you really think he's
that bad? Satan?"

"I've always said that he isn't what he seems," Virginia said.
"The devil is in the details, and I can sense the tiniest details from
a thousand miles away. Some men are diamonds in the rough, but
Leyton? Cow manure in a field of green. Trust me, sweets, I know
men."

"There's never been a truer statement," Julianna answered,
thinking of the men who had clamored for the attentions of Virginia

Rose Fleming. Her smile was a magnet, her words liquid gold pouring over men like a rush of riches. She made even the most awkward of suitors feel unique, but her courtship journeys hadn't been free of sharks and wolves.

"Tell your parents the truth—that you'd rather dine with slugs than marry Leyton," Virginia advised. "It's not too late, not until you say 'I do'."

Julianna shook her head. "Sometimes I'm afraid it's already too late. Leyton has made himself the son that Father always wanted, and Mother thinks our banks will fail if Leyton were to leave."

"Oh, good night!" Virginia said, as she sent the butt of her cigarette sailing into a hedge ripe with pink blossoms. "Daddy says your father is a brilliant businessman who will never let your banks fail." She lit another Lucky and went through her face-fanning routine. "What I don't understand is why you feel like it's your job to solve these issues for your parents."

"I never thought of it as solving things," Julianna said. "I was just living life the way I thought I was supposed to, the way I've always been told I should. But marrying Leyton?" She shuddered and hugged herself as though a cold breeze had swept through. "The closer the wedding gets, the more I feel like the expectations are too high. Even if I wasn't seeing bits of the devil in some of the details, there's the fact that I don't love him. Even if he was divine, that one thing is reason enough not to go through with it."

"Bingo!" Virginia shouted. "You've seen the light!"

"I'm seeing a lot of lights these days," Julianna said as she slumped against the swing, her expression brooding. "I've told you how Father and Leyton discuss business at the dinner table, talking like Mother and I are no more alive than the silverware?"

"Hmmm."

"Wait until I tell you what they did a few days ago," Julianna said, suddenly sitting up straight and turning towards Virginia.

"You know that farm down the road? The family has been loyal bank customers for twenty years, but times have been hard lately and they fell behind in their note." Another shudder racked her body, but this one was brought on by anger. "What do you think Father and Leyton did?"

Virginia blew a smoke ring. "Flogged their granny?"

"Auctioned the farm, Virginia. They sold everything out from under that poor family."

Virginia shook her head, saying nothing.

"Leyton actually oversaw the auction," Julianna continued, the words tasting as bitter as a dissolving aspirin on her tongue. "He stopped the bidding before they'd gotten full price then made up the difference by selling the furniture, tractors—even a litter of newborn pigs." She smacked the swing. "All his talk about helping the farmers avoid auction, all his talk about working out something with customers—empty words and outright lies." She smacked the swing a second time. "It makes me so angry I could scream."

"Ignore what I said about the devil in the details," Virginia said. "It sounds like the horns of Leyton-Satan have officially popped out."

They swayed quietly for a few minutes, Julianna looking about the estate and the long driveway lined with magnolias, their white blossoms reminding her of stars. Tears wet her eyes, making everything look wavy, as though she were seeing the world through a fishbowl.

She glanced at her watch. "Mother will send out the search dogs if I don't get back."

Virginia stood and smoothed out the backless, gold lamé gown she had dared to wear to today's conservative affair. "I should get back to my date—he must be bored senseless by all the stuffed shirts at your party. No offense."

Julianna nodded, thinking of Virginia's date. She never kept company with society's purebreds but opted for the companionship of wildcards instead. Her latest, Captain Cloud, was an aviation daredevil, a wing walker who performed to the oohs and ahhs at air shows. "He's really handsome, Virginia."

"He's a barnstorming bean brain, but yes—he's precious in his bomber jacket and goggles," Virginia said. "He's a good kisser, too."

"You've been steaming up the car windows?" Julianna teased.

"A little," Virginia admitted with a shrug. "But you know me—only feed a man hors d'oeuvres." She stepped into her shoes. "Men leave the table when their stomachs are full, so don't even put the main course on the menu."

"You, Virginia Fleming, are profound."

Virginia tossed her cigarette off the veranda and took a lipstick from her purse. She colored her lips and smacked them, then offered the lipstick to Julianna. "Want some?"

Julianna took the lipstick and drew it across her own lips. Handing it back to Virginia, she said, "Go rescue Captain Cloud. I'm going to stay here a few more minutes—take some deep breaths before facing the lions."

"I'll hold your mother at bay," Virginia said as she started for the front door. Pausing, she placed a hand on Julianna's arm. "The wedding is still two months away—we'll think of something."

Julianna smiled sadly, wishing she could find realistic hope in Virginia's words. She felt trapped, though, unable to see an escape hatch. Well, at least not a graceful one. As Virginia slipped into the house, Julianna went down the front steps and along the walkway, not caring that the cement pricked her silk stockings. She strolled aimlessly about the grounds among towering oaks and magnolias and weeping willows so overweight their branches scraped the grass. There were pink and blue hydrangeas and gardenias perfuming the air. It had only been a few months ago that the blooms were missing from this country paradise as the hosts slept through the winter until springtime nudged them awake. New color and sweet fragrance followed, nature's message and reminder that life renews when the season is right.

To every thing there is a season, and a time to every purpose under the heaven. The scripture from Ecclesiastes 3:1 came to mind, and she began to check off the specifics it went on to mention. A time to love, to hate, to weep, to laugh. There were many, coming to her in no particular order. A time to mourn, to dance, to speak up, to be silent. Her thoughts paused. Was now her season to speak up about not wanting to marry Leyton? To speak up about all the things that were bothering her? And did the Good Book say anything about there being a season to run away and disappear?

How peaceful it was out here—if only that were true inside her own mind. The flowers and trees weren't burdened by whether or not they should have bloomed, for they knew their purpose and existed for it. The sun and sky above never questioned what they were supposed to do next. The two wrens that just flew overhead were free to fly wherever they chose.

She, however, had no idea what her purpose was, what she needed to do next, and how she was ever going to take flight from the branch she was currently stuck on. She really couldn't even compare herself to a bird on a branch, though. She was more like one locked inside of a cage, one that was starting to bang against it and try to lift open the door. As if to confirm that she wasn't like them, the two wrens took flight from their branch and soared high over the roof of Dreamland.

Suddenly, the quiet around her shattered, the still air ripped by the blare of a car horn that sent chilling alarm through Julianna. Her head jerked in the direction of the horn, and she gasped, realizing that she had wandered into the road and was standing in the path of a car, its black body speeding toward her like a bullet.

Dirt swirled. Brakes squealed. And the stench of smoke rent the air. The car skidded sideways, trying to miss Julianna.

A scream froze in her throat and her knees buckled just before a black shade was yanked down over the world.

When the car came to a stop, the People's Bandit sat stunned behind the wheel for a second then smacked his forehead.

First a mule, now a woman.

Fear twisted his stomach as he jumped from the car and hurried to the woman. I didn't hit her, he assured himself. I'm sure I didn't hit her. She must have fainted.

She was on her side, cheek resting on one arm that was stretched straight above her head. The Bandit knelt beside her and eased back the hair that was fanned across her face. Seeing the face, he smiled softly and lifted her head, cradling it against his chest.

It was her. The one he had walked away from two weeks ago, leaving her standing on a rooftop. Now they met again, this time on a roadtop.

"Miss? Are you all right?"

Her eyes fluttered open, revealing magnificent green marbles glazed over with shock. He imagined that he was wavering in and out of her focus, until she gasped. That's when he knew she was seeing him clearly.

"It's you," she whispered. "Jace McAllister."

He jolted, nearly losing his hold on her, but catching her just before her head fell back on the road. "I—I said no names, remember?" His voice sounded as dazed as his head felt.

"I peeked in your wallet when you went to request a song," she said, gently rubbing her forehead. "I'm sorry." She sat up now and glanced about their surroundings. "What happened?"

"You were standing in the road for some reason," he answered. "I almost hit you. Can you stand?"

She nodded and let him help her slowly rise to her feet.

"Do you feel dizzy, miss?" he asked as he cautiously released his grip on her.

"Yes, Mr. Mc—" She stopped and laughed. "Mister and miss is rather formal for two people who," she glanced away then back, blushing, "kissed like we did."

Recovered from his initial shock, Jace's voice prickled with irritation. "I still don't want to know your name and I wish you'd forget mine, miss."

"That's Miss Sheffield," she said with a hint of defiance. "Miss Julianna Sheffield."

"Sheffield," he muttered under his breath, then shook his head, not believing what he had just heard her say.

"You recognize the name," she noted. "Do you know my father?"

"Richard?"

"Yes—how do you know him?"

He looked to the sky and laughed, still shaking his head. "What are the odds?" he wondered, more to himself than to her.

Police sirens whined in the distance, pulling Jace from disbelief to reality. He stared in Julianna's eyes, Caribbean clear in the sunlight, a window into a sweet soul, deer-like and gentle but clearly perplexed by his strange reaction to her question. He wished he could give her an answer. But he couldn't, just like he couldn't explain his mysterious ways the first night they met.

Suddenly, he felt like he was back at the Downtown Panache. Deja vu surrounding him, he said, "I have to leave you."

"But why?" she asked, voice cracking. "Why must you run instead of stay?"

As he started to turn, she grabbed his arm. He liked the way it felt, even though it was detaining him. He liked that she didn't want him to go, even though he had to.

"Jace, have you at least thought about me since that night?

He smiled, as he always did when the memory starred in his mind, which it seemed to do like film that hadn't been cut, but instead was a loop that played over and over again.

"Do you?" she asked again. "Think about me?"

"Every conscious moment," he said, and they were the most honest words he had ever spoken to a woman.

"Then stay—"

He cut her off, grabbing her shoulders and pulling her to her tiptoes, then pressing his lips to hers. The kiss was quick but rich. When he pulled away to look at her, she seemed breathless, her face flushed a pink.

"I wish there could be something for us," he said as he stepped away and moved toward the car.

He felt her eyes burning into him as he hurried to drive out of her life. But then she threw something at him. Not the rock he was sure he deserved, but words that stung even more; they stung his soul.

"I'm getting married in two months."

Guarded hope came over Julianna when she saw him pause, saw his hand freeze before opening the car door. His shoulders stiffened, and she knew her words had affected him. Maybe, just maybe, some corner of his mind had considered the possibility of someday having a place for her in his life.

But when his shoulders dropped, so did her hope. Without turning, he called, "What do you want me to do?"

She looked anxiously at the mansion then back to him. Heart thundering and throat dry, she realized exactly what she wanted him to do. "Take me with you."

The words sounded like they came from a movie, like Julianna was sitting in a theater hearing them spoken by an actress. Julianna couldn't believe they had come from her, but she felt no desire to call them back.

Now Jace looked at her. "We have a serious conflict in interest, Miss Julianna Sheffield," he said. As if on cue, the sirens wailed again, announcing that they were drawing near. Jace nodded toward the sound and continued, "You'll figure it out soon enough."

He flung open the Chrysler's door and slid behind the wheel. Before tearing away, he lowered one arm out the window, his hand pointing a silver revolver to the ground. He shook it open, revealing an empty chamber. "It's not loaded. It never has been."

She didn't know what he was talking about and could only gape, arms wide open to her sides. Anything she might have said would've been drowned out by the roar of the Chrysler as he sped away.

He's done it again, she thought, watching the Chrysler's tail lights. As the car disappeared around a bend, she grabbed a rock and hurled it.

It only fueled her frustration, and there was no damming the tears that were destroying her face powder and splashing onto the bodice of her gown. She ran toward the mansion, feet pounding the ground so hard that each step echoed in her head, causing it to throb. The pain didn't slow her down, though, because she was desperate to get inside and dash up to her room, where she could sit and think, where she could try to make sense of Jace McAllister.

When she reached the front door of the mansion, it flew open and she was nearly trampled by her father, Leyton, and a few other men from the bank. They charged past her like a stampede of incensed cattle, and right behind the herd was her mother, arms waving frantically and mouth forming a perfect "O" as though she was about to scream.

Seeing Julianna just outside the door, her mother stopped and stood rooted to the floor. She grabbed Julianna's shoulders and pulled her into the foyer. "Oh darling, we've just gotten wretched news! We've been robbed again! The same man as always—"

"Julianna!" Her father broke from the pack of men and dashed into the foyer. "How long were you out front?"

She glanced at her watch. "A half hour, maybe?"

"Did you see anyone?" Rage shook his voice. "The police said he was headed out this way, witnesses claim the car was black, a Chrysler—"

Leyton and others from the bank were in a Packard sedan, waiting for Julianna's father to join them for a frantic ride downtown. When they blew the horn, her father bolted without getting Julianna's answer.

I didn't hear Father right, Julianna thought, her skin turning clammy. Her heart seemed to fall to her stomach, landing like a brick, and her breathing was quick and raspy. She closed her eyes and tried to concentrate on her breathing, on bringing it under control. As it slowed, she remembered the words of Jace McAllister, spoken over the wail of police sirens.

You'll figure it out soon enough.

She slumped against the staircase but grabbed the banister in time to steady herself. Slowly, she sat on one of the lower steps and rested her head against the spindles of the banister.

Jace McAllister. The People's Bandit.

Her mother was talking to Cassie Spraggs, the family cook and housekeeper, who had hurried from the kitchen to the foyer when the commotion began.

"Oh Cassie, I hope nobody was injured by that man."

Julianna lifted her head and said quickly, "No one was."

The words came unexpectedly, leaving Julianna as surprised as her mother and Cassie. The women gave her curious looks, and her mother said, "I hope that's true, but how can you sound so sure?"

"I—well, it's just that he's robbed us before and no one was harmed."

Her mother and Cassie exchanged glances then nodded in agreement. Julianna sighed, glad they weren't going to press her with more questions. It was true—the People's Bandit had never shown violence, but that wasn't why she had spoken up. It was Jace McAllister's gun with the empty chamber, something that had made no sense at the time. Now she knew he was trying to tell her something, something about himself.

She didn't have to ponder it long. There could only be one reason why Jace McAllister wanted her to know that his gun was never loaded. Despite his actions, he wasn't all bad—and it mattered to him that she knew that.

She smiled sadly as a disbelieving, half-laugh escaped her. What a day. From the frustrations of Leyton to the shock of Jace, she suddenly felt depleted, like she could nod off to sleep given the chance. Instead, she watched her mother compose herself before the foyer mirror then float graciously down the hall and back to her party. Like a queen greeting her subjects, she flung open the doors and was swallowed by a sea of worried faces. "All is well," Julianna heard her say as the doors closed. "Richard and Leyton are taking care of everything."

All is well, Julianna scoffed silently to herself. She had just discovered that the man she couldn't stop thinking about was a bank robber. And not just any robber, but the one who fancied the banks that belonged to her family. All was definitely not well.

Julianna had always walked the upright way and obeyed the rules of life and law. But what about the rules of love? Wasn't love supposed to cover a multitude of sins? She wanted it to, but felt certain that some secrets didn't fall under that Biblical passage. She had crucial information that the authorities needed to know. Of course she would tell them. Well, of course she should tell them, but just as she knew the difference between right and wrong, she also knew the difference between would and should.

"You going back to the party, Miss Julianna?" Cassie asked, breaking into the moral dilemma that was beginning to wrestle with Julianna's thoughts. "People've been askin' where you took off to."

Hoping her face didn't show signs of the thoughts in her head, ones that nobody would believe, Julianna tried to appear collected as she flipped her hand in the direction of the party. "I'll go back, but the whole thing should be wrapping up soon."

"Shoo boy, and won't I be glad." Cassie chuckled as she edged her big bottom in between Julianna and the banister. "Lord help, my kitchen done imploded on itself." She put a cushy arm around Julianna's shoulders. "Rest your head against me, child. It's not been a dandy day, not dandy-do at all."

Julianna snuggled against the familiar bosom of Miss Cassandra Baptista Spraggs, the dear woman who had been with the family for thirty years. She was a mountain of a woman whose five-foot-ten-inch frame jostled three hundreds pounds of sass and honey. She was fifty-three, wore her gray-streaked black hair in a tight bun against the back of her head, and had smooth skin the color of cocoa. When complimented on it, she always said, "We Negress women don't get them crepe-paper wrinkles like whites. Don't know why the Lord made us that way, but He did and the glory goes to Him."

Cassie was a fierce warrior for the Lord. Except for the Bible, she was uneducated book-wise, but she was a sharp observer of people and their ways. She kept life simple and to the point and was the wisest person Julianna knew. Next to Virginia, she was Julianna's dearest friend.

Cassie sighed and stroked Julianna's hair. "Your daddy and Leyton—they was madder than plucked roosters when they left here. Won't be no gettin' along with them for a while."

Julianna covered her face with her hands. Her shoulders trembled.

"There now," Cassie said. "Cryin' helps."

"I'm not crying," Julianna said, words muffled.

Cassie shifted position and peeled Julianna's hands away from her face. "No, you're laughin'." She reared back her head, studying Julianna curiously. "What? The bank gets robbed again, and here you sit—findin' it comical?"

Julianna stopped laughing, and her expression turned to pain, the way she imagined that farmer down the road must have looked when Leyton sold his possessions. The way she suspected a lot of people looked when their homes, farms, businesses, pride, and dignity were snuffed out by the People's Standard National Bank, the bank that took and took.

"I wasn't finding it comical," Julianna said. "But Father and Leyton have taken so much from other people. Maybe, Cassie, maybe they deserve a taste of their own medicine."

Jace slammed his fist on the steering wheel, hitting it so hard that he almost lost control of the car and had to yank it out of a swerve.

Julianna Sheffield.

He tried to scowl as he thought of her name, hoping to make it ring with distaste.

She was a woman who brought trouble. A woman who made a man reconsider his wandering ways, who made him think about tomorrow and of babies who looked like him. Things Jace had not allowed himself to think about for quite sometime.

It was why he had left her on the rooftop of the Downtown Panache. He hated himself for not being more gallant, but what a relief to think he would never have to see her again.

"Ha!" Jace hit the steering wheel again. If only he'd known the future.

Take me with you, she had said, and Jace wondered if he should have done it. How he'd love to see her hair blowing wildly about her face as they sped along the twists and turns of these country roads.

How he'd love to continue what they'd started on that rooftop . . .

He slapped his mask back over his face, hard, ready to knock himself senseless for drifting into fanciful thoughts. When it came to Miss Julianna Sheffield, he just needed to concern himself with one thing.

She was the only person on earth who knew he was the People's Bandit.

Some men might have taken her for just that reason, but Jace knew better. A man moves faster when he moves alone, so why travel with a woman the whole country would be looking for? The Sheffield Princess, gone missing right after the bank was robbed and the gunman escaped in the direction of the Sheffield mansion.

No matter that Julianna volunteered to go; her desperate request told him that she would not have skipped into the house, packed a bag, and kissed her family good-bye before jumping into the Chrysler.

Add kidnapping to my list of sins, Jace thought, knowing that Julianna's picture would have been plastered on storefronts and in the newspapers. The reward for her safe return would have been more than most men earned in a lifetime. She would lead the bloodhounds right to him.

Not that she wasn't doing that anyway, he knew. The self-described dutiful daughter was probably spilling his name and a detailed description to the police right this moment.

On the other hand—and Jace always considered the other hand—he had detected in her a rebellious streak. But was it enough to keep her silent?

No, it was too much to hope for. Too much for him to ask.

Right now, he could only try to stay ahead of the police. They must have fanned out around the countryside, because he was hearing sirens everywhere.

He topped a blind hill, just as a police car topped it from the other side. The outlaw and the lawman traded looks, and never had Jace seen such fury fill another man's face. He turned so red, so suddenly, that Jace half expected to see his cheeks explode off his face. The cop raised his fist and clenched it into a shaking ball.

I'll get you! it swore to Jace. I'll get you!

Jace left the cop behind in a cloud of choking dust and pushed the Chrysler hard. No doubt the cop was making a quick U-turn and would soon be in heavy pursuit, probably bringing friends. Jace looked at his watch, grinning when he saw that it was just minutes before five. Julianna had cost him time, but he might just make it out of this after all.

He had mapped out this area of farmlands and meadows. Now, passing a red barn with a fresh coat of paint, he knew a railroad crossing was just a mile up the road. The closer Jace got to the tracks, the louder he heard the whistle of a train, telling him that the good ole five o'clock freight was making her daily amble toward town.

Right on time.

It was a long train of boxcars and flatbeds, as slow and lumbersome as a snail crawling through molasses. Anyone who didn't beat the train was doomed to an aggravating wait, unless they used the time to read the paper or maybe knit a sweater. Jace didn't plan on doing either.

He checked his rearview mirror and saw three police cars in the distance—a high-speed little posse intent on catching one bandit.

The tracks were straight ahead now, and the black coal engine was in view, drawing closer to the crossing at the same time as the Chrysler. The ground rumbled with warning, but Jace didn't brake. He floored the pedal, moving so fast that every inch of the car shook and plumes of gray smoke poured from the exhaust pipe.

Jaw set and eyes unblinking, Jace leaned back in his seat and braced the steering wheel. Jace's thrill of escape mixed with terror as the Chrysler's front tires hit the tracks, striking with such speed that he thought the car would somersault. It held its grip, though, and kept all four tires on the ground.

The face of the massive engine was a mere few feet away from the Chrysler. Crossing before it, the car was swallowed in darkness as the train's black shadow loomed ominously above, and its horn battered the quiet country with a long earth-shattering blast. A quick, intense chill radiated up and down Jace's spine.

Suddenly, daylight returned and Jace felt the springy jolt of the car's tires bouncing off the tracks and back onto the road. He laughed, loud enough to wash out the sounds of his heart banging against his chest.

Behind Jace, the train rolled like a lazy river, the great divider between him and his pursuers. As the police sat trapped behind the long line of metal and steel, Jace drove away, rounded a bend in the road, and came to a rocky driveway that led to the abandoned, lopsided house that concealed a holler.

The holler was like an enchanted haven, so cool and dark that the crickets were already singing even though nightfall was hours away. Ethereal black-and-yellow monarchs swooped in and out like circulating air, and a young red fox roamed on soft beds of fallen pine needles.

A babe in the woods, Jace thought, suddenly reminded of Julianna, though he didn't want to be. If he could have his way, he'd forget she existed. But he knew he wouldn't get his way. Something told him that the beautiful girl he barely knew would be like an unsettled ghost, haunting his mind more often than not.

But not right now. Right now, he had to get out of this holler, this town, maybe this state. Moving quickly, he transferred the briefcase from the Chrysler to his own maroon Auburn, a sporty two-seater with a boat-tailed body. Next, he grabbed a casual shirt and pair of pants that lay folded in the Auburn's backseat. He yanked off his mask and dropped it to the ground, then sent buttons flying as he ripped away the tailored suit and dress shirt he'd worn during the robbery and chase. He tossed the suit onto the Chrysler's hood, where one pant leg snagged around its silver hood ornament.

The last things to come off were his black nondescript driving gloves. They were the first articles he put on when dressing before a robbery, and he wore them from start to finish, making sure that no steering wheel, cuff link or button could bear the signature of his fingerprint.

Now dressed in pleated trousers and a short-sleeved silk shirt, his maskless face clean and tan, he drew attention only because of his good looks. Not a sane soul would point a finger at this man and accuse him of being on the wrong side of the law.

The train was still slogging along, and Jace knew from timing it earlier that the tracks would be clear in another five minutes. He slid behind the wheel of the Auburn and began a bumpy jaunt down the drive, turned onto the road, and sped along until he came to a fork. It formed a Y, and he sat idling in its middle.

If he went to the right, the road would take him on a curvy journey that led back to the home of Julianna. If he veered left, the road was a straight shot away from her.

Take me with you. He wondered if the offer was still good, wondered how crazy it would be to take his chances and go back for a woman his memory couldn't shake.

Trouble, he reminded himself. Trouble.

He hesitated a few more seconds then mashed the accelerator and tore to the left.

CHAPTER

FOUR

Four Saturdays after the robbery, Julianna and her secret sat at the dining table in Dreamland, eating the noon meal with her parents and Leyton.

Since the holdup, talk of it had dominated every conversation until today, when the men were starting to refocus on business as usual. Julianna and her mother, as expected, ate in silence as though such discussion was of no interest to them.

Julianna, though, tuned in to catch every word. She had been listening closely ever since that journalism class gave her a degree in social awareness, and not the kind that involved etiquette and debutante balls.

"I hear that seizing Miller's Diner was uneventful," her father said to Leyton.

"It was," Leyton confirmed. "There wasn't much the man could do to save his shop or even his salt shakers."

Julianna's mouth dropped open. She had never spoken up about the men's business dealings, but now she couldn't stop herself. The farm auction down the road had been the straw that bent the camel's back, but the diner was the one to break it. She adored the kind Mr. Miller, had eaten food prepared by his hands, and listened to the stories he was fond of telling customers who sat at his counter while he slapped lettuce and tomatoes on delectable sandwiches. "The bank took Miller's Diner? But the man is blind and his wife is ill. He told me so himself."

"When did you speak with Zeb Miller?" her father demanded.

"A couple of weeks ago when I stopped in for a sandwich." She looked from her father to Leyton and back to her father. "He also said that his brother had passed away and willed him some money, enough to pay off debts."

Leyton chuckled and dabbed the corners of his mouth with a napkin. "I believe he told the same tale to our loan officers."

"Then why did the bank seize the diner?" Julianna asked. "Mr. Miller said his brother's estate would make distributions next month."

Leyton's eyes glazed over with boredom, and he sighed heavily. "People say a lot of things to buy themselves time—you would be flabbergasted by some of the sad sack stories your father and I have been burdened with."

"You've been burdened with?" she asked sharply. "What about the people living those sad sack stories? The people you once said you wanted to help?"

Annoyance flashed across her father's face. "The bank's method of doing business is of no concern to you, Julianna."

Leyton smiled at his future in-laws, then took Julianna's hand and patted it. "Perhaps Julianna should be better informed about the bank's operations. After all, she's a grown woman now, and a caring one, too. Zeb Miller is a kind man—I understand Julianna's distress over our decision to take the diner."

Julianna burned at his patronizing tone but managed to keep her voice smooth. "I realize he was late on his note, but he could have paid it off if he'd been given another month."

Her father laughed. "Leyton, my boy, now you see why I could never put Julianna in charge of the banks." He took a sip of water. "She's softer than butter."

Leyton joined the laughter. "I'm afraid she is, sir." He winked at Julianna and gave her hand a squeeze. "But that softness is what I love about her."

She turned crimson, angry and embarrassed by the men laughing at her like she wasn't there. Virginia would never stand for this, and Julianna wished desperately that she could think of a snappy, Virginia-like comeback that would put the arrogant peacocks in their place.

Leyton turned in his seat so that he faced Julianna. "I know we appear harsh, but it's business." He bit his bottom lip and sighed sadly. "Trust me, love, on a personal level, I don't like taking things from people, and I know I told you that I had ideas that might help us avoid those measures. " He dropped his eyes as though speaking to the napkin that was neatly folded in his lap. "Unfortunately, they just couldn't be implemented. Not at this time." He looked up and moved his head slightly in the direction of her father, as if sending her a secret code that he was the reason those plans would not be put into action. Next, he leaned over to brush her cheek with a kiss and her ear with a whisper. "It wasn't my decision."

Maybe the decision was all on her father, but maybe it wasn't. Julianna just didn't know, but what she did know was that Leyton was sitting here appeasing her father while trying to pacify her. Two-faced, double-talking. So Leyton thought she was too dense to catch on. Perhaps deep down, Leyton didn't like taking things from people, but the fact that he still did it showed her that he cared more about himself than he did others; that when given a choice, he would choose what best benefitted him. After all, actions spoke louder than words.

"Excuse me," she said tightly as she pushed away from the table. "I'm going out to the gardens for a while."

"We're still on our salads," her mother protested. "You can't excuse yourself yet."

"I'm not hungry," she answered abruptly as she hurried across the room.

"Honestly, she's been so feisty lately," her mother complained to the men then laughed. "Wedding jitters. It's best just to humor a bride-to-be."

"Feisty," Julianna murmured as she left the room. Playful kittens were feisty. Little girls pulling pigtails were feisty. Julianna was far beyond that; she was furious, mainly at herself because her wedding to Leyton was now three weeks away—and she was doing nothing to change it.

She was furious, too, because the man she really loved was beyond reach. Jace . . . The irony was not lost on her that he too had stolen from others, but at least she had reason to believe he cared about his fellow humans. She knew from the radio and newspaper reports that he threw cash out the car window. She knew from him directly that the gun he carried wasn't loaded. But Leyton . . . Well, any man who would take a blind person's salt shaker and auction off a litter of piglets struck her as one who didn't have much mercy, as one who would squeeze every last thing he could out of people.

She also felt some degree of satisfaction at the poetic justice that Jace's thefts directly impacted Leyton and her father. Oh, she knew they weren't suffering in the material sense or that any money was missing from their pockets. After the crash in twenty-nine, the FDIC had been established, so bank money was now insured. Those two crowing roosters couldn't suffer the panic of a woman losing her home in the dead of winter, or the humiliation of a man watching his business be taken away, but at least they felt the bitter sting of being robbed and of being powerless to stop it.

Yes, some facet of her enjoyed what Jace had done, which was one reason why she carried his secret and always would. Legal, moral, and ethical concerns hovered about her thoughts, but she never allowed them in, never let them take away the gratifying fact that her father and Leyton deserved what they got. If the truth about Jace ever came to light, it would not be from her. The secret was in her heart, a bond she would forever share with him.

She knelt before a gardenia bush and pressed one of its snowy-white blossoms against her nose. Its sweetness was the only joy she had known today, and she was savoring it until a shadow fell across her. She looked up and saw Leyton.

"Get up," he ordered, grabbing one of her arms and jerking her up toward him. She stumbled and turned her ankle before she was fully standing.

"Leyton!" She was shocked by his forceful intrusion into her quiet moment. He had shown his less-than-gentle side before, but never had his manner been this rough.

He pinned her against the brick wall that surrounded the gardens, his hands pressing hard against her shoulders. His face leaned in close to hers as he said, "How dare you challenge me."

Her heart tightened at the tense delivery of his words and at the threat she saw in his eyes. Their normal gray had darkened to the color of slate. They flickered, like embers that could flare up into a burning rage if she wasn't careful. Two instincts collided inside her head, one telling her to fight and break free while the other said to freeze and comply. Don't scream and you won't get hurt. Wasn't that what the bad guys always said to their victims in the movies? But the deep pressure in her shoulders had to stop. The thought sparked her own anger. How dare I challenge him? How dare he assault me!

"Take your hands off of me," she demanded in the same tone he had used with her. But he only put more weight against her. She winced and cried out. She tried to move her arms but was only able to bend them at the elbows and smack weakly at his sides.

After a few seconds, he lowered his hands from her shoulders and gripped her wrists together in front of her, as though in handcuffs. "I'll let you go as soon as you understand something," he said, his voice firm. "The final decision to take the diner was mine. It was a last resort, not the first choice, and I'm very sorry it had to happen." He tightened his hands around her wrists. "But here is what you need to know, Julianna—no wife of mine is to question my judgment, especially not in the presence of her father, who happens to be my employer."

He released her then and stepped aside, giving her a clear path to walk away. And as if the encounter had not even happened, he looked at his watch and happily announced that he was due at the tailor shop to be fitted for his tuxedo. "The one I'll wear in our wedding, love, so I must be off." With a deep bow at the waist and a grand sweep of his arm, he smiled, winked, and said, "You're free to go, my lady."

Free to go, my lady? Honest to Heaven, she wanted to smack him. The scene replayed in her head. He shoved her against a wall, lectured her, and now he was bowing like a crown prince, inviting her to just glide past him and carry on with her day? Or was he mocking and dismissing her without discussion, implying that only his thoughts counted in this matter? Just minutes ago he had been threatening and confining, but now he was lighthearted and playful. His monologue switched from admonishment to attire in just a few breaths. Dr. Jekyll and Mr. Hyde, she thought, the chilling comparison stabbing her heart like an icicle.

Watching Leyton walk away, Julianna hugged herself to stop her quaking. What was it Virginia had said about his horns officially popping out? Julianna was sure they had just emerged a little more. She stayed in the garden until she heard him drive away from the mansion then hurried inside. Ignoring the slight ache from turning her ankle, and hoping she would see no one, she ran for her room. But Cassie was coming in from collecting the mail, and Julianna smacked against her, the older woman's size stopping Julianna like a tank. Bills and letters flew in all directions.

"Lord, help!" Cassie grunted. "I know I bounce when I walk, child, but I ain't made of rubber."

"Oh, Cassie, I'm so sorry!" Julianna began gathering up the mail. "I wasn't looking where I was going."

"And your head is hard as a rock," Cassie said, rubbing her chin. She looked at Julianna. "You're shakin' like a mouse cornered by a tomcat. What's wrong?"

"Leyton," Julianna said, sounding like she had just swallowed a spoonful of castor oil. "We had a fight. Well, he did. I mean, he did all the talking."

"What kind of fight?" Cassie eyed her suspiciously.

Julianna shuffled the mail into a neat stack. "Here."

"Forget the mail," Cassie said, not taking her eyes off Julianna. "That man hit you?"

"No."

Cassie touched Julianna's face then wiped a tear as it escaped from one eye. "You're scared, child," she said softly. "I can't picture you bein' scared if you and Mr. Leyton just had a spat. What is it you need to tell me?"

Julianna hugged herself and rolled her eyes toward the ceiling. "He—he pushed me against the wall, held my wrists . . ."

"Lord have mercy," Cassie whispered. "I knew that man was no good."

"You and Virginia," Julianna sniffed. "You both warned me."

"Lord have mercy," Cassie repeated, this time louder and underscored with anger. "You listen to me—if a man gets rough before you're married, he gonna follow through and get rougher after you're married, on that you can mark my words." Her chest was heaving, her coffee eyes bugging from her head. "My sweet Jesus says a man's to treat his wife like Jesus treated the church—and you didn't see Jesus roughin' up the church, no sir." She threw the stack of mail on the floor. "No sir!"

"I can't marry him, Cassie," Julianna said, voice cracking. "No matter how happy it makes Mother and Father, I just can't."

"No, and you got to tell your mama and daddy right now." She began leading Julianna down the hall. "C'mon—they's still in the dining room."

Julianna shuddered. The thought of finally breaking the long overdue news to her parents was nearly as dreadful as imagining life married to Leyton. "They won't understand," she warned Cassie. "They're blinded by his charm."

"Well, Cassie here is gonna give 'em some eyeglasses."

To her surprise, Julianna felt a sudden surge of hope. This was about more than her lack of love for Leyton now. Her parents might try to convince her otherwise, assuring her that she was merely suffering from pre-wedding jitters and cold feet. No, this was about him threatening her and actually assaulting her right outside in their own garden. It was a sign of character that was not up to par, a preview of what was to come once the wedding certificate was signed and sealed. This carried things to a different level, and surely . . . surely her parents would not stand for it nor expect her to. "All right," she said to Cassie. "You're right—they must know."

Cassie linked her ample arm through Julianna's, and they entered the dining room, where her father was reading the newspaper and her mother was nibbling at a second helping of pecan pie.

Cassie didn't wait to be acknowledged, but instead drove straight to the point. "Mr. Richard, Miss Audrey, I been with this family thirty years now. You both know I've always been one to say what's on my mind."

Julianna's father—well aware that Cassie was a straight shooter—still gave her a stern look, his eyebrows tensing into a straight line. "What is this about?"

"That man—Mr. Leyton—he's no good, no good at all, sir."

Julianna cringed at Cassie's boldness, dreading the reaction it was certain to raise from her father.

He was on his feet immediately. He smacked the table so hard that the crystal goblets wobbled and the silver utensils clanked against the plates. "And what, Miss Spraggs, gives you the right to raise any questions about my future son-in-law? I won't hear such talk from you."

"You got to hear me, Mr. Richard. Please." Cassie stood with her shoulders back, her eyes looking squarely into those of her employer. "That man's got the devil's grin, and it chills my bones, Mr. Richard, always has. But today he and Miss Julianna fought in the gardens."

As Cassie squeezed her to her side, Julianna became keenly aware of the cliff her dear friend was about to dive off of. Maybe she had been mistaken about her parents, especially father, siding with her. Whether it was his blind eye to Leyton or Cassie's brusque approach, Julianna sensed he was not going to take this well. There would be no turning back for Cassie once the words were out. They were all Father would connect her to from this point on, which might even affect her being able to keep working for them. Julianna had never known life without Cassie, and the idea of her being fired over this was so horrifying that it overpowered her fear and sent adrenaline surging through her. Julianna knew she should have addressed this with her parents long ago, but she had lacked the courage and now it had come to this. No, she would not allow Cassie to deliberately stand in front of a freight train just to save her.

Julianna broke away from Cassie's grip, stepped forward, and faced her father, ready to deliver news that she feared might raise the roof off of Dreamland. Giving herself no time to reconsider jumping off the tracks, she opened her mouth and let the facts rush out. "Father, don't be angry with Cassie. She's only reacting to something I told her. It's…it's because she loves me. You'll understand when I tell you." She took a quick but deep breath and continued. "Leyton . . . he . . . pinned me to the wall, held my shoulders, my wrists . . . and made me turn my ankle."

Julianna's mother let out a small scream. She jumped from her seat and hurried to Julianna. "Darling, is this really true?"

Julianna nodded, and her mother, looking bewildered, turned to Julianna's father. "Richard, she says it's true."

Amusement played on his face as he focused intently on Julianna. "He made you turn your ankle? How did he make you turn your ankle?"

She almost wilted beneath his stare. His expression seemed to say, Now, this I've got to hear. She knew she had some work to do if she was going to convince him that this wasn't an exaggerated fish tale or some other embellished story he might hear at the men's club.

"The ankle isn't the main thing," she told him, trying to redirect his attention. "I turned it because he yanked me off the ground."

"What were you doing on the ground?" her mother asked.

Rolling around and ruining my dress, Julianna wanted to say, frustrated by the interruption. It was hard enough to stand here and speak without questions that delayed her getting to the most important facts. Nor did she know how much nerve she had before it would run out. She didn't need distractions taking up valuable time.

"Smelling some flowers," she answered quickly and irritably before giving her full attention back to her father. "My ankle rolled when Leyton yanked me up. It . . . happened . . . but him yanking me, pinning my shoulders, and then holding down my wrists didn't just happen. Those were deliberate."

Her father walked to a window that overlooked the gardens. Hands behind his back, he stared outside for a minute then asked, "When Leyton did these deliberate things, what was the nature of your conversation?"

She closed her eyes in dismay. "Do you think I provoked him?" she said quietly. "Is that what you're asking?"

Now exasperated, her father turned from the window and waved his arms. "No, I'm just saying that I don't know what kind of fight this was! You say he jerked you off the ground, but he might say he was helping you up and accidentally pulled too hard. You say he restrained you, but he might say it was to keep you from flailing or running away. I don't know, Julianna, because I wasn't there." He lowered his arms as well as his voice. "He didn't actually strike you, did he, Julianna?"

She gaped at her father, feeling like she was being cross-examined by Leyton's personal attorney, who was doing his best to put doubt into the minds of a jury and have all charges against his client dropped. She wasn't surprised, not really, considering her father's fondness of Leyton. But still, a piece of her heart ripped and her throat ached with tears. To her father's question, she could only shake her head.

"There now, everything is fine," her father said, calmer, crossing the room and patting her shoulder. "As long as he didn't hit you, then this is probably nothing more than him not realizing his own strength. I'm sure that after today he knows he'll need to be gentler around you. He isn't the first man who would need to learn that in regard to the weaker sex."

Julianna couldn't look at him, so shattered were her feelings. She looked at her mother instead, seeing that she was struggling with what to make of the situation. Her face was a puzzle, and Julianna knew that it was hard for her to see beyond the safeness of her own world, hard for her to grasp anything if she couldn't imagine it happening to herself. She looked to her husband for guidance. "Are you sure, Richard? Yanking, grabbing—well, it sounds barbaric."

"Barbaric?" Julianna's father scoffed. "A bit dramatic, don't you think, dear?" Now he patted his wife's shoulder. "It's nearly one o'clock—don't you and Julianna have a meeting with the caterers?"

"No!" Julianna suddenly screamed, the outburst taking her by surprise as much as it did the others. She felt hot inside and out, as though blazing with fever, and her frame tensed from head to toe.

"Julianna!" her father snapped. "What on earth—"

"I'm not marrying Leyton!" she shouted. "Even if he held my wrists so he could drape them in diamond bracelets, I wouldn't want to marry him!"

Now it was her father's turn to gape at her. Her mother followed suit as Julianna's announcement seemed to echo throughout the bottom floor of the mansion. When it faded, Julianna looked at them pleadingly and said, "I ha, hate him."

There was a minute of awkward silence then her father laughed. "Does this remind you of anything, Audrey?" He looked at his wife with a knowing expression. "Didn't you say you hated me, too, that you couldn't stand the thought of marrying me? And wasn't that right before our wedding?"

"Well, yes," Julianna's mother answered hesitantly. "But you weren't threatening me, and I don't recall shouting it—"

"It was nothing but pre-wedding strain," Julianna's father said. He lifted Julianna's chin. "And that's all it is for you. Believe me, in an hour this tirade will seem silly." He retrieved his paper from the table and started from the room.

Julianna had never stood up to her father, but she couldn't let him leave on such a flippant note. She took a deep breath to gather strength then said, "I meant every word, Father. I don't want to marry Leyton."

He went rigid in the doorway, his back to her. "Leyton is a good man," he said, his tone thick with impatience. "He'll make you a good husband, and that's the end of this conversation." He left then, his footsteps fast and loud as he walked away.

Julianna's hands slapped to her sides and she looked helplessly at Cassie.

Julianna's mother took her hand. "Darling, I don't know what to say."

"Don't say," Cassie advised. "Listen." She thumped her chest with her fist. "Listen to Julianna, 'cause her heart knows the truth and your head needs to hear it."

"This is just so sudden," Julianna's mother whined. "It upsets everything—Leyton and Richard are so close, and Leyton has been so helpful at the bank."

Julianna jerked her hand free from her mother's and folded her arms across her chest. "No, Mother, I refuse to think that Leyton saved our banks from collapsing. That's what you believe, but Father is perfectly capable of running our banks. Besides, times aren't as hard as they used to be. People trust the banks again."

"I know that," her mother snapped, miffed. "I listen to President Roosevelt's Fireside Chats." She brightened as quickly as she had darkened. "Leyton so seems to adore you."

"Oh, yes'm," Cassie broke in. "Reckon that's why he pinned her 'gainst the wall out there?"

Julianna's mother glanced anxiously between Julianna and Cassie. "Do you honestly think he's a wolf in sheep's clothing?"

"Yes," Julianna and Cassie answered in unison, but Cassie went further. "Little by little, a sheep peels away its layers." She shivered. "Wickedness, Miss Audrey—it's like a pot on the stove. Can simmer a long time, then one day, it just blows to kingdom come."

The analogy was lost on Julianna's mother. "The wedding invitations are set to be mailed on Monday," she fretted, flecks of panic dancing in her eyes. "Maybe, Julianna, if you talk to Leyton

about what you don't like—if your father and I talk to him—maybe
he'll change."

Now Cassie snorted. "That man won't change nothin' but his
underwear."

Julianna stifled a laugh, but her mother was too preoccupied to
hear any humor. She spoke slowly and carefully, her face a mask of
worry, "And then there's the other thing, Julianna."

Julianna sighed. "Mother . . ."

"Well, Leyton accepts your . . . delicate condition," her mother
said, voiced hushed, eyes heavy with pity.

Julianna sighed again. It was true. The memory played through
her mind, and she rested her head in her hands, rubbing her temples.
It had happened four years ago at the Thanksgiving parade. She had
accidentally scared a policeman's horse. The animal had knocked her
down, then reared its hooves again and again, striking her abdomen
each time it landed. A heroic onlooker had pulled her to safety, but
only after the damage was done. She had sustained massive injuries
to her female organs—repairable, but leaving her with heavy scar
tissue and cycles as erratic and unpredictable as springtime weather.
Children, the doctors agreed, just weren't likely.

Julianna shook her head fiercely. Did her mother honestly think
Leyton's acceptance of this was enough to warrant her marrying
him? Would every other man on the planet consider her damaged
goods? "I can't believe a man wouldn't marry me because—not if he
really loved me. Couples adopt children all the time."

"You're right," her mother whispered, head dropping. "I'm
despicable to have implied otherwise." She was quiet a minute,
seeming to melt in shame. "I'm still reeling from your news, that's
all." She looked up hopefully. "Don't you think your father might be
right? This is all pre-wedding strain?"

"No. Father is wrong."

Her mother wasn't ready to give up. "Let's go meet with the caterer anyway. We'll see how you feel—"

"I'm not going to the caterers," Julianna said firmly. "I don't want you to go either." She started to leave the room.

Her mother reached after her. "Please, Julianna."

Julianna didn't answer. She left the dining room and fled upstairs to her room, where she fell on the bed and hugged a pillow to her chest. Pictures of Rafaela angels smiled from the walls; she stared at them, thinking of nothing, thinking of everything.

Ten minutes passed and she heard a car start in the driveway. She scrambled from the bed and ran onto the small balcony off her room. Her mother's car pulled away, traveling through the arch of oaks and magnolias then turning toward town.

Julianna's shoulders sagged as she walked back into her room. Her mother, her last hope, had just left for the caterers to discuss cakes and entrees and champagne for the biggest wedding of the year.

Later that day, Julianna took a large bouquet of yellow daffodils to the Colby Street Mission. Freshly cut from the Dreamland gardens, they added a spot of brightness to the gray-white walls, scuffed floors, and heavy air of hard-luck tales.

The mission wasn't much to look at. A large house, once grand, it had been donated to the town for charitable purposes. The neglect of hard times showed, though, and the house had weakened to a rickety structure, its tin roof weighted with rust and its wobbly porch rail just barely hanging on.

Julianna was working the soup line, ladling out tomato soup to men stripped of their pride, women who were younger than they looked, and eager-eyed children who hungrily thrust their bowls toward her.

"Thanks for coming in, Julianna."

"No thanks necessary," Julianna said to Lilly Armstrong, who ran the mission with her husband, Micah. Both in their mid-fifties, the couple were former missionaries and dependent on donations and helping hands to keep the mission operating. Julianna had first learned about the mission from her journalism professor, who had encouraged his students to volunteer. After seeing how many were suffering in her own town and wondering if any of them had once been customers of her family's bank, Julianna was eager to get involved. Anything she could do to make their lives a little better, anything she could do to ease the suffering her family, or other families like hers, might have caused some of these souls.

Julianna really liked spending time with Lilly, too. She came from a wealthy background but had abandoned it when she met Micah and felt called to join him in the mission field. Full of stories against the backdrops of Africa, India, and South America, of humanitarian journeys that brought her more blessings than money could ever buy, Lilly was one of the most interesting and inspiring women Julianna had ever met. Her dedication and joy showed Julianna there was more than one way to be rich in this life. Julianna got a taste of it every time she served at the mission. It was one of the few places she felt she made a positive difference in someone's day. She learned that even a small act of kindness could inject hope into another's heart, and she felt like her time was well spent and that she had done something that actually mattered.

Julianna fed the last hungry mouth then untied her faded green apron and tucked a few wayward strands of hair back into the loose pile atop her head. She was wearing a plain, sky-blue cotton shirtwaist dress. She always dressed down when she came to the mission, careful not to show any hint of her wealth in front of people who slept on cots, people her father and Leyton might have put in this place to begin with.

"Sad, isn't it?" Lilly asked, looking about the room.

Julianna followed her eyes, seeing both the young and the old, those who traveled as a family and those who walked alone, people who were once comfortable and people who had never known an easy day. "You really run the gamut here," she said, knowing this would be the last time she saw any of them. The shelter was closing in a few days because donations had dried up. She knew Lily had been working very hard to find the residents temporary housing at other shelters, but from what she said, it was no easy task and some would return to the streets.

"I just wish I had a few more weeks to get them all squared away," Lily said. "Then I could close the doors and not lose sleep."

"I guess I'll start washing dishes," Julianna said, feeling terrible about Lilly's situation.

"You should head home," Lilly suggested, nodding toward a window. "It'll soon be dark, and the sky looks like it's going to open up and pour."

"I don't mind staying a while longer," Julianna said. She was in no rush to get home where her parents and Leyton were expecting her later for a game of pinochle while the Wonder Soap Playhouse aired on the radio. She glanced at her wrist, saw it was bare and remembered that she didn't wear her expensive watch to the shelter. It was a fact she was fully aware of, but what was it about Leyton and her parents that always made her automatically check the time? The very thought of them seemed to be a reminder that she always had an appointed place to be at an appointed time. Worse, she knew tonight would be tense, as everyone ignored the day's events and tried to carry on as if the pink elephant wasn't hunched in the corner. They would talk about the bank, the country club, society gossip, the wedding.

The wedding, Julianna thought as she tossed some dirty spoons into the sink, and was startled by how loudly they clattered. She realized then that she had actually thrown them, an action that went along with the way she was suddenly gritting her teeth. She knew the wedding was still on. The revelation to her parents had not altered anything, and she would be forced to sit and listen to her mother recount every detail of her visit with the caterer. Her father and Leyton would pat each other on the back and say they were now only weeks away from becoming family. Cassie would quietly slip in and out to refill drinks and replace snacks, her warm hand sympathetically squeezing Julianna's shoulder when she passed by.

Julianna turned on the sink faucet and waited for the water to get hot. Holding her hands under the stream, she found its steady flow and growing warmth to be calming, but not enough to wash away her dread of the night ahead. Instead of facing what awaited, she wanted to crawl onto a pallet here in the mission, where she could listen to Lilly read a story to the children. She could just close her eyes and drift off to sleep as Micah played slow tunes on his harmonica. Dreamland, with all its opulence, seemed like a penitentiary compared to the mission with only its bare necessities. Here, she wasn't Julianna Sheffield. She was just Julianna, the nice young lady who came in to help.

How freeing it was to be disconnected from the suffocating rules and expectations of higher society. How much more it made her think and ponder when she was outside of that realm, where she had lived untouched and unaware for so many years. It had made her one-dimensional when it came to her knowledge of how many different kinds of people wove together the tapestry of the world. It had suppressed her compassion from reaching the depths it was capable of reaching, because she hadn't known the need for it was there. Now she did, though. Now she felt like there could be more to Julianna Sheffield than the same high tea road her mother had taken, and her mother before her. Oh, her mother would call her a black sheep, but at least she wouldn't be a blind sheep. If only she knew how to break the cycle, she would. But how? She feared she was destined to remain trapped within the circle of her birth, stuck riding round and round and round on the carousel with Leyton.

"Don't forget that you're not parked out back today," Lilly said, breaking into her thoughts.

"Yes, Mommy," Julianna teased. As always, she had driven the servants' old Model A instead of her own newer, nicer vehicle. Others might resent her, and who could blame them for it if she showed up at the mission in her expensive clothes behind the wheel of her expensive car? Tonight she'd had to park the car a block away because of a fallen tree blocking the entrance to Colby Street.

As Lilly predicted, the rain came hard, pelting the roof so hard Julianna feared it might cave in. There would be no leaving right now, so she huddled in the kitchen with a couple of other volunteers, cringing every time lightening sizzled close by or thunder seemed to rock the foundation. The basement flooded, sending Micah and other able-bodied men clamoring downstairs with bailing buckets. If it hadn't been for the extra work it meant for the men, and the fear it put into the faces of some of the residents, Julianna would have prayed for the storm to last until well after the pinochle game had ended.

As it turned out, the storm moved on within an hour, and even though night had settled by the time Lilly walked Julianna onto the front porch, it hadn't grown too late for her to miss the entire plans awaiting her at home. "You shouldn't venture out by yourself," Lily said. "I'll have Micah walk you."

"Micah's still bailing water," Julianna said with a casual flip of the hand. "I'll be fine."

"I suppose," Lilly said, not sounding convinced. "And Julianna, thank you."

"Oh, I don't mind coming in."

"No, thank you for the gift."

Julianna turned on her way down the steps. "What gift?"

Lilly smiled at what she thought was modesty. "I was waiting for us to have a minute alone before saying anything. Honestly, I'm not sure you even want me to say anything, but Micah ran out to his truck to get another bucket and saw the flag on the mailbox was up. I guess you slipped out and back in before the storm hit, but he found the envelope. Honestly, I wasn't trying to squeeze money out of you when I talked about closing."

"Lilly, what are you talking about?" Julianna asked, truly perplexed, as a raindrop splashed on her cheek. Lightning flashed on the horizon, and the rumble of distant thunder sent tremors across the sky. "Well, whatever it is, you're welcome. I'm going before it starts raining again."

Lilly waved her on and Julianna hurried down the sidewalk. Darkness enveloped the street, and she prayed for protection as she rounded the corner. She had the unsettling sensation that she wasn't alone. Fear knotted her stomach and she sped her steps. She sighed with relief when she saw the Model A, believing she would soon be safely locked inside it.

Her relief was short-lived. A jolt of petrifying fear shot through her as a drunkard stumbled from a door stoop and swayed before her. Julianna screamed, hand flying to her heart, but she quickly reined back her senses, realizing that the dizzy-eyed man was too sloppy to harm her.

She tried to step around him, but he blocked her way, his grungy, unshaven face peering into hers. He smiled, showing a space between every tooth in his head.

"Wellllll," he slurred. "Hey there, honey pot. You're a pretty one. Gimme a kissie?" He closed his eyes and puckered his lips. Despite the unsafe surroundings, this inebriated fellow was so comical and cartoonish that she had to stifle a laugh.

She tried again to step around him. He grabbed her arm, but she yanked it away, her swift movement causing him to lose his balance and topple against a trash can.

Now another man appeared, this one from an ally just ahead and off to Julianna's right. There wasn't anything humorous about him as he came closer, looking like a menacing villain from a movie as he emerged through the steam of humidity rising from the sidewalk. Julianna wasn't sure if he was sober or not, but she could definitely see that he was a stocky, smirking thug, his oily face dotted with blemishes, his chin marked with a jagged scar. When he stood before her, he looked her up and down and wet his lips. "Look what the storm washed in," he said, touching her hair. "A live dame."

She recoiled from his touch and stepped backward into the drunk, who had picked himself up from the ground and the garbage. He yelped as Julianna's heel spiked his instep but still tried to stake his claim. "She's with me," he said with a belch.

"Says who?" The thug asked as he reached again for Julianna's hair. She smacked away his hand, so filthy it's knuckles and palm lines appeared to be encrusted with tar.

"Like it rough?" He hissed. "Well, there ain't no broad I can't tame." He grabbed her shoulders and tried to kiss her, but she whipped her face in the opposite direction, feeling only the abrasive stubble of his beard growth.

Then, like music from a dream, Julianna heard another voice. A rich voice of authority that said, "The lady is with me."

The words were followed by the ominous click of a gun.

The thug and drunkard scurried away as Julianna turned to see her rescuer. At first he was just a tall shadow with a strong presence, but then he stepped closer.

A smile spread across her face. "Good evening, Mr. McAllister."

He stared at her for a long minute then gave her two options.

"You can marry the other guy," he said. "Or you can come with me."

CHAPTER
FIVE

He was waiting for an answer.

Julianna clutched her key ring with trembling fingers. She gave him her decision by fumbling with the fastener on her purse, finally getting it open and dropping the keys inside.

"Good," he said quietly as they fell into step along the sidewalk. It began to rain again, but this time it was only a shower. Warm and sweet, as though readying the earth for something new to grow. "I see you aren't wearing your watch tonight."

"No, no I'm not," she said, a smile of realization rising on her face. She wouldn't need it because she had nowhere else she needed to be. "How long have you been following me?" she asked, shivering from the disbelief of this night. She sounded cold, as if it was January instead of July.

"Since you left your house this afternoon," he said. They reached the Auburn, and he opened the door on the passenger's side. Before Julianna slipped inside, he placed a hand on her arm and searched her eyes for doubt. "Once you get in this car, life will never be the same."

"I'm counting on that," she said, taking her place in the passenger's seat. Her legs shook, not from fear, but from the enormity of seeing a dream come to pass. This dream that had felt so impossible only moments before.

He began driving them through the city, the lampposts setting the wet streets aglow. The rain was gentle, the windshield wipers soothing. Julianna felt herself start to relax.

"Julianna?"

She knew what he was going to ask before the words came out.

"Why didn't you turn me in?"

She looked at her hands in her lap. In her imagination, answering this question had been so easy. Now, in the flesh, she could not control his reactions.

"Some people might think it's for revenge on my father and fiancé," she said. "I hate the way they run our banks."

"That's what some people might think," he agreed. "But what do you think?"

A passing car came dangerously close, and Jace swerved to miss being hit. It was over in a split second and they were riding safely again.

We could be killed in two seconds and he'd never know how I really feel about him, Julianna thought, and it struck her as sad. Now was not the time to inch around the heart of the matter. And why bother with careful answers? Hadn't she already thrown caution to the wind? Already crossed the line of no return?

She shifted so that her back was against the door and she could see his profile. "I didn't turn you in because—because I've been in love with you since the minute I saw you."

He was quiet, and it stripped her naked. Never had she felt so vulnerable, and it was evident in her voice. "I'm hoping you came back because you have the same feelings for me."

Jace sat still for a moment. Then he seemed to decide something. He looked over at Julianna, his heart in his eyes. "I tried to avoid any feelings I had for you, Julianna, and I'm still struggling to accept them."

"Because you robbed my family's banks."

"Reason enough, isn't it?" He asked. "And I don't get how you can trust me, knowing what you know."

He had slowed the car and was watching her more than he was watching the road. She turned and stared out the windshield, knowing she had to find a way to explain what would seem crazy to most people.

She saw how Jace gripped the steering wheel, and though she hated to keep him in suspense, she was truly struggling to find the right words.

Finally, she looked away from the world outside the car and turned her eyes back to him. "I really don't know how to explain it except that—" She paused and smiled gently. "The heart has reasons that reason cannot know."

He nodded and loosened his grip on the steering wheel. "Shakespeare?"

"Pascal."

He nodded again, whispering the quote to himself. He seemed to agree that it justified nothing yet explained everything. "I think that's the best answer you could have given me."

"Maybe it will even help explain why you robbed our banks," she said, still smiling. "I know you didn't pick our banks because you liked our customer service." Now the smile vanished. "The robberies were personal, Jace, and I can only imagine why. Our banks have abused their power and hurt a lot of people."

"I'll tell you everything," he promised, "but do you trust me enough to wait?"

She hesitated, hating the idea of waiting for anything more with Jace. She felt like she had been waiting since the night she first saw him. Yet, what was she to do? Get out of the car and tell him the plans—whatever those were—had to be called off? Relenting, she said, "I can wait, but just answer one thing. Are you planning to rob them again?"

"There aren't any left to rob," he said.

Julianna laughed. She was relieved, too, thinking the conversation had gotten too tense. But Jace, his hands choking the steering wheel again, didn't seem to share her feelings.

"Didn't you hear me, Julianna? I robbed all of your family's banks." He ran a hand through his hair. "I've got no right to want you, no right to barge into your life like this. You should have handed me over to the cops, and it amazes me that you didn't. I've been laying low in small town motels, wondering if my name and description were going to end up in the papers and on the radio."

"They weren't, though," she reminded him. "My silence should have spoken volumes."

He whipped the car off the road and killed its engine. He pulled her across the seat and gathered her into his arms, their faces only inches apart. "It did, Julianna—so I came back for the same reason you didn't turn me in."

Julianna felt a delicious blend of joy and relief surge through her veins. "I'm glad we agree on that," she whispered.

"We have to," he said. "Whatever journey we're starting—and I'm not sure what that is—it would be impossible to finish if we don't agree on that."

She shook her head, amazed. "We really know so little about each other, yet . . . we know we need to be together. Is this how love at first sight works? Two people just know, so their beginning is really the middle?"

"I guess," Jace said, leaning his head against the seat and pulling hers to his chest. "I guess. Does that scare you?"

"A little," she admitted. "But it doesn't scare me nearly as much as the thought of us not being together."

"Yeah, I know," he said. "That had something to do with me coming back. I figured I could spend my life loving a woman I don't really know, or getting to know a woman I already love." He fell silent for a second, then laughed. "I'm not sure if that even made sense."

"I don't know if it did either, but I completely understand what you mean," she said then laughed with him.

They listened to the rain for a few minutes, now a strong and steady downpour. Julianna knew she wasn't getting out of this car. She'd be washed away, and not just by the pounding rain. To leave the man in this car would be to go back to the man waiting for her at Dreamland, where she would lose herself and any chance to see how this love with Jace would finally come to make sense. Because he was here and holding her, she trusted he wasn't leaving this car either. Whatever there was still to know, they were both ready to begin finding out. And for right now, she decided that was enough. It must be enough because it was all they had, and wherever they were going from here, they were going together.

"Julianna?"

She lifted her head and looked up at him.

"You know so little about me," he said, "but you still know more about me than anyone else in the world."

He kissed her then, with more intensity than before. Her breath caught, and she tossed back her head as his lips slowly explored the tender plane of her neck while his hands released her hair from the pile atop her head. The waves tumbled to her shoulders, and he tangled his hands among the cascade.

"Jace . . ." His name came from deep within her, and she was surprised by the sensual tone of her own voice.

His lips returned to hers, and he pressed her as close to him as the small confines of the car would allow. A golden warmth spread through her as her own lips matched the passion of his. She closed her eyes, wishing only to languish in the kiss, serenaded by raindrops pattering against the windshield.

Suddenly her heart began to thud against her chest, bullying her, reminding her how unschooled she was in the ways of love. Afterall, her mother had drilled into her that nice girls waited until their wedding nights, that no man wanted a bride he couldn't teach. Julianna knew girls who allowed a fiancé more liberties, but Leyton's interest had never gone beyond a simple kiss, so she really knew nothing of intimacy with a man. She struggled to hold the kiss now between her and Jace as her mind fretted over the journey he spoke of, a journey that included the feelings of passion that were so new to her, their intensity scaring her almost to death.

He pulled away and laid his head on her chest. "What?"

"I'm sorry," she whispered, flustered. "I want to continue, I do, it's just . . ."

He lifted his head and smiled into her eyes. "You bring out all the man in me, Julianna, but you don't have to be afraid of that."

She placed her hands on the sides of his face then ran them back through his hair. "I must seem so young, so prudish."

"Neither," he said, shaking his head. He sat up and started the car. "Until something is right for both of us, it's not right at all. You set the pace."

"When will it—whatever it is—be right for us?" She wanted his honest thoughts, but she also knew she was testing him, trying to find out how far into the future he was looking.

"I don't know," he said as they pulled back onto the road. "I can't even guess what will happen tomorrow. The only thing for certain is that I'm driving away with you tonight—and for some reason, that feels right."

They traveled in silence for a few minutes then Jace said, "We're almost out of the city limits. Do you need to call anyone?"

"My parents," she answered, wishing she could cut off her arms instead. She knew, though, that the Model A would be discovered empty in a bad part of town. Everyone would fear the worst, and Julianna didn't want to burden them with that. She also didn't want them launching an all-out manhunt to track her down.

Jace stopped the Auburn at a phone booth outside of a gas station that was closed for the night. He walked her to the booth and waited outside while she made the dreaded call.

"Ju-lee-anna!" her mother cried into the phone. "Where are you? It's after ten—your father, Leyton, and I are doubled over with concern."

"Mother, I have to tell—"

"Get home this instant, darling! It's neither safe nor proper for you to be roaming about this time of night."

This was it. For twenty-two years, she had lived to please them. Until this past year, she didn't think she minded doing that. It was what she knew and what she did, but their satisfaction now required something she just couldn't give. The fact that she didn't want to marry Leyton was all the reason they should have needed to tell her it was okay. But it hadn't been enough. They'd proved it that afternoon, when even his threats and aggression were not enough to let her call it off. She had always believed that they had her best interest in mind—but what did their pitiful response to the garden assault have to say about that? Today was the straw that broke the camel's back. Tonight she would walk away.

Julianna took a deep breath then let the news out. "I'm not coming home." A second later, she knew she had released more than the words. She had also released the anchor that had been weighing her down for . . . how long? She didn't really know. It had been unseen, but definitely not unfelt. She just didn't know how heavy it was until it was gone, and she suddenly sensed the freedom she had only imagined bursting through the surface.

There was a pause of stunned silence. Julianna pictured her

mother cradling the phone close to her lips and turning her back to the men. When she spoke, her voice was low and hushed. "Darling, I know you're upset about quarrelling with Leyton, but he confessed everything to your father and me—begged our forgiveness. He's also brought you a gift in a bitty box." She giggled. "Bitty boxes behold big baubles."

Julianna didn't respond to her mother's tongue twister. "It was more than a quarrel," she insisted. "But it doesn't matter—it's not the only reason why I'm leaving."

"Leaving?" her mother gasped, then giggled again, only this time nervously. "You sound so . . . so permanent."

Suddenly, her father was on the phone, barking so loudly that Julianna had to hold the receiver away from her ear.

"What kind of nonsense are you saying?"

Despite her new sense of freedom, her father's voice made her chest tight with anxiety. As it tried to chip away at her nerve, she had to gather all of her concentration to keep her voice from quivering. "I told Mother I'm not coming home," she said. "I'm . . . leaving. Leaving town, tonight."

"Ah, so you're just up and leaving," he mocked. "And just where are you up and leaving to?"

She said nothing. The real fact was that she didn't know where she was leaving to.

"Don't sit there like a mute!" he ordered. "Where are you? The bus station?"

"I have a ride," she said.

"Well, that's splendid," he told her. "What are you planning to do? See the world in that pitiful jalopy the servants call a car?"

"No, the Model A is parked on Patterson Avenue, near the Colby Street Mission. Someone needs to pick it up."

"Oh, so you are at the bus station," he assumed incorrectly. "Well, fine—go ahead and get on the bus. Go to the coast, the mountains—

wherever you need to go to get this ridiculous bout of cold feet out of your system. But when you come dragging home in a few days, don't expect a party."

She took a shuddering breath. "Good-bye, Father."

As she was about to replace the receiver, he screamed, "Good-bye? Don't you even want to speak to your fiancé?"

She answered with a click, followed by a dial tone.

Before leaving the phone booth, she made a call to Virginia's house, knowing her vivacious, in-demand friend wouldn't be lounging at home on a Saturday night. She spoke with one of the family's maids.

"Emmie, please tell Virginia that I've gone away but not to worry. I'm happy, I love her, and I'll be in touch." Before disconnecting the line, she added, "Oh, and please have her give this message to Cassie. I'm not sure if she'll hear it right from Mother."

That done, she stepped out of the phone booth and smiled up at Jace. "I'm ready."

"You're sure?"

"I'm sure." She glanced back at the distant lights of the town they were about to drive away from, the town of her parents, of Leyton, of Dreamland, and of the only life she had ever known. To everything there is a season. A time to plant and a time to uproot. "Oh yes, I'm sure."

They returned to the car and then to the road. It seemed to stretch forever, especially through the hills and valleys of the countryside. The rain had moved on, and the nighttime air was sweet and heavy with the scents of a world refreshed. The wind rushed through the car windows, bringing with it a mixture of honeysuckle and jasmine, spearmint and clover, as Julianna's hair whipped about her face in a tangled, wayward, and wonderfully free mess.

"Where are we going?" she called to Jace.

"Home," he answered.

❯❯ ❮❮

The home Jace spoke of was six hours away, by the ocean in a bungalow overlooking dunes, sea oats, and the olive-green Atlantic.

The house was a shell-colored stucco with a black shingled roof. River rock pillars supported the overhang of the front porch, a sand-dusted retreat offering a stunning view of the Ambrose Point lighthouse, which towered nearly two hundred feet above waves crashing against the bluff of the point.

The lighthouse was a spectacular sight along the southern shore, a cone-shaped structure built from cast iron and painted in red-and-white spiral. Its beam cut sharply through the night, reminding captains that the shoals could deal fatal blows to the hulls of passing ships.

It was long after midnight when Jace drove into Ambrose Point, casting quick smiles at the sleepy girl beside him, watching her lose the battle to hold her eyes open. He turned off the road that snaked between the coast and a forest of pines and oaks, parked the car behind the house, and lightly tapped Julianna on the shoulder.

"Hey . . ."

She stirred and murmured, "What time is it?"

"Some call it the middle of the night, some call it the wee hours of the morning," he said. He got out of the car and went around to her side, opened the door, and helped her stand.

Soft mounds of beach and grass were a mat to her feet, but as she trudged wearily toward a back porch, the sand seemed to take on the weight of lead. Jace steered her across the porch and inside the house, where all she noted in the dark hour was the hollow slam of the screen door as it shut behind them.

"You'll sleep in here," he said, guiding her into a pale-blue bedroom. "It's not the royal chambers, but it's com—" He stopped as

Julianna collapsed onto the simple oak bed and curled into the fluffy folds of its feather mattress.

She didn't budge until noon, awakening to Jace's hands massaging her shoulders. She rolled onto her back and brushed the hair from her eyes. "Hi."

"Hi yourself." He smiled down at her. "You like root beer and Mr. Goodbar?"

"Love them."

"Today's special." He stood and extended his hand. She took it and let him pull her to her feet, looking pleased here in these new surroundings.

"Where's the—"

"Across the hall," he said, pointing toward the green-and-white tiled bathroom.

She joined him in the kitchen where, as promised, soda and candy awaited.

"I've got other things," he said, nodding toward the icebox.

"No, I'll have what you're having." She unwrapped a candy bar and broke off a piece.

As the chocolate melted in her mouth, she looked around the small kitchen, admiring its oak cabinetry. A breakfast room was adjacent, with a window that opened to the beach.

Looking at a couple of market bags on the table, she asked, "You've already been out?"

"While you were sleeping." He reached into one of the bags and pulled out a toothbrush and a bar of scented soap. Handing them to her, he said, "I don't know what you like, but this beats what you had when you got here, which was nothing."

Julianna picked up the soap, holding it to her nose. "Thank you," she said as she sniffed the soap. "Violet—my favorite."

She set it on the table, then glanced down at her rumpled, slept-in dress. She would need some new things and mentally added the bills and change in her purse. Not enough for too much, but maybe a sunsuit, some culottes . . .

After eating, Julianna returned to the bathroom to wash up. Face scrubbed and teeth and hair vigorously brushed, she felt more presentable, despite her dress. She walked into the front room, liking its hardwood floors, built-in bookcases, and river rock fireplace. The décor, though, brought a smile to her face.

"Jace, did the checked sofa come with the striped chair, or do you just appreciate contrast?" she teased, walking among the room's overstuffed furniture.

"I appreciate comfort." He was on the front porch, calling through the screen door.

"I can respect comfort," she said, thinking of Dreamland's fussy Victorian chairs. She picked up a coaster on an end table, her eyes widening when she saw it was from a promotional set given by the bank last year. Their green-and-gold logo was emblazoned on the front.

"Jace," she called, waving the coasters at him. "Did you steal our coasters, too?" She walked to the door and looked out, seeing that he was sitting on the steps, his bare feet resting in the sand, his dark hair tousled by the wind off the water.

"Steal them? The sign in the bank said 'free'." He smiled over his shoulder, and her heart skipped a beat. He was a beautiful man, and even more so here, surrounded by the sand and sea.

"May I look at your 78s?"

"Help yourself," he said as he stood up. A few seconds later, he was inside and joined her at the phonograph in the corner of the front room, a stack of 78 RPM records next to it. Kneeling, she flipped through the records while he leaned against a nearby chair and watched her. Louis Armstrong and His Orchestra, Jelly Roll Morton's Red Hot Peppers, Jimmy Durante's Jazz Band . . .

"I'm glad to see we like the same bands," she noted when she had gone through the stack.

"Does that mean you'll stay?" He sounded serious, but his eyes twinkled with humor as he extended a hand to help her stand.

"It would make it very hard to leave," she teased back.

Holding her hand, he began leading her through the living room and towards the hallway. "You've pretty much seen the house, except for my room. That's where you'll learn the most about me."

A warm blush flooded her cheeks, causing him to laugh. "Not like that, Julianna. Well, I hope like that, but not right this minute. I really just want to show you my collection of movie tickets."

"Oh," was all she could say, blushing even more.

The walls in his room were painted off-white, a simple backdrop for his pine furniture. There was a bed, two nightstands, a valet and dresser, where movie ticket stubs were tucked in the frame of its attached mirror. Animal Crackers, Horse Feathers, and Duck Soup, all starring the Marx Brothers.

"This is your collection?"

"This is it."

"You've been to three whole movies?"

"Maybe a few more than that, but I really liked these."

"Let's see what else I can learn about you," she said as her eyes fell on two framed photographs on a nightstand by the bed. She crossed the room and picked up one of the pictures, her heart leaping at the sight of Jace dressed in naval attire, a massive ship looming in the background. Jace's arm was resting across the shoulders of an older man Julianna guessed to be his grandfather, judging by the family resemblance and the man's advanced age.

"You're in the navy?"

"Was in the navy. I'm out now." Quickly, he added, "Honorably."

She lifted the second photo and smiled tenderly at the barefoot boy standing in the tide. He appeared to be about four years old, looking back at her with a youthful version of the same dark eyes that had mesmerized her from across a room. She knew the boy in the picture was Jace, and that the woman standing behind him could only be his mother. She was young, stunningly beautiful as the wild coastal wind whipped her hair back from her face, and she gazed upon Jace with the exclusive love a woman reserves for her child.

"They say a picture paints a thousand words," she said, "but these just raise a thousand questions I want to ask you."

"Let's go outside," he said as he headed from the room.

She started to follow him, but stopped on the way out of the bedroom, her attention caught by a stack of newspapers piled on the floor of one corner. She knelt and looked through them, reading that every headline sang praises to Babe Ruth. The Babe Breaks His Own Record! The Sultan of Swat! One Hundred and Thirteen Home Runs!

So far today, Julianna had gathered several glimpses into the life of Jace McAllister. And all of it gave her good cause to shake her head in wonder, perplexed by the man whose alias was the People's Bandit.

As she restacked the newspapers, she heard the screen door open and close and knew he was back outside with the wind and the water. She hurried to join him, but stopped just short of going onto the porch, her hand poised on the door handle.

Who is this man? she wondered as she looked out at Jace, the wind billowing his shirt back as he stared at the sea and fiddled absently with a twig while seated on the steps that separated the porch from the sand. This man who collects jazz, follows Babe Ruth, likes the Marx Brothers, keeps family photos, served his country, has bad taste in furniture and . . . oh yes, does some bank robbing from time to time?

After a few seconds, Julianna stepped onto the porch and sat beside him, wrapping her arms around her knees to keep the skirt of her dress from flapping in the gales. She followed his gaze and sighed when her eyes rested on the lighthouse. "It's so beautiful. How tall is it?"

"One hundred and seventy-eight feet," he answered. "The original was only eighty."

"What happened to it?"

"Mother Nature." He snapped the twig he was toying with and tossed the broken pieces on the sand, where the wind picked them up and sent them scampering toward the shore. "It was built from wood in the late 1700s, so the wind and rain had nearly beat it down by the turn of the century."

"And that's when this one was built?"

"No, there was another one," he told her. "It lasted until the Civil War, then the Confederate soldiers blasted out its steps so the Yanks couldn't use it as an observation tower."

Impressed, she said, "That's quite a history."

He nodded toward the lighthouse. "This one's been here since 1876. It's automated now, but it had a first-order fresnel lens—its beam shot twenty miles out to sea."

She gave him an inquisitive look. "You know a lot about that lighthouse."

"Yeah," he said, smiling as he stood. "I'm a regular tour guide."

"So that's what you do when you're not robbing banks."

"When I can fit it in," he said. "I've got my international spy duties to think about, too." He rolled up his pants legs and started toward the waves. "Come on."

They made their way across mounds of soft sand before coming to where it was solid and packed down by the tide. "I want to show you something," he said over the roar of wind and water.

"The lighthouse?" she asked hopefully.

"Later," he promised as they headed for a surf-beaten dock in the opposite direction. When they reached it, he led her underneath it, and they waded into the low tide. He stopped beside one of the support posts and pointed to a pocketknife carving in the wood.

Jace 1910

"I was eight when I did that."

"You've been around here a long time."

"Most of my life." His eyes caught something small bobbing just below the surface of the water. He reached in and scooped up a white sand dollar, then held it out to Julianna. "Ever held one?"

She let him place the sea creature into her hand, where its tiny legs tickled her palm. "My friend Cassie says the five marks on a sand dollar represent the five wounds Christ suffered on the cross." She returned the sand dollar to the water and watched it merrily bop away before disappearing into a swell. "Have you ever heard that before?"

"Yeah. I have, actually," he answered. "From my grandfather, the man you saw with me in the picture."

"How long were you in the navy?"

"Eight years."

"And what do you do when you're not sailing the seven seas?" she asked. "I mean, besides the spy job and pirating my father's banks?"

He laughed at her choice of words. "Rob tourists—and anyone else who needs to charter a boat." He glanced at the horizon. "If we stay out here long enough, you'll see Ambrose Annie coming back, full of tourists who paid way too much money to go deep sea fishing."

"Ambrose Annie?" Julianna asked. "I'm assuming she's a boat."

"Sister to Amy, Abbie, and Allie," he said. "We own four charter boats—we being me and three guys I've known since I was a kid. When tourist season is over, we go looking for shrimp."

Julianna shook her head. "Bank robbing to boat charters. You are a very . . . complex man, Jace McAllister."

"Varied interests, that's all," he told her. "And anyway, it all works together to make a story. You'll get it." He leaned against the post that bore his carved name then pulled Julianna close so that her back was against him. One arm encircled her waist and the other pointed down shore toward the lighthouse. "See that red brick house next to the lighthouse? It used to be the keeper's quarters."

"I see it," she said, loving that he had pulled her against him without any hesitation. It felt as though he had done it without thinking, just as the waves were rolling in without thinking, but were instead responding to a natural current. Intimacy, she was realizing, must not be exclusive to passion. It was about two people connecting on a deeper level. Jace was doing this—showing her his trust by opening windows into his life.

"I grew up in that house."

Intrigued, she looked at him over her shoulder. "Yours was a lighthouse family?"

"Three generations." He put both arms around her waist and rested his chin on her head.

"Was your father one of the keepers?"

"No. My mother."

"Your mother?" Now she was deeply intrigued and turned in his arms. "Amazing."

"Not really." He shrugged. "A lot of women kept lighthouses, made daring rescues."

"Not mine." Julianna laughed at the very thought of the primped and pampered Audrey Sheffield sloshing through choppy waves in a dinghy to pull shipwrecked souls to safety. "I don't think she's rescued anything except for a hat that was accidentally put in a pile of old clothes to be thrown out."

Jace was looking down at her, his expression amused but distant. She smacked his chest. "Did you hear anything I said?"

"I really did," he said, "but when you're standing this close to me, it's hard to," he brushed her lips with his, "concentrate." He kissed her softly then, causing a warm glow to rise within her, one that was in sync with the wind that suddenly picked up and brought a shower of salty spray off the water. Even their surroundings seemed to be in rhythm with their movements. Was she crazy to think that nature itself was sending them signs, showing them that this was the right way for things to be? She was going to accept that it was, that it was confirming what her heart already knew.

Julianna drew back first, her fingers playing in his hair. "Lighthouses, bank robberies, your name carved on a dock . . . tell me something, Jace McAllister."

"What?" he murmured, his lips buried in her neck, still kissing her, holding her so tightly against him that her back arched.

She lifted his head and gently embraced both sides of his face. "Who are you?"

》 《

He was the great-great-grandson of John Delaney, a man whose soul was charged with a mariner's zest for the sea, and a high-spirited sailor who became a naval hero in 1819.

Jace saw the interest sparkle in Julianna's eyes.

"What did he do?" she asked. "To earn that kind of an honor?"

"Went head-to-head with some pirates," Jace answered, smiling fondly at the story and the adventurous images his mind had created when he first heard it. He had been five years old, standing in the lighthouse tower with his mother and watching the waves dance with the morning beams of a saffron autumn sun.

"He was in the navy," Jace went on. "Spent most of his time on an American warship that patrolled the Gulf of Mexico looking for pirates and smugglers."

"Sounds exciting."

It had always sounded that way to Jace, too, especially when his mother told the story. There had never been a better storyteller than his mother, who dipped her words in color and enhanced them with a spectrum of facial expressions and gestures as she moved about a room. Jace never grew bored hearing about John Delaney and how his ship had come upon pirates overtaking a merchant's vessel en route to New Orleans. The sea bandits had been vicious in the inky, restless waters of the Gulf that night, their swords piercing unarmed men, and their rugged, scarred bodies forcing themselves on terrified women.

The navy attacked, swarming over the pirates like hornets, and a battle was underway, blood mixing with saltwater on the deck of the merchant's vessel. Fires exploded at every turn, crackling demons against the black night, their flames rising and their tips reaching for other objects to set ablaze. The wind was wild, announcing that the hurricane-plagued Gulf would soon be under the siege of a massive storm.

Waves lunged against the rails of the ship. Relentless, they pounded it until one wave made the leap, its force so great that it sent seven of John's shipmates careening across the deck. Three were tossed up and cast into the furious sea.

John dove into the swells and would later say he had gone over by the will of God, for only God could know that when John burst to the churning surface, he would be two feet from a lifeboat that had disengaged from the merchant's vessel. He clamored aboard and, guided by fiery pieces of floating wood, found his fellow sailors, each exhausted from fighting the waves and barely hanging on to buoyant debris.

The rescue made John a hero, and years later his bravery was honored when he was named keeper of the Ambrose Point Lighthouse.

"And that's when the family legacy started," Jace told Julianna as they looked toward the lighthouse. "My great-grandfather, Collin, was the next one to take over."

"Was he a pirate hunter, too?"

Jace caught a strand of Julianna's hair as the wind snapped it toward her eyes. "Sort of," he said with a smile. "He was in the Navy African Slave Trade Patrol, looking for people who tried to get rich off human bondage."

"My family seems so boring next to yours," Julianna said.

Hardly, Jace thought, but said nothing. He'd get to Julianna's family later.

"Tell me about you and the lighthouse," Julianna said.

He shrugged. "I lived there with my mother and granddad. My father—" He hesitated and looked to sea, wincing with regret. Not regret over something done, but regret over something he hadn't been able to do anything about. "I never knew him."

"What . . . happened?" Julianna asked, and Jace could hear caution in her voice, like someone treading carefully through water to test its depth.

Jace didn't want to tell her. Truth was, he was scared she'd feel sorry for him and his family, and that was the last thing he wanted. His family had been strong and done all right.

"Jace . . ."

"He was in the navy, too," Jace said, knowing he owed her a complete history, knowing he couldn't have remote corners that excluded Julianna, this woman who loved him despite his actions against her family. "But his ship went down near Cape Hatteras—it hit a shoal, and the hull split in two. Nobody made it out."

"Oh, I'm sorry," Julianna said softly. "How old were you?"

"Ma didn't even know she was pregnant," Jace said, dreading the expression that was sure to come to Julianna's face.

Alarm sprang to her eyes and her hand covered her mouth. It was just the look Jace had feared. Feeling uncomfortable, he focused on the breaking waves. "I don't think Ma ever accepted his death. Not completely."

Jace could see her in his mind, standing in the lighthouse tower, scanning the watercolor horizon in search of a ship that would bring her husband home. Or pausing in the middle of a chore to gaze at the Atlantic, long waves of dark hair whipping in the gales. Dreamy and distant, she had watched the water a lot, as though the monster that took her great love would somehow be the hero to give him back.

Julianna tugged gently on his shirt sleeve. "You look so far away."

A quick shake of his head and the sad memory fell to the back of his mind. He smiled down at Julianna. There was plenty of time to tell her about his life. Plenty.

"Come on, there's a barbecue shack down the beach," he said, immediately feeling better. He pulled her from underneath the dock and into the dazzling mid-afternoon sun.

For now, Jace McAllister had said all he was going to say about who he was.

CHAPTER
SIX

See Captain Cloud—The Wing-Walking Wonder!

Leyton scoffed at the promotional signs plastered on the fence surrounding the fairgrounds, the site of the Star-Spangled Air Show.

The Wing-Walking Blunder is more suitable, he thought. *The man has a fool's profession.*

He hurried across the dusty grounds and toward the bleachers, where he was sure that one Miss Virginia Fleming would have a front-row seat. If anyone knew of Julianna's whereabouts, it would be her best friend.

Leyton knew that Richard wouldn't approve of the conversation he was about to initiate with Virginia. "This is a closed family matter, and there's no need to raise speculation," Richard had said. "It will only cause talk of a kidnapping, which will draw the press. Or worse, people might suspect running away or insanity, which would bring scandal on the Sheffield name."

Richard believed that Julianna would abandon the idea of leaving home and drag back with her head low. He was willing to give her a week before devising a plan to find her. Leyton, though, was itching for answers, some kind of lead that would take him to Julianna now.

Virginia's movie-starish looks made her easy to spot, and she was the picture of style in her cuffed and pleated pants, silk blouse, and sunglasses. Her hair glowed like fired bronze as she sat in the sun-drenched bleachers, sipping Coke and minding her own business while waiting for the show to start.

Leyton paused at the bottom of the bleacher's steps and studied Virginia for a minute. Her blue eyes had always guarded him with suspicion, her demeanor never warm. At best, she was stiffly cordial, but Leyton hadn't seen her best very often.

Ah well, he wasn't fond of her either. Her feisty temperament prickled his nerves and reminded him of the bratty girls who had made fun of him in school. He also concluded that she was fickle, her attention span like that of a flea as she jumped from boyfriend to boyfriend. How different she was from his Julianna! And that was why he was so puzzled by the recent turn of events. Julianna was the woman he trusted to be present, the one he could count on to follow the expected path of dependability. Yet what had she done? Vanished into the night, just as his mother had done so many times. Every time he made that comparison, his blood simmered.

Today he was not going to offer Virginia his usual polite tolerance because of who her parents were. Today there was too much business at hand, starting with Julianna's escapade and how to remedy it. So much for the sweet girl he thought her to be. She was not, was not, going to leave him at the altar looking like a pathetic sap. Nor was she going to deny him the stable life he envisioned, which included the fortune that was just at his fingertips and all the plans he had to go along with it.

Leyton jammed his hands into the pockets of his trousers and strode up the bleachers. Standing directly over Virginia, who was sitting on the first row, he dispensed of proper formalities and said firmly, "I need to know where Julianna is."

Virginia slowly raised her sunglasses and gave him a lingering look of haughty contempt, clearly not pleased with his tone. Her eyes spoke for her, seeming to ask, Surely you can't be speaking to me?

Annoyance burned the back of Leyton's neck, and he wanted to shake that look right off of Virginia's face. "I'm sure Julianna has contacted you since she left two days ago."

"You're casting a shadow on my view," Virginia said coolly as she lowered her sunglasses back over her eyes. "So please, get thee behind me, Satan."

His jaw tensed and his hands, hidden inside his pockets, tightened into fists. Who does she think she is? This pampered daddy's girl, speaking to me in such a manner? He helped himself to the space next to her. "I'll say it again, Miss Fleming, I need to know where Julianna is." His voice simmered with anger. "Where is she?"

Virginia lit a cigarette and blew a white puff of smoke into the air. "I don't know."

Scowling, he fanned away the smoke as it drifted in his direction. "I can't understand your coldness," he said. "What have I done to you? What makes you detest me to the core?"

Virginia paused in the middle of a smoke ring and gazed hard at Leyton. "I don't like the way you treat Julianna," she said bluntly. "Compliments mixed with insults, the way you grab her arm just a little too roughly for it to be in fun." Her gaze changed into a glare. "The way your eyes follow other women, especially anything blond and thin."

Leyton sat straight and rigid. "Julianna is the only woman who interests me."

Virginia laughed and drew on her cigarette. "And donkeys are going to sprout wings and fly in today's air show." Her laughter stopped like water suddenly dammed. "You only care about her family's money. I know—I've dated men like you."

He grinned smugly and folded his arms across his chest, his eyes flickering with challenge. "So, you can read me like a book, then?"

"I don't have to read you," she said. "The way you paw and fawn all over Julianna's father makes your intentions obvious. Like I said, I've dated men like you. I've dated a lot of men, and I know what money-hungry looks like."

He gave her a quick survey with his eyes. Yes, she had a dance card that was filled, but Leyton couldn't see what the excitement was about. Oh, he supposed she was pretty, if one preferred the company of a copperhead—and he meant that as in snake, not hair color.

"You never dated me, though, did you?" He couldn't resist the jab and a tiny sneer. "Because I never asked you."

"And it's good for your ego that you didn't. I would have said no."

He reddened as if sunburned and stood abruptly. "You're impossible to talk to, but don't think that being difficult will buy you any silence regarding Julianna's disappearance." He wagged an authoritative finger in her face. "I'll speak with you again."

Virginia sprang to her feet, her face as red as the stripes on the American flag waving above the fairgrounds. Leyton took a small step back and considered her with an amused sweep of his eyes. It must have been the finger-wagging that set her off, he guessed. A spoiled princess like Virginia expected men to clamor about her feet, not shake a finger in her face demanding that she do anything besides smile her toothpaste-ad smile. Maybe most men did clamor, but Leyton wasn't like most men—and Miss Virginia Fleming had best get used to it. Leyton Drakeworth planned to stick around for a while. A long while.

Nothing, though, was going to work out if he didn't find Julianna.

"One last time, Miss Fleming. Where is—"

"I don't know," Virginia said through gritted teeth. "But here's what I do know—if Julianna wanted you in her life, then you'd know where she is. The fact that you're out in the cold should," she waved her hands in the air, —"oh, I don't know, perhaps, hint that she doesn't want to see your face again?"

"I'll not indulge you in a childish fight of scratch-and-kick," he said, his own teeth now gritted. He wondered if it was possible to break a tooth this way. His molars felt like they were cracking under the pressure of his clenched jaw. Blood rushed to his face, making it feel hot and swollen, and he swore that he would experience spontaneous combustion if he didn't do something . . . anything to release the pressure.

He turned on his heel and shoved Virginia as he did, shoved her hard enough to make her stumble back into the bleachers. Onlookers gasped, and two men jumped to Virginia's rescue, steadying her before she fell.

"Lousy jerk!" one of the men called out as Leyton walked away, shoulders back and eyes staring straight ahead.

"That's right, Leyton!" Virginia added. "If the shoe fits, wear it!"

Leyton glanced over his shoulder and saw one of Virginia's shoes sailing through the air. He quickened his steps, but the pointed heel struck him squarely in the back, raising a chorus of snickers from those in earshot.

Leyton yanked down a poster of Captain Cloud as he passed through the gates of the fairgrounds. He trotted through the gravel parking lot and jumped into his Duesenberg, knowing he needed to calm down. But he also knew it was too late—fury overtook him sometimes, whenever someone set him off like a bottle rocket. It was too bad, just too bad, for anyone who got in his way.

Flooring the accelerator, he tore away, creating a storm of dust and gravel as he passed a family walking toward the entrance. Glancing in his rearview mirror, Leyton saw a boy of about fourteen yelp and clutch his rib cage, obviously struck by a piece of flying gravel.

Snorting a laugh, Leyton drove faster and fishtailed out of the parking lot and onto the main road that took him to town and to the bank. Richard wanted him to function as though nothing were amiss at Dreamland, so Leyton would assume a brisk, business-as-usual demeanor just as soon as he got to work. Until then, he could only think of Julianna.

Somehow, some way, he would find her, and then . . .

Oh yes, then . . . he thought as he released the steering wheel for a second, the time it took to smack his fist against his palm.

A few days after bringing Julianna to Ambrose Point, Jace took her to the boardwalk, finding it crowded with tourists. They had just gotten a couple of hotdogs when a man in the crowd made a sudden grab to keep his small child from darting away. The movement seemed to startle Julianna. She fumbled with her hot dog and put a small smear of mustard on her new white cotton blouse.

"Oh, look at this . . ." she said, scowling at the bright-yellow stain. She turned to Jace, seated next to her on a bench. "Clumsy me."

Concern flashed across his face. "Why'd you jump like that?"

"He startled me, that's all," Julianna said, biting into her hotdog.

"Yeah, but the way you flinched when that guy—" He looked away, then into her eyes. "Are you sure that Leyton never hit you?"

"I told you he didn't," she assured him. Yesterday, as they sat on the porch watching the sun sink away, she'd told Jace of her days with Leyton. "He got pretty aggressive that one time in the garden, but he never went as far as hitting me."

Jace didn't feel relieved. Instead, anger darkened his features as he stood and stepped a few feet away to a railing that overlooked the ocean. He gripped the railing so tightly that his biceps flexed. "Maybe he didn't actually haul off and hit you," he said, voice tense and controlled, "but his hands must have really scared you. Otherwise, you wouldn't be jumping out of your skin because some guy reached for his kid."

Julianna went to him and slipped her arm around his waist. "Leyton can't hurt me now."

"I wish I could guarantee that, Julianna, but I'm an outlaw—can't promise you much of anything."

He watched her smile at his self-description.

"That's what I am," he said, his voice matter-of-fact. He stared at the evening sea, its gold-tipped waves hitting the shore. Now his face fell pensive, and if he could have let Julianna into his mind, she would have heard his thoughts of the sea, the ones telling him that maybe he should have stayed there, surrounded by the rage and glory of deep waters. In some ways, it was safer, much safer, than land. It was only when a man left the freedom and isolation of the sea that his heart could wander into trouble.

Like his had done.

Look where he had landed. Living, for the first time in his life, without any kind of a plan. Existing minute-to-minute with a woman he was terrified to love but more terrified of losing. A woman he had to have but who created a big dilemma.

Now that he had her, what was he supposed to do with her?

Jace thought of his granddad, Abel Delaney, wondering how the old man would advise him, were he alive. Granddad's heart, too, had wandered into trouble, and Jace had told Julianna about it yesterday, had told her all about the man whose slight heart murmur had kept him out of the navy but not out of the sea.

Bronzed and rugged, Abel had worked on everything from the lightships of Nantucket to the salvage boats of Key West, hunting for sunken treasures. There were many harbors and many women. Abel swore there wasn't one who could anchor him to land, and he never promised to return to any woman's arms. Lord knew, he was an honest man, though as wild and free as the waves he sailed.

Only one woman had gotten to Abel's heart. The daughter of a sponge fisherman in Key West; she was as kind as her name implied— Charity. Once in love, Abel struggled like a fish on a hook, then escaped back to sea where grueling labor and tumultuous waters helped him forget her smile.

But the smile came back to find him.

Six years passed, and Abel had grown weary of happily allowing women and wine to lead him astray. The Holy Bible and the North Star—that was all a man needed to stay peacefully on course, and he returned to Ambrose Point to take over the lighthouse.

Then the letter came.

I chance writing to you at Ambrose Point because Charity once mentioned your connection to it. As her dearest friend, it saddens me to tell you that she has passed away from the fever. Yet . . . she leaves you a part of herself . . .

Though the letter didn't explain, Abel knew why Charity never told him that their sultry nights of reckless love had resulted in a daughter. She hadn't thought he would welcome the news, and it pained him to know he had left her with that impression. Maybe she would have been right, for he had been playing with the devil in those days. Now he was of God, as strong and solid on the inside as he was on the outside. His new heart insisted that he be a man, that he do the right thing.

He went to Key West to meet his daughter—a child named Meredith—who looked at him with his own eyes, watching him suspiciously as she clutched a patchwork doll to her chest.

"I'm your father," he had told her, and with the words barely past his lips, she dropped the doll and came to him, tiny arms wrapping around his waist.

He brought Meredith back to Ambrose Point and raised her on his own. She grew to be tall like him, with flowing dark hair and Charity's quick and easy smile. She was an enjoyable girl, with a musical laugh and a good story to tell, and she never complained about the work the lighthouse demanded. Everyday at sundown she climbed the steps—all one hundred and ninety-two of them—to the tower where she lit the lamp. At midnight, she made the same trip to replenish the oil; at sunrise, she extinguished the light.

Abel loved her more than life itself. When she married a sailor at sixteen, it broke his heart—but it broke even more when that sailor died at sea, and Abel watched Meredith stare at the ocean, her face mirroring the lonely emptiness of the water.

It was nine months before he saw her smile—Charity's smile—again. It was the day Meredith gave Abel what would become the greatest joy of his life. A grandson named Jace . . .

Now, as Jace stood on the boardwalk, remembering his granddad's life, Julianna waved a hand before his face. "Hello in there."

"Sorry," he said, looking away from the water and giving Julianna an apologetic smile. His mind was half on her and half on his granddad, but as Jace gazed at Julianna's face, he realized there was a lot to be said about the heart wandering into the trouble of love. Such trouble had its blessings. Just as Granddad had been blessed with Meredith, Jace was blessed with Julianna. He'd figure out what to do with her.

"Let's ride the Ferris wheel," she suggested, eyes shining like green jewels.

He let go of the railing and took her hand. "Easy enough," he said as they started weaving their way along the crowded boardwalk, dodging scampering children and stepping around strollers.

As Jace led her along, Julianna thought of his contemplative mood, wondering if his thoughts were in line with hers. Questions nipped at the back of her mind. Where did she and Jace go from here? What were they to do with each other? The past several days had felt like a vacation, with Jace's strong hands gripping her in the ocean, lifting her into the swells of the waves so that the current could surf her into shore. He had shown her how to bait a hook, and they fished from the end of a pier, the sun turning her skin tawny and highlighting her brown hair with streaks of honey-gold. They had driven to a nearby inlet, just as the crab fishermen were returning with their catch. She had learned to break crab legs and eat the meat straight from the shell, laughing as she imagined her mother's disgust. Every day brimmed with the wish that something could last forever—and was shadowed with the knowledge that it couldn't. She and Jace would have to make a turn, take another step, but what was it to be? She didn't know, didn't want to ponder it. Not now anyway. Now she just wanted to ride the Ferris wheel.

The tourist season at Ambrose Beach was in its prime, seeming oblivious to hard economic times. Its arcades, carnival rides, and food vendors were lively, catering to affluent families traveling in small packs, well-to-do couples strolling arm in arm, and groups of highbred young women flirting with groups of highbred young men.

People mother would approve of, Julianna thought as she took in the women, most of them wearing colorful silk short sets or sailor dresses with matching tams.

"If I ever talk to Mother again, I'll have to tell her that I'm in a place where people dress well," she said to Jace. "That will actually make her feel better about things."

The Ferris wheel was a starring feature in the amusement park across from the boardwalk, and a beautiful attraction with scrolling gold-painted bars and twinkling red lights.

"No rocking," Julianna teased as they waited in line to ride.

"That takes the fun out of it."

"Ah, I should have expected that from you," she said. "You like to live on the edge, Jace McAllister, though you still haven't told me why you've made yourself an outlaw."

"Boring story," he said, eyes traveling to the top of the Ferris wheel.

His discomfort with the subject was clearly painted on his face, and as much as Julianna needed to know all the details of his life, she knew this wasn't the time or place. She rested a hand on his arm. "When you're ready to talk, I'll be ready to listen."

"But will you be ready to hear?" he said quietly, then tried to cover his concern with a quick smile. "It's our turn to ride."

She caught the worry in his voice, and it sent a tremor through her heart. When the time was right, she knew this man had something big to tell her.

They boarded the Ferris wheel, and Jace snapped the metal bar across their laps as the ride began to move. Each time they sailed over the top, Julianna could see most of the Ambrose Beach resort. The bustling boardwalk was at its heart, and from there stemmed pink and white hotels, romantic seaside cottages, and an assortment of souvenir shops and quaint boutiques.

"Look at the point," Jace said when their car stopped at the top.

It was a good five miles away, shimmering gold in the lingering rays of the sun. The waves rolled gently, lapping against the pedestal bluff of the lighthouse, and were mirror-like as they reflected the lavender of twilight's velvety sky.

"Is it hard for you to look at it?" Julianna asked, her eyes and voice gentle. "I mean, does it make you miss your mother?"

"You never stop missing someone," Jace said, "but my memories of the point are mostly good." He shifted in the seat and pulled Julianna's head to his chest. "The storm that killed Ma . . . she'd never want that to wipe out all the good times we had."

"She doesn't sound like someone who would," Julianna said, though she didn't know how Jace could avoid it. When he'd told her about the tropical storm that hit Ambrose Point when he was seventeen, he'd spoken with such vivid detail that Julianna almost felt like she was in the midst of nature's wrath herself. The storm, like an angry demon, had moved across the ocean, jagged veins of lightning sizzling from raven clouds. After filling the tower lamps with oil, Jace and his mother had rushed down the winding stairs and into the courtyard that separated the lighthouse from the keeper's quarters. Rain and hail pelted them like daggers and the wind seemed to weigh a hundred pounds. Jace said they forced their way through it, feeling like they were moving in slow motion.

In the center of the courtyard was a large metal bell mounted to a wooden post. It rang wildly in the wind, until one tremendous gust freed it from the post and sent it catapulting through the air. Seconds later, it was rolling on the ground, its flight broken by Jace's mother. Jace hadn't stopped to check her injuries, but swept her into his arms and finished making his way into the house. Only then did he see the horrific blood shooting from her leg like a geyser. An artery was severed, and there was nothing Jace or his grandfather could do, though they had tried to stop the blood, which left her so quickly that her life slipped away in twenty minutes.

After the storm, the Lighthouse Board automated the Ambrose Point tower, ending the legacy of Jace's family. That was when Jace and his granddad built the bungalow on beach property passed down through the family.

Julianna looked up at Jace. "I'm glad it doesn't haunt you," she said.

"Julianna," he said suddenly, as though breaking from a trance. "In all my bank robberies, I never killed anyone."

Well, he definitely hadn't been thinking about his mother, and the statement—so out of the blue—brought a surprised laugh from Julianna. "I know that."

"I just wanted to make sure you did."

He kissed her then, slow, soft, and deep, until the music and laughter around them faded with the sun, and they were aware only of one another. They were still kissing when the ride ended, not realizing they had come to a stop until the people in line started to applaud.

They rode the roller coaster four times and the tilt-a-whirl twice, then returned to the boardwalk, finding it in high spirits as an all-girl harmonica band was finishing up on the bandstand, then made way for a jazz band.

Inhibitions tossed to the wind, people began to dance before the bandstand, stepping forward and backward, kicking their legs and crossing their arms over their knees.

"Look! They're doing the Charleston!" Julianna exclaimed.

Jace held up his hands in protest. "I only slow dance."

"Mind if I go?"

He shook his head as she shot into the lively group and tried to match her dance movements to theirs. She hadn't danced the Charleston in years and felt self-conscious about her steps. For the first few minutes, her eyes were pointed at her feet, as though watching them would prevent them from doing something out of sync.

When she relaxed and looked up, laughing, the last thing she expected to see was a face from home.

There it was, though, by the cotton candy vendor. Francine Marst, a fixture on her parent's social circuit. Seeing Francine, the laugh caught in Julianna's throat, and her hands slapped to her sides as she froze before the bandstand.

Another dancer accidentally smacked Julianna with a wayward hand, waking her like she'd splashed cold water in her face. Julianna quickly threaded her way through the dancers and pressed herself inside a store's doorway while she collected her thoughts.

She didn't see me, Julianna hoped as her heart drummed in her ears. I'm sure she didn't.

Julianna took a cleansing breath, deciding then not to worry Jace with something that was probably not worth a second thought.

Francine had been busy with her children, picking flakes of cotton candy from the youngest one's Shirley Temple ringlets. The odds of her having spotted Julianna in that brief moment were low, way too low to hide in a doorway over.

Even if she saw me, so what? Julianna reminded herself. I'm an adult, here because I want to be.

She wanted to get away from the boardwalk, though, wanted to do whatever it took to avoid having her father and Leyton discover her whereabouts and bring on a confrontation. It was bound to happen sooner or later, but the later the better. She hurried back to Jace and tugged playfully on his arm. "Let's go back to the house and listen to the radio."

"Gets my vote," he said, sounding glad to get away from the crowd.

They walked toward the car, taking the beach instead of the road. Julianna carried her sandals in her hands, relishing the cool sand as it squeezed between her toes. The wind wrapped her hair around her face, and she pushed it back and looked at Jace. He seemed to be lost in thought again, a place he had spent a lot of time in tonight.

He returned her look and shouted over the wind and waves. "Julianna—marry me."

She thought the gales had distorted his words. "What?"

He stopped her in her tracks and pulled her to him, burying his mouth against her ear.

"Marry me," he repeated. "Tonight, tomorrow . . . as soon as we can."

It seemed surreal, his words echoing throughout her soul, as though they had come to her in the twilight phase of sleep. He led her out of the wind and up onto the grass behind a cluster of palm trees where his voice didn't have to compete with nature.

"I've been trying to figure out what to do with you, and the answer's been coming together all night," he said. "Getting married might sound crazy, but I know it's right. I love you and can't see my life without you, so that makes it right, Juianna. And when your last name changes, it might be harder for Leyton to track you down. I'll have legal rights as a husband, ones that will let me protect you."

She pressed a finger to his lips. "Do you think you know me well enough?"

"I know that you know I'm the People's Bandit—and for some reason, you still love me."

He was right, so right about that. She smiled and toyed with a button on his shirt. "When I saw you I fell in love, and you smiled because you knew."

"Who said that one?"

"Shakespeare, Romeo and Juliet." Her smile turned wistful. "I want to marry you, Jace, but not if it's just because you think I need protecting."

He drew her to him and rested his chin on top of her head, now his comfortable, standard position whenever he held her. "You know it's more than that."

"I can't have children," she blurted. There. It was out, the hollow state of her womb, her delicate condition that marvelous, self-sacrificing Leyton was so willing to accept.

He didn't flinch at the news. "So it'll just be you and me," he said. "Or we'll adopt ten brats from somewhere." His lips nuzzled her neck. "Julianna, I don't care."

She dropped her head and closed her eyes, wanting to cry from relief. She'd always trusted that if a man really loved her . . .

"I'll tell you everything about me," he said. "Before we're married, right now if you want me to."

She took his hand and pulled him down to the grass, where she leaned back and looked at the sky, catching pieces of the Big Dipper that flickered through the swaying palm leaves. At last, he was ready to fill in the empty blanks, to explain all the why's and how's that had brought them to where they were.

He stretched out on his back, arms folded behind his head. "Your father won't be paying for this wedding."

She laughed. "Oh, that's for certain."

"No, I mean he won't be paying for anything." He stared up into her eyes. "Any money you see me spend . . . it's not from your father's banks. That money is gone, but—"

"What?" Julianna broke in, sensing that he wanted to get a burden off his chest.

He snapped a long blade of grass and ran it through his thumb and forefinger. "I never thought I'd pay that money back, never wanted to, but you and I won't be free until I do. We'd know the truth, Julianna, and it would chase us for the rest of our lives."

She remembered realizing the truth about Leyton then trying to bury it beneath her parent's approval. It had risen, like a monster from a grave, bent on torment. "I think you're right about that," she said softly.

"It could take a while, though," he said. "Until then, we carry a big secret between us."

He sounded so solemn that it scared her. Her own voice wavering, she said, "As long as you're trying to make it right—"

"It'll still be a big secret," he said. "I don't want it getting so big that it drives us apart." He tossed the blade of grass and ran his hand up and down one of her forearms. "I don't want to pay for my sins by losing your love."

"My feelings for you are forever," she insisted. "Let me prove it."

He shook his head. "You don't need to prove anything."

"But I'm going to," she said, "by not putting conditions on us taking the next step. You don't have to tell me about the robberies until after we're married."

He laughed. "Oh yeah, yeah I do."

"No," she said. "Cassie says to listen to your heart, and mine knows that nothing you say will change the way I feel about you." She rose to her knees. "I'll always love you, Jace," she said as she leaned down to kiss him, her lips moving slowly over his while her hair brushed against his chest.

CHAPTER

SEVEN

Julianna and Jace interrupted the justice of the peace as he sat in his porch swing, ear cocked to the radio, counting down the innings of a baseball game. They forced back smiles as he married them, his voice annoyed and his manner anxious, shifting his feet as if he needed to visit the outhouse.

His wife sat at the piano, banging out an off-key version of "Wedding March," then sprang from her bench to fling hefty handfuls of rice at their departing backs. They dove into the Auburn and sped away, Julianna holding her ring up to the late afternoon sun, marveling at how its facets winked at her.

The ring was a half-carat diamond marquis, set in white gold and flanked by two small rubies; it had been given to Jace's mother by his father. Julianna considered it the most beautiful ring in the world.

"You didn't have any flowers," Jace said as he whipped off the road. Letting the engine idle, he got out of the car.

"Leaving me already?" Julianna teased as she watched him slip below an embankment and into a field of tall grass and wildflowers.

He returned a few minutes later and leaned in her window. "I usually only go into fields when I'm outrunning the cops, but here." He handed her a small bouquet of buttercups. "Flowers for the bride."

She laughed, pressing the flowers to her nose. "Look at you— elusive bandit, presumed all-around bad boy—picking buttercups in a field." She laughed again, this time adding a tender caress to his cheek. "If J. Edgar Hoover could see you now."

They drove to the inlet and met the crab boats then savored dinner while sitting on the far end of the dock, feet dangling over the waves as they broke against its wooden posts. By the time they returned to the bungalow, dusk had surrendered to night and lightning illuminated clouds in the distant sky. The house greeted them warmly, its only light coming from a small table lamp that cast a honey glow on the front room.

Jace fiddled with the radio dial, looking for a station that played ballads. Watching him, Julianna felt a shuddering sigh run through her from head to toe. Soon, very soon, he would be touching her as he never had before.

When the music and light came together, she was eager for his embrace but trembling slightly. Though she could tell desire shot through him, too, he took his time, drawing out a kiss while unfastening a few buttons on the back of her dress, then lowering it to her shoulders. His mouth slowly pulled away from hers, then began to explore her neck, the hollow of her throat, and the curve of her shoulders, tantalizing her skin with feather-light brushes from his lips.

More than anything, she wanted to please him, but when she tried to unbutton his shirt, her fingers fumbled over one another, like a child trying to maneuver a pencil for the first time.

"I'm not very good at this," she whispered.

He smiled down at her. "I think you're doing fine."

Her hands dropped from his shirt. "I've never been with a man," she said quietly. "Not—not in this way."

Gentle eyes caressed her face. "It'll be all right," he said then led her to his bedroom where his touch was a languished, unhurried expedition, his passion a tender match to the serene rhythm of the waves beyond the house.

She relaxed beneath him, but her breath caught sharply as they united.

"Do I need to stop?" he murmured.

She shook her head and gripped his shoulders, pulling him closer to her. After a few minutes, her discomfort began to fade and she melted into the intimacy of the night. Every sound, every touch, seemed of a deeper dimension—the feel of his skin as her fingertips slowly massaged his back, the whisper of her name, falling softly upon her ear. She saw the fire in his eyes just before they closed and he buried his face in her neck, his hands raking through her hair and clutching the pillow that cushioned her head.

Afterward, she felt his heart beating against her chest, as though it was trying to physically mesh with her own heart. Her throat tightened with emotion and a lone tear descended on her cheek.

He lifted his head from her neck and took a deep, catching breath. "I love you," he said, smiling until he saw the tear. "What's this for?" he asked, brushing it away.

She found her voice, husky as it fought through the myriad of feelings that seemed to have settled in her throat. "It really was like becoming one person," she said. "I felt like you could see straight into me."

"To your soul," he said, settling beside her and pulling her into the crook of his arm.

She nestled against him, and they lay quietly for a few minutes, listening to the steady music of the ocean. His hand dropped to her stomach, where it made slow, circular caresses. "Sorry about kids," he said, voice flat and drifting, heavy with the desire to sleep.

"Me too." She sighed, then threw him a teasing look. "I feel better, though, knowing we're going to adopt ten."

"All boys."

"I'd like being the only woman in the house," she said, taking his hand from her stomach and massaging it between hers. "Jace, when people find out we got married after only five days together, will they say we're crazy?"

"Yeah," he answered. "Do you care?"

"No," she said, turning on her stomach and resting her head on his chest. "Let's think up ridiculous names for our ten boys."

He gave her a slight, tired smile. "Harpo . . . Groucho . . ." he said, voice fading just before he fell asleep, his arm draped across her back.

She lay with him for a few minutes, enjoying the easy rise and fall of his chest as the white cotton curtains billowed in the window over the headboard. The breeze waltzed in, its cool breath a scintillating contrast to the warmth of their skin. She slipped from his loose embrace and scooted to the head of the bed so that she could look out the window. The sky was black satin, with the moon reigning behind scattered strips of thin clouds. It was beautiful but dim compared to the beam coming from the lighthouse. Sharp and golden, it cut through the night like scissors through paper.

She looked from the lighthouse to her husband and again felt emotion well up inside of her. He had taken her beyond herself tonight, to a new frontier of closeness.

She was so glad she had waited for him instead of satisfying her curiosity with other men. It could never have been the same with anyone else, any man other than the one God had chosen for her.

Smiling, she stretched out beside him and closed her eyes as the curtains lifted above her and another breeze floated across her face.

Tonight.

She wouldn't have missed tonight for the world.

Leyton brought the Duesenberg to a screeching halt in front of the headquarters of The People's Standard, a stately, red brick building with five stories.

It was Friday morning, nearly a week since Julianna's departure, and Leyton was tight with frustration. He leapt from his car and made a brisk entrance into the bank's lobby, where his erect stance was as intimidating as a schoolmaster's switch. Conversations stopped in mid-sentence and eyes glued themselves to paperwork as Leyton walked about, peering at the activities of each employee.

Normally, he paid little attention to the Nobodies, but right now they were taking the edge off his tension. Enjoying the nerve-racking effect he had on them, Leyton strutted around the lobby several times before heading to his office on the fifth floor. He paused in the doorway of Richard's office and greeted him.

"Leyton, my boy, how are things going?"

"As well as can be expected," Leyton said, his tone even and efficient so Richard's secretary wouldn't suspect they were referring to anything besides business.

"Good." Richard smiled from behind his mahogany desk. "Are you free around eleven?"

"If I need to be," Leyton answered, wondering how Richard could be so calm, so normal, when his daughter had stolen into the night like a common thief.

"How about some golf?"

"I'd love that, sir," Leyton said. "My thoughts have been rather occupied this week."

Richard nodded, and Leyton thought he saw a hint of sympathy in the older man's eyes. "I assure you the outcome will be satisfactory."

Leyton went to his own office and closed the door. He looked at Julianna's picture, smiling from a brass frame on his bookcase.

"I thought you would have come home by now. Begging my forgiveness, ready to start new. I need you, love, more than you know."

It embarrassed him in front of Richard and Audrey that she hadn't come home, and it was getting harder to move through his daily routine as though nothing were unusual. A red canvas flashed before him, and he knocked Julianna's picture to the floor where it lay face up. He stepped on it, loving the scratchy crackling of the glass as he ground it beneath his heel.

Julianna sat on a kitchen chair, wearing Jace's white terry cloth robe and watching him make pancakes at the stove.

"Very good," she said, clapping, as he tossed a pancake high into the air, where it made a perfect flip then landed back in the skillet.

He put it on a plate with some others then threw another pancake toward the ceiling. When it didn't return, Julianna laughed. "It looks—lonely up there."

"C'mon." Jace motioned it back with a spatula. When it fell, he caught it in the skillet and dumped it onto the plate. "That one is yours," he said to Julianna. "For laughing."

When they finished eating, Julianna carried the dirty plates to the sink. Seeing the telephone sitting at one end of the kitchen counter, her jaw tightened. She had called her parents a couple of nights ago to let them know she was still alive and well. Barely had she said hello to her mother when her father snatched the phone, raging about her despicable behavior, threatening that she had better come home or else. She had expected his anger, but he wouldn't even let her squeeze a word in. Furious herself, she had slammed the phone down so hard that its bell sounded. She would call her mother next Wednesday, when she knew her father was away at a golf tournament. In the meantime, Mother knew she was breathing.

Jace stood from the table, smiling as he stretched. "Get dressed. Let's go to the lighthouse."

As they walked the quarter mile of shore that led them to the point, Julianna stole glances at Jace, loving the way he looked with the wind rustling his pants and blowing open the collar of his shirt. He caught her eye and smiled then draped an arm around her shoulder.

When they reached the point, it was another quarter mile to the lighthouse. A dirt road had been cut and was well maintained by the National Lighthouse Committee. The outside walls of the point were packed with large gray rocks, slippery after being battered by the waves.

The lighthouse itself was surrounded by a six-foot chain-link fence. Undeterred, Jace scaled it quickly and stood on the other side. Julianna, though, carefully maneuvered her feet in and out of the small holes until she finally sat balanced on the top of the fence.

Jace reached for her. "Jump to me."

She pushed herself from the fence and he caught her, setting her safely on the ground. She had never been so close to a lighthouse before and was awestruck as her eyes took in the full height of the brilliant red-and-white cone. "It's magnificent."

The door was locked tight, but Jace jimmied it open with the smallest blade in his pocketknife. Just inside, steps curved above them, seeming to lead to Heaven.

"I can't believe your mother climbed these three times a day," Julianna said as she started up. Jace behind her, she wound around and around, passing three oblong windows on the way. "I'm not going to look out of them," she said. "I'm saving the view for the tower."

"Well, on a climb like this, you need something to look forward to."

It was the most stunning sight Julianna had ever seen, a panoramic view that took in both water and land. The ocean seemed infinite, a constantly moving body that stretched beyond the light-blue horizon. The land, too, looked eternal, starting with the town of Ambrose Beach and turning into an endless canvas of green farms and fields. Julianna saw miles of shore, some parts still and deserted, other areas awake with sunbathers and children playing in the surf.

"Worth the climb, isn't it?" Jace said quietly.

She looked at the ocean, sparkling like sapphire beneath the late morning sun. "It seems so calm and contented."

"It can be a hell-bent vixen, though."

She watched his eyes go from the water to the land just beneath them, particularly to the keeper's quarters. A faraway expression came over his face, the face of someone whose mind was traveling back, reviewing the regrets and glories of the past.

Her heart squeezed for him as she, too, focused on the keeper's quarters. He had lived in those quarters for seventeen years. He had seen his life forever changed on those very grounds, forcing him to become a man while one tender foot was still in boyhood.

"The memories you must have," she sighed.

"You want to hear some of them?"

She leaned back against him, comfortable as his arms went around her.

"Yes," she said. "All of them."

CHAPTER
EIGHT

Had his dreams panned out, Jace would have been a writer. One like Herman Melville, who satiated his thirst for adventure then wrote about it.

"Melville was a sailor, like us," Jace's granddad had said when he handed Jace a copy of Moby Dick on his twelfth birthday.

Melville had been Jace's inspiration to write stories about the sea, and it blended perfectly with his other plans to sail, like his ancestors before him. From the time he fought imaginary pirates trying to overtake the point, Jace had never considered not going to sea.

Granddad offered his blessings, along with his warnings.

"Sometimes it's better to put your roots in the land, so don't let the ocean steal your heart," he had said as they stood at the depot, waiting for Jace's train to be called. "She will if you aren't careful."

Jace was barely eighteen and promised Granddad that he was only committing four years to the navy. After that, he'd give the land a fair shake then decide where to seek his gold.

Jace sailed on the USS Panther, where the hard physical labor added more definition to his muscles and erased all boyish traces from his face, replacing them with the chiseled features of a man. He gained two more inches in height during his first year on board the massive floating city as it quietly cruised the deep, dark blue Atlantic, from north to south and back again, hundreds of sea miles from any shore. She was a ship groomed to fight, but had no one to do battle with—pirates had faded into history and the Great War was over. Still, the navy was America's foremost line of defense, bettering their submarines and further developing the aircraft carrier. Jace was proud to be part of it, though the work left him dead tired, too tired to write the novel that lived in his head. Instead, he kept a journal of quickly jotted notes recorded for future use.

His four years were up in 1925, and he returned to Ambrose Point ready to carry out the second part of the promise he had made to Granddad.

"These days, a man needs college," Granddad had suggested as they sat on the front porch, watching a ship glide past the lighthouse.

Jace nodded, as he had been thinking the same thing.

Granddad pointed to the clouds, translucent pink as the sun went down. "Your opportunities are sky-high."

"I still want to write," Jace said.

"But you don't want to starve."

Jace knew that Granddad was leading him to a safe and reasonable place. "Something to support you while the dreams are being built, something to fall back on should the dreams crumble to dust." While Jace couldn't argue with the sensibility of it, he wondered if he could really get the apple if he didn't go out on a limb.

His heart was restless, telling him that his dreams and the sea were better companions; still, he packed a duffel bag and left for school, sensing that he was dangerously off course.

By the winter of twenty-nine, he was midway through his senior year, very near a degree in finance when he saw an advertisement on the bulletin board outside one of his classes.

Paid Internship. Southern Gold Brokerage Firm.

Needing the money and the experience, he applied and was accepted. Southern Gold was one of the largest brokerage houses below the Mason–Dixon, claiming that all Americans could know prosperity. Their brokers were an aggressive lot of salesmen, pitching stock to everyone from housemaids to millionaires, which accounted for the observation rooms always being filled with investors, mesmerized by the mechanical music of the stock ticker. The eruption of cheers was a frequent sound in those rooms, while the brokers kept the phones and cable wires jammed. The firm even had branch offices on several cruise ships, where short wave radios and ship-to-shore phones kept passengers close to their beloved market.

The most prized client of Southern Gold was an old and trusted name, one of the most respected in all of Dixie.

The People's Standard National Bank.

And the General Manager of Southern Gold was a young shooting star in the world of finance.

Leyton Drakeworth.

Julianna's disbelieving voice interrupted the story, "You're telling me that you worked for Leyton?"

"The one and only," Jace said.

She shook her head in stunned amazement. "This is unbelievable."

"And I've only just begun."

Drakeworth didn't fraternize with the brokers at Southern Gold, wouldn't recognize them if his life depended on it. The only exceptions were those brokers who had made it to middle management and oversaw others, like Jace's boss, Benjamin Halstead, a thirty-five-ish, overzealous broker who was overwhelmed with filing and phone calls.

Initially, that was what Jace helped him with. After a few weeks, the grunt work was caught up, and Halstead's desk was dissolved of its haphazard mountain of papers and crumpled cigarette packs.

"McAllister, come here," he said one afternoon, motioning for Jace to sit down on the other side of his desk. "I've got a project for you."

He shoved four file folders across the desk. "These are some of our smaller accounts, and I'm going to let you work with them." He fired up a cigarette and leaned back in his chair. "You can't buy or sell without my approval, but I want you to keep up with these clients. Give me your ideas, tell me what you think we should do with their money. If we agree, I'll let you make the calls and do the talking. Sound good?"

Jace picked up the folders. "Thanks for the chance."

Compared to some of the portfolios managed by Southern Gold, Jace's clients were probably considered among the least important. By Leyton Drakeworth, anyway. To Jace, though, Antonio Costiano, Sally Jackson, Jared Adams, and Robert Willows had become like friends, and he looked forward to seeing them peer eagerly through the observation window. He came to know more about them than their files told, like why they were in the market and how it wasn't something they played for adventure. These were simple people, like Ma and Granddad, with humble plans, risking as much as they could to see their hopes unfold.

Jace finished school in June and was brought on full-time by Southern Gold. At first, he could only buy and sell with supervision, but that trickled away over a few weeks and he was given five more small portfolios to manage.

Most investors bought on margin, paying only ten percent of a stock's price and borrowing the rest from their brokers. By late September, the brokers' loans tallied over six billion dollars. Economists shouted that financial devastation was in the cards, prices declined, and hoards of rich players fled from the market as though it was a building gutted by fire.

"I should pull my people out," Jace told Halstead, dismayed while watching the ticker tape machine. "The market is plunging."

"These things happen," Halstead said through a haze of cigarette smoke. "Ride it out."

"I'd rather get out."

"Trust me, it'll pass." Halstead mashed out his cigarette in an ashtray overrun with butts. "Besides, Drakeworth says we're to talk people out of leaving the market."

"Why's that?"

"Because." Halstead struck a match and lit another cigarette. "If everyone starts falling for this crap Depression-talk, it'll become a self-fulfilling prophecy."

"All right," Jace conceded. "I'll give it a little longer."

In early October, U.S. Steel dropped in value by eighty million dollars, and other large corporations watched the same thing happen to their own worth. As prices declined, brokers were unable to sell at prices high enough to cover the loans they had given their investors. The phone lines began to burn, with brokers begging investors for more margin to cover their debts.

A lot of small investors couldn't cover the extra margin, leaving brokers no choice but to dump the shares on the market for whatever they could sell for. Jace was lucky. Of his nine clients, only four had bought on margin and three were able to cough up more. Only Jared Adams couldn't stay afloat.

"I can't cover it," Adams said. "What . . . what does this mean?"

Jace could tell from the way Adams's voice cracked that he knew exactly what it meant.

"I have to let it go," Jace told him, wishing he could place his hand on a hot stove instead. "I . . . man, there's nothing else I can do."

"But my kids, you know?"

Jace winced behind the phone receiver, hating that this furniture-maker had invested in the market to give his kids a few of life's nicer things. Nothing wrong or greedy about that. So, why him? Why Jared Adams to lose everything?

Southern Gold continued to show faith in the market, encouraging investors not to jump ship. Jace didn't get it, no matter how hard he tried to figure out Drakeworth's thinking. It just seemed that the signs of disaster were there—for those who wanted to see them.

The construction industry slowed down, as did steel production and car sales. People picked up their paychecks only to learn that it was their final one, accompanied by a pink slip and best wishes. For Jace, the days were nervous and the nights sleepless until, finally, he couldn't stand the anxiety anymore. The weight of responsibility bearing on his shoulders was too heavy. He gathered up his remaining eight portfolios and began making calls, pulling his clients from the market, which he likened to a shuddering giant about to fall. He had gotten through five clients when Halstead strode up to his desk and leaned in close.

"McAllister, what are you doing?"

"Selling off."

"I figured." He glanced about, hoping that other brokers hadn't heard. "What're you trying to do? Start a panic? Look, it'll smooth out."

"When?" Jace asked. "These people are losing money every day."

Halstead didn't answer. "How many did you yank?"

"Five." He looked at the clients he still had to pull: Costiano, Jackson, and Willows.

Halstead looked at his watch and nearly gloated. "Market's closed."

"Great," Jace muttered. He hadn't realized how late it had gotten.

"It is great. Now you can go home and calm down. Tomorrow's another day."

It was Thursday, October 24, and the market opened with heavy trading.

"Market's all crazy," Halstead gushed as he watched the ticker. He gulped the last swallow of his cold coffee. "Gets my blood racing. What about you, McAllister?"

Jace was green, his stomach in knots. "It makes me sick."

"Wonder which way she'll go?" Halstead mused. "Time'll tell, huh?"

At ten thirty that morning, the market plunged. Straight down, like a tremendous weight plummeting off the ledge of a windowsill.

Panic drove brokers into a wild selling rage. Amicable coworkers yesterday, they became screaming savages, every man out for himself as stock prices dropped five or ten points between each sale. Fearful investors began pounding on the window of the observation rooms and yelling for brokers to unload both good and bad stocks.

Forty-five minutes passed and the market didn't stabilize. For the next hour, prices sank with such speed that many stocks became worthless, unwanted orphans that no one would buy at any price.

For many small investors, that was the bitter end. Counted among the losses were the last of Jace's clients.

Jace couldn't pin down what he felt when he realized that everything was gone. He only knew that he had to get out of the broker's room, away from the commotion and cursing of the people around him. He shoved past the other brokers and hurried by the observation room with his head down, avoiding the looks of flat-busted investors.

Despair thickened the air like smoke, making Jace feel like taking another breath would be impossible. He jerked his collar loose, sending a button ricocheting off the wall. Reaching the door that led outside, he slammed it open with his shoulder and stumbled into the noonday sun, joining the zombie-like crowd gathered outside. Investors, brokers, curious onlookers, all shaking their heads or staring into space, stunned by the news and fearful of the future.

"Excuse me, Mr. Broker?" The voice was soft but shaky with age.

Jace snapped from his daze and looked down at Sally Jackson, tears trickling through the valleys of wrinkles that creased her face.

"Yes, ma'am?" It was all he could say to this client, a childless widow living on her dead husband's insurance money and whatever her arthritic hands could earn from sewing. She only wanted to keep her house up, fearing she'd have to live in a Hooverville if the house collapsed.

"When will you get my money back?"

Jace glanced away, guilt making it impossible for him to look at her trusting face.

And as he looked away, he saw Antonio Costiano, his pained face sending Jace a message that all hope of sending his only son to college were gone.

"I listened to you!" He glared at Jace as his wife steered him down the steps.

Jace couldn't summon any words, but maybe his face showed the regret he was feeling. Maybe it collapsed as harshly as the market because Antonio's glare melted. "Ah, it was a gamble," he said, shrugging as though he'd merely lost a dollar in a poker game. "You, my friend, aren't to blame."

Jace sensed Antonio's forgiveness, but self-absolution seemed impossible as he bolted to the sidewalk, cursing himself as he hurried away from Southern Gold. Why hadn't he done something? Like pull his clients in late September? If only he had moved forward on his hunches and the warning signs around him, even Jared Adams would have been spared.

Halstead. The name was burned into Jace's mind. Halstead had waved away all of Jace's worries about the market, had followed Drakeworth like he was the Pied Piper. At least Jace had that excuse to rest on, but he wondered how long it would hold him. New kid or not, he'd known that he needed to take better care of the people who trusted him with their money.

He longed for the ocean and his days among the frothy swells. He ached to go back, regretted ever leaving, and sadly recalled the day he returned to land. He'd known that day that he was stepping off course. Even then, his hunch had been right.

On Monday, October 28, Jace witnessed history in the making as the ticker announced the worst losses ever felt by the stock exchange.

"People are too spooked to move," he said as he watched the sinking prices.

And it was true. Investors sat on their money, refusing to buy anything, while those who still held stocks weren't interested in keeping them. Prices fell all day, a dire descent that carried into Tuesday, forever branding the day as Black Tuesday, robber of dreams and proof that the strong didn't always survive.

That evening, eating at a small diner that was on his walk home, Jace fumed over Drakeworth. Why had he encouraged people to stay in the market? And what about the company's top investor, Richard Sheffield? What was his financial portfolio looking like right now? In all the day's stories of millionaires sliding onto skid row, nothing had been said about Sheffield hitting the rocks. Nothing, and Jace wondered if he had instructed Drakeworth to liquidate his investments and sell his stock before the disaster.

He stood abruptly and tossed a few bills on the table, enough to cover his meal and tip the waitress. Then he stormed from the diner and headed back to Southern Gold, his eyes wanting to confirm what his gut was feeling.

Except for the janitors, the building was deserted. Jace banged on the back door until one came into earshot and let him in. Jace nodded his thanks then hurried to the second floor. Compared to the heel-scuffed, coffee-stained, cigarette-littered brokers' room on the first floor, the second story was like the Taj Mahal—hallways and foyers polished to a blinding sheen, marble windowsills, and cherry furniture.

As Jace strode down the hall, he wondered what he was hoping to accomplish. Even if he found proof to support his suspicions, what was he going to do about it? Turn in a man for selling his stocks?

The truth was, he couldn't do anything. It was only a curiosity he needed to satisfy, maybe because he wanted to be angry at someone besides himself.

Drakeworth's office was at one end of the hall, its door open and lights on, though he wasn't inside. Jace walked in as though he had been invited, letting out a low whistle as he took in plush upholstery and floor-to-ceiling bookcases. One wall was graced with an oversized print of an Old World globe while another held a panel of windows overlooking the street.

A file cabinet sat beneath the print, and Jace guessed that was where he would find information on Sheffield's interests. Approaching the cabinet, he wondered if it was locked.

He would never know the answer. As he was about to test the handle on the top drawer, voices cracked the silence in the hallway. Jace recognized the jovial sound of Drakeworth's and Sheffield's voices, and they were making a straight line for Drakeworth's office.

Jace knew there was no way to escape unseen. His eyes darted about, finding the only place to hide—Drakeworth's coat closet. Quickly, he took cover, hoping that neither man had outerwear to hang up.

Jace listened as the men moved about Drakeworth's office. First there was the sound of a key turning in a lock and a drawer sliding open, followed by the clatter of ice cubes tumbling into glasses. Next came the thick splashes of liquid cascading over the ice.

"I like a man who doesn't participate in Prohibition," Sheffield said.

Drinks filled, the men lit cigars, the aroma rich and heavy. A moment passed, and Jace imagined the two men taking deep, satisfying draws on their cigars.

Sheffield spoke again, his voice booming and as full of as much cheer as his glass was. "Well, she came crashing down, just as we suspected."

"But we're better off because of our suspicions, sir," Drakeworth said with a laugh. "Ah, the sweet rewards of finding opportunity in the face of disaster."

"Yes," Sheffield agreed puffing loudly on his cigar. "Sweet."

Jace knew that for men like Sheffield and Drakeworth, the unregulated stock market was a target for manipulation, a game of forcing prices up or down and netting millions in mere months. Anyone with enough money and know-how could do it.

The men were like roosters strutting about the office and crowing over their success, reveling in the brilliance of their strategies. As they reminenced and laughed over this move or that move, Jace was able to put the pieces together. Others had done it, too, and those in Jace's profession knew there was a dirty side to the business. Before the market turned skittish, they had formed a stock pool made up of Sheffield and several officers at the People's Standard National Bank. With Drakeworth as their broker, they bought shares of stock in companies not considered valuable, then made phony trades amongst themselves, causing other investors to think the stock was more valuable and sending the price way up. When it peaked, the men would grab their hefty bank roll, pull out, and send the stock price tumbling—leaving stunned investors to count their losses while the pool members cheerfully split the profits, minus a generous broker's fee for Drakeworth.

Later, when the market started to decline, they pounced on its vulnerability by selling short. They borrowed stock from Drakeworth on ones they believed would go down in price. When the price dropped, they would buy new shares at the lower price, return to Drakeworth what they had borrowed at the higher price, and pocket the difference. And Drakeworth's prize for cooperating was a bloated broker's fee, along with Sheffield's promise of job security and continued comradeship should the bottom fall out.

Anger was eating Jace alive. Every limb was threatening to flinch or strike out at something, but he ordered himself to do nothing more than clench his fists and bear down on his teeth. Intellectually, he knew he couldn't blame the market's collapse on the men outside the closet, glorifying themselves as they puffed their expensive cigars and downed their poison. Yet, he could never believe that their hands were absolved of all blood, not when he had heard them laugh as they admitted to manipulating the market. They had driven prices down and made at least some contribution to the crash, but what scorched Jace was that they had known the economy was slowing and taken advantage of its ails, lining their wallets at the expense of others.

Jace couldn't fault a man for mining the gold before it was gone. But this. He pressed his fist against his palm. This kind of financial wisdom was about self-preservation, the greed of advantaged men who already had more than most would see over a lifetime.

Jace stopped talking, perplexed by Julianna's lack of reaction.

"There's not much about Father and Leyton's business dealings that could shock me," she said, looking to the horizon. "I've seen them take a man's last penny, not to mention his dignity."

"I never knew my father," Jace said as he followed her gaze. "And I think I'd rather have it that way than to feel like you do about yours." He brushed away a lock of hair that had blown across her cheek. "It must be hard."

"Hmm," she murmured, distracted as she continued looking across the water. "There's one thing I can't figure out."

"What?"

"Well, if Leyton and Father believed the end was coming, why did they talk up the market? If their customers and associates took heavy losses, wouldn't the People's Standard and Southern Gold suffer because of it?"

"You'd think."

"Then why didn't they advise people to take their money and run?"

It was a good question. One that Jace, too, had wondered about while squashed in the coat closet. And one that Drakeworth and Sheffield had given him the answer to.

"These are the finest cigars available," Sheffield had said. "A gift from Abbot Tinley."

"He's a man of impeccable taste," Drakeworth said. "And an impeccable customer of your bank. I'm grateful he took your advice and left the market last summer, as did many of your most valuable customers."

"Other men are now sitting on empty," Sheffield said with a chuckle. "Fortunately, they're parked in front of my competitors' banks."

"May the strong survive," Drakeworth said between puffs on his cigar. "I can say with confidence that we—excuse me—you will survive the collapse quite nicely."

"Absolutely." Sheffield spoke arrogantly. "No doubt some smaller customers won't fare so well, but my most prosperous customers are solvent."

So you warned the big guns, Jace realized. Why not the little guys?

Sheffield continued, "And you were correct in saying we."

"That pleases me, sir."

"I said I would make a place for you in my bank," Sheffield stated matter-of-factly.

"I never doubted you," Drakeworth said. "And I'm positive that I'll soon be in need of employment."

"I assume that Southern Gold took a hard hit. "

"Many clients saw losses," Drakeworth mused. "The powers of Southern Gold will hold me responsible. I stand firm, though, that I was correct in directing my brokers to encourage most of their clients to stay in the game."

"Oh, absolutely. Panic and predictions only fulfill people's fears of recessions and depressions," Sheffield said authoritatively. "Nobody wanted to see today's events unfold."

"Of course not," Drakeworth replied. "I hoped that optimism would keep the market breathing, that it would rally and return to good health."

"We all did, but naturally, men such as myself can't risk being too optimistic."

"Correct again, sir," said Drakeworth. "I made sure my managers understood the differences that exist between clients." He paused to take a drink. "After all, when the barber down the street loses his piddling of a savings, it's not a devastating event at large. But when men of great means are financially shattered, the effects are widespread."

So that's it, Jace fumed. They let the smaller potatoes support their hopes while protecting the fat cats just in case.

It was called hoping for the best but preparing for the worst. Not a bad philosophy, but this had to be the most self-serving example Jace had ever heard of. And the ugliest part was that little clients, like the ones who trusted Jace, had been the sacrificial lambs of the two arrogant creeps strutting outside the closet.

Sheffield finished his drink. "I thank you for the fine scotch and equally fine cigars."

"As always, your company and conversation have been a pleasure," Drakeworth said.

"May I escort you out, sir?"

Jace stayed hidden until the men left the office and their voices dissipated in the corridor. He left then—fast.

Returning to his apartment, he yanked his duffel bag from the closet and tossed it on the bed. He pulled the drawers out of his dresser and dumped the contents into the bag, hurrying as though getting out of town would make him forget Sheffield, Drakeworth, and the four people whose lives he had played a part in ruining.

He especially wanted to forget all traces of them.

He stepped into the night and carried his bag seven blocks to the bus station, where he bought a seat on the first bus that was heading anywhere near Ambrose Point. He would have to make a transfer somewhere along the line, but that was fine, just as long as he could break out of this town—this life—tonight.

When the bus lurched from the terminal, he felt some relief, but it was not the flood he was hoping for. And no matter how many miles the bus put between him and Southern Gold, four ghosts stayed in hot pursuit.

Costiano, Jackson, Adams, and Willows. They haunted him with guilt and regret, a thousand should-have's and if-only's.

For the first time since his mother died, Jace McAllister cried.

CHAPTER

Jace and Julianna were walking back to the bungalow, the scorching noonday sun prickling their shoulders like hot needles.

"Did you ever think of turning in my father and his cronies?"

"Many times," Jace told her. "But for what? Selling short, stock pools . . . it was the twenties and the market was unregulated. Everyone for themselves."

They reached the house and went inside, escaping the sun and its blistering heat. She got a couple of Cokes out of the icebox and handed him one, which he finished in three swigs as he looked out the front window.

"So you got on a bus and left town," she reiterated for him, taking a sip of her Coke. "What happened next?"

"I came back here," he said, remembering that Ambrose Point had never looked so good—and never looked so bad.

The local bus terminal was small, not much more than a bench on Main Street. When Jace stepped off the bus, he saw that little about the town had changed. The same flag waved over the courthouse, the same old men sat sparring around the barbershop, and the same tarnished bell was hanging in the steeple of the First Baptist Church.

"The town had pretty much stood still in time," he told Julianna, "but Granddad hadn't. It was pretty clear his health was going and his days were short. The next few months were about taking care of him. He stayed inside most of it, but there were some days here and there when he felt like walking on the beach." In his mind's eye Jace could still see those days, slow and ambling, with Granddad once saying, "Don't hate that I'm dying, Jace, 'cause I'm not. I'm just going to my real home."

Jace had hated it, though, and answered by not answering. He had only looked at the ocean, her swells high and pewter. She could be the most beautiful creation in the world, or on days like that one, the saddest sight in all of nature.

"Granddad said that sometimes people can only get well by going to Heaven," Jace recalled. "He told me to celebrate after he was gone, to do it by throwing his medicine bottles out to sea."

"And I'll bet you did exactly what he asked you to."

Jace nodded. "It happened just before Easter, right inside this house. I stayed with him till the end." He turned from the window. "Have you ever heard of people seeing angels right before they die?"

"I have, Jace. Cassie, knows a lot about the Bible and spiritual things. She's mentioned that it's been known to happen. Well, at least according to some people's last words."

"Yeah, Granddad pointed up and asked me if I could see him— the angel." He laughed softly. "All I saw was the ceiling, but when I looked back at Granddad, he was gone and the ocean outside was calm."

Julianna, who had been sitting on the sofa, now joined him at the window and wrapped her arms around his waist. "I can't imagine how hard that must have been for you."

"It was," he said, stroking her hair, appreciating that she wanted to comfort him. It had been a while since anyone had done that. He'd heard a lot of the typical condolences at first—Sorry for your loss and He's in a better place—but those faded away with time, which was fine because they really didn't help that much anyway. He'd appreciated the good intentions but had never said more than thanks, never talked to anyone about Granddad's passing, especially about the angel that supposedly showed up at the end. He wasn't sure if people really wanted to hear the details, but Julianna was listening, and it felt good to finally say some things out loud.

"But I'm glad he's not sick anymore. I really can't be anything but happy for him when I look at it that way." He thought of the small seaside cemetery a few miles away, overlooking the surf as it hit the golden shores below. "I buried him next to my mother, boarded up this place, and went back to sea, which is a place I probably should never have left."

"Your granddad encouraged you to, though," she said. "It must have made him happy that you tested out your land legs."

Now Jace laughed loudly and kissed the top of her head, loving that she was trying to encourage him and see the positive side of his decision to come ashore, but certain things couldn't be overlooked. "Yeah, Julianna, he would have been real proud if he'd lived to see those land legs take me away from the scene of my crimes."

"Oh Jace, you know what I mean," she said, playfully smacking his chest. "You went to school, you had a good profession—it was just a horrible time for the economy. You did the best you could for those people."

That was true, but his good intentions didn't absolve him of his guilt, didn't pay the bills or restore the savings for those people who had trusted him. He'd failed them, failed himself, and as far as he was concerned, had failed Granddad by not doing better with his advice to give the land a shot.

"Granddad didn't know about what happened with Southern Gold," Jace told her. "I might've told him if he hadn't been so sick, but my burdens were too much to put on him. Not then."

He did tell him later, though, on his way out of town and back to sea. Duffel bag slung over his shoulder, he made his way to the cemetery to say what he suspected would be a long farewell to his mother and Granddad. It had only been a few weeks since Granddad had passed, and his grave was still a mound of dirt with remnants of flowers scattered about. Jace dropped his bag, sat beside the grave, and poured out the whole story.

"I promised him I'd make it up to them. I didn't know how or when, but I swore that I'd figure it out."

Julianna turned so that she was facing him, her arms still circled around his waist as though holding him in a dance. He knew what was coming next because the need-to-know was written in her eyes. "And just how, Jace McAllister, did you figure it out?"

"It started at sea," he said, "where I picked up that habit my mother had of watching the water." He thought back, recalling how quickly he began to suspect that there was a big difference between what he saw and what his mother must have seen when staring upon the temperamental sea. He felt nothing that provoked the sad, faraway quality that veiled the eyes of his mother. What he felt was the water at its worst, angry and agitated, raw from salt and hardened from gales.

"I'm not sure what she thought about," Jace said, "but I thought about self-preservation and how forgetful men can be when their sense of well-being is threatened." He gently broke their embrace and turned back to the window, staring hard at the waves rolling upon the sand. "They forget about other people and about fair play." He fell quiet for a few seconds then added, "They even forget about God's wrath."

"And I'm sure that Leyton and my father were at the center of those thoughts."

"You have no idea," he said, remembering how he had so often compared the Sheffield pool that had gained so much to the four clients who had lost it all. Anger had boiled his blood while guilt tormented his soul, and after a while . . .

"It just seemed like I'd never find peace until I used my anger against them to absolve my guilt over the others." He turned back to her and looked at her straight on, deep into eyes that didn't seem to harbor any judgment. Instead, they were soft, encouraging him to continue, assuring him that she understood exactly what had driven him to do what he did. "And that, Miss Julianna Sheffield, is when the idea of robbing the Sheffield banks was born."

It was a thought he'd dismissed at first. He'd laughed in its face and pushed it away, but the thought wanted to grow, as though it had taken root the second it entered his mind. Why not? he finally asked himself.

"At that point, Julianna, I had no one left to love and nothing I cared about losing."

Julianna listened, amazed at how events had woven her and Jace's lives together long before they knew of the other's existence.

He was still standing before the front picture window while he talked, but she was now seated in a corner of the sofa, hugging a small pillow in her lap. He turned, his eyes imploring hers.

"Do you think I'm a madman?"

"No," she answered firmly. "I think you struck back where you knew it would hurt."

"Granddad would call it doing the wrong thing for the right reason."

"What do you call it?"

"I call it creating my own poetic justice."

She nodded in both agreement and understanding, remembering how she had thought about poetic justice the last day she was in the Dreamland gardens. She knew her father and Leyton deserved some, and by then she was aware that Jace was delivering it. Now she longed to know how he did it, and more importantly, what exactly happened after he did it. She squeezed the pillow more tightly to her, knowing that a huge revelation was about to come her way.

Jace began his confession.

His first leave from the navy was during the spring of 1931. Unlike his shipmates, he didn't travel to a woman's arms or a mother's fried chicken. Instead, he embarked on a mission that would have to be accomplished in a few weeks.

Jace had saved most of his earnings from his first year at sea, plus Granddad had left him his life savings. He bought the Auburn and returned to the city of his unraveling, where Sheffield had four banks—the headquarters and three branches.

Four banks to take from, four clients to pay back, Jace thought, amused. Four banks fit nicely into his plans, which weren't about an eye for an eye. They were only about giving back what he believed had been wrenched from his clients' hands.

The first robbery would be for Sally Jackson.

Jace checked into a motel, then watched the south branch of the bank, taking a week to get familiar with its comings and goings and with the way the lobby and its outskirts were designed.

Next, he searched the countryside for a place to stash the Auburn, settling on the back side of an abandoned farmhouse, its neglected fields high enough to swallow a man whole.

When the day of the first robbery came, he left the Auburn behind the farmhouse then cut through a field of sunbaked weeds. Minutes later, he emerged on the other side, facing railroad tracks that interrupted the still, country landscape, leading trains into the city that Sheffield and Drakeworth called home.

He ducked back into the fields and waited for the coal engine to make its daily, noontime amble into the city. Right on time, its face appeared from around the bend, lugging a caravan of open-door boxcars. As it lumbered by, Jace darted from the field and ran alongside the train, keeping pace with the sawblade-sharp wheels, chiseling against the sparking metal tracks.

He ran faster, edging as close to the train as he could without losing a leg. In one swift, forward spring, he hurled himself into the boxcar, landing stomach-down on the floor. His legs hung free, but he brought one foot to the door frame and pushed against it, maneuvering himself safely into the car.

Head resting on bended knees, he sat until his breathing returned to normal then looked about the boxcar and saw that he had a traveling companion in the form of a hobo sleeping on a piece of cardboard. Jace then stood and made his way to the door, where he watched the flowered countryside give way to the concrete city.

The train slowed as it approached its freight yard. There were tracks and roundhouses, and the heavy stench of fuels mixed with coal, which woke the hobo. As though he had done this many times before, he rose from his cardboard bed and quickly gathered his scant belongings.

"Better jump," he advised Jace. "Town's got laws agin' hoppin' trains. You'll do jail."

As they passed through a graveyard for old cabooses, Jace leapt from the boxcar, his feet landing hard on the rumbling ground. His soles tingled from the impact, but he moved fast, zigzagging in and out of the retired cars and hurdling a couple of weedy tracks. He was out of the freight yard then, safely on city pavement where he could walk freely.

He walked the three blocks back to his motel and let himself into the small room he had rented. It was time to dress for his first day at his new profession, and he began by pulling on a pair of black leather driving gloves. If he went down, it wouldn't be because of something small and overlooked—like a fingerprint on a button of his black double-breasted suit. The gloves came first, the mask last.

For now, he tucked the mask inside his jacket and hot-wired a black Ford that had been parked in a nearby lot for days.

The south branch of the People's Standard was on the corner of Oak and Maple, facing the latter. Oak was one way, short and narrow, no more than a glorified alley. Its name puzzled Jace, as not a single tree shaded its skinny sidewalks. Oh well, it was a skip from the bank and would make a good escape route, so that's where he parked the Ford.

Dense hedges lined the front of the bank, parting for the walkway and steps leading to the main door. Behind them, Jace duck-walked his way to the porch and crouched beside it, watching a customer hurry down the walkway and turn, the clipping of her high heels growing fainter. Carefully, he peered over the porch and through the glass door of the bank, spying the guard seated just inside. The guard was facing the lobby but saw only the black print of the newspaper he held open.

Now was the time. Jace slapped the mask over his face and dashed into the bank, sticking the cold barrel of his .38 against the nape of the guard's neck. The man stiffened and dropped his paper, its pages scattering about the floor.

"No one will get hurt," Jace said to the guard, his tone easy and unwavering. "Please tell everyone not to make any moves, and kindly lay your gun aside, sir."

"Stay calm!" the guard called to the ashen-faced tellers who lined the far wall, arms paralyzed at their sides. "Don't move—the man has a gun."

"Don't forget your gun, sir," Jace reminded him. "You were going to lay it aside."

"Friendly fellow, aren't you?" the guard growled as he lifted his gun from the holster at his hip, leaned over in his chair, and placed the revolver next to his feet.

"I hear you get more with honey than with vinegar," Jace said as he removed his gun from the man's neck. He stepped to the guard's side, positioning himself so that his eyes could rove easily between him, the tellers, and the front door. His back was protected, facing a wall with no doorways or windows, only a trio of oil paintings showing coordinating landscapes.

"I just came to get what I came to get," Jace said. With his gun, he motioned for the guard to stand.

The guard complied, though without enthusiasm. "What?"

"Lock the door and pull the shade, please."

The guard did as told then looked to Jace for further instructions.

"Take this," Jace said as he tossed a black briefcase at the guard. "Have the ladies fill it. Quickly, please."

Under the threat of Jace's revolver, the guard hurried across the lobby and to the first of five tellers. He held the briefcase open, and she emptied her money tray, and so it went the rest of the way down the line, quickly, precisely, rhythmically, as though they had undergone numerous dress rehearsals for this great performance.

Jace's gun wasn't loaded. This hold up was only about making things fair and square, only about righting some wrongs. Never would the end justify the means if someone got shot along the way.

That included himself.

He quickly scooped up the guard's revolver and dropped it in his coat pocket. No point in taking a bullet as he ran from the bank.

The guard returned, holding the briefcase in both arms. "Here's your loot," he snarled.

Jace nodded and took the briefcase. "If you'll unlock the door, I'll be on my way."

"I've done everything else for you, haven't I?"

"That you have," Jace said as he backed to the door, his gun still controlling every movement in the lobby.

He swung the door open and sprang back into the sunshine, knowing the tellers were already dialing the police. He tossed the briefcase into the Ford, fired the engine, and shot down the alley with an ear-shattering screech of his tires. At the end of Oak, he rounded onto a road called Mason and careened briefly toward a lamppost but quickly steadied the wheel.

He stayed on Mason until it turned into a dirt rural route, nestled among fields instead of buildings, empty of people and cars that caused him to swerve or slow down. There were no sirens in pursuit yet, but he hurried as if they were, his fingers wrapped tightly about the steering wheel, and made a safe escape back to the farmhouse.

The next morning, he read about the robbery in the newspaper. He heard about it from the radio. And at the diner he liked to eat at, the regulars had turned into They Sayers.

"They say he waltzed right in and out," said one gray-haired old-timer who gnawed on a sausage link while perched on a counter stool a few seats down from Jace.

"They say he was so dang polite," said the old-timer's even older-timer of a friend.

Head down, eyes stuck on the newspaper before him, Jace had smiled to himself.

"Yeah," mused the sausage-eater. "They say he made a clean break. They say nobody will ever see that money."

Again, Jace had smiled, knowing that someone would indeed see that money.

"I remember that robbery," Julianna said, interrupting the story. "Father was horrible to be around."

"And Drakeworth?" Jace had to know.

"He seized it as an opportunity," Julianna recalled. "A chance to show Father how he could take charge. He screamed at the police, fired the guard—"

"Wait." Jace stopped her. "He fired the guard?"

"Awful, isn't he?" Julianna said. "He said the guard should have tried to stop you."

"The guard did the only thing he could have done," Jace said, feeling terrible that he'd gotten the guy canned.

"Most people would agree with you," Julianna said. "But Leyton is not most people."

CHAPTER

TEN

Leyton was not most people, and he was glad of it.

Leaving the Midwest had changed his life—charmed it, or so it seemed. He didn't know why, but things had a way of working out for him.

This morning would prove to be a splendid example.

He was about to play eighteen holes when he ran into Geoffrey Marst in the locker room of Sweet Creek Country Club.

"Drakeworth!" Geoffrey exclaimed, landing a friendly punch to Leyton's shoulder. "Francine and I are looking forward to the wedding." Another friendly punch. "By the way, what is Julianna doing in Ambrose Point?"

Ever cool, Leyton didn't flinch at this shocking news. "How did you know she's in Ambrose Point?"

"Francine and the girls just returned from there," Geoffrey said. "Francine saw Julianna on the boardwalk, though they didn't get a chance to speak."

"Ah well, I'll mention to Julianna that Francine saw her."

"Out of curiosity, why is Julianna vacationing now, what with all the wedding preparations?"

"She's there for a friend's wedding," Leyton easily lied. "Serving as a bridesmaid. You know all the girlish festivities that go along with that."

"Do I ever." Geoffrey said, glancing at his watch. "Women and weddings. Have to run, but I'll see you at your wedding."

"Absolutely," Leyton said when Geoffrey had left. "Absolutely, you will."

He walked through the club like a man hurrying to claim a million dollars. Outside, the spring in his step turned into a sprint as he headed for Richard, who was waiting for him by the greens.

Later at Dreamland, Richard rummaged through some papers in a file cabinet in his study. "Audrey and I were in Ambrose Point a few summers ago. I'm positive I've got a map of the town, showing every nook and cranny." Locating it, he gave it to Leyton.

"This will be most helpful," Leyton said, settling into a chair to study the map.

Richard sat behind his desk. Arms folded behind his head, he reclined, ever contented, in his chair. "Now remember, not a word to anyone that you're going to Ambrose Point. I don't want Audrey to get her hopes up, just in case you don't find Julianna."

"I feel like I will find her, sir."

"So do I, but Audrey will be crushed if you don't. Besides, she would want to go with you, and I think you and Julianna need time alone to settle matters."

"Most definitely," Leyton said, folding the map and putting it in his pants pocket. Time alone with Julianna. They certainly needed some of that.

"You'll leave first thing in the morning?"

"Yes, sir."

Leyton stepped from Richard's study, feeling downright giddy. Julianna's little disappearing act hadn't worked, and he was going to be a member of this family after all.

As if to make it seem all the more real, he strode into the kitchen to help himself to a snack. There was nothing quite so nice as making oneself at home.

Cassie was at the counter, rolling dough.

"Hello, Cassie," Leyton greeted her as he took an apple from a basket on the counter. Cassie looked up from her dough. "I was plannin' to use those apples in a pie, Mr. Leyton. You can see I don't have many, and Miss Audrey likes her pies nice 'n fat."

"Oh, I didn't know," he said, teeth cutting through the glossy red skin.

"Well, fine!" Cassie set the rolling pin aside and placed her hands on her ample hips. "You tell Miss Audrey why there ain't no apples in her apple pie."

"Calm down, I'm only having one," Leyton said, chewing with exaggerated chomps.

A few minutes passed then Cassie said, "Mercy, you're gratin' at my nerves!"

"What?" He held the apple in midair. "I'm enjoying God's fruit. Is that a sin?"

"No, but you chomping like a mule sure annoys me. Makes me tempted to commit a sin."

Leyton smiled and tossed the half-eaten apple into the trash can. He took another apple from the basket. Cassie grabbed for it, but he held it high over his head.

She opened a counter drawer and took out her Bible, prompting a snicker from Leyton.

"Scripture for my sinful soul? Something to make me a better person?"

"Nope, gonna read something that will make me a better person," she said, flipping through the well-turned pages. "Here it is—Thou Shalt Not Kill."

Leyton returned the apple and smiled. "I'm sorry, Cassie. I didn't mean to fluster you. I'm just trying to have a little fun, so let's you and me get along. I am practically a member of this family."

"Me too," Cassie said. "Been here since Mr. Richard was a young man. He knows I've got the big mouth." She looked at his hands. "Don't you take anymore of my apples."

He nodded at the Bible. "I don't know a lot about that book you're so fond of, Cassie, but it's always intrigued me that it's been rejected by many a brilliant man."

"Been accepted by many a brilliant man, too, probably 'cause they took the time to read it," Cassie said, picking up the basket of apples and whisking it to the other side of the counter. "Maybe they was smart enough to figure out who give 'em their big brains to begin with."

Leyton opened his mouth to answer, but no words came. Not too many people got his tongue. Turning as red as the apples, he strode from the kitchen and left Cassie to her pie.

Jace didn't know the first thing about raising a girl, but he couldn't imagine a father pushing a cad like Drakeworth on his own daughter.

He voiced this to Julianna as they walked to the dock, seeking refuge from the sun. Its heat was nearly unbearable, turning the house into a sweatshop. Beneath the dock, they would find blue shadows and cool surf.

"Father wanted a son," Julianna said with resignation, fanning her sun-pinkened face. "Someone to play golf with and turn the banks over to. I wasn't the heir who fit into his plans."

"But Leyton would have been—if you'd done what you were told," Jace finished dryly. "He's a hard man."

"He always has been," Julianna said. "When I was six, he wouldn't watch my ballet recital because I didn't get the starring role of Snow Princess."

Jace smiled. "I can't believe you weren't the Snow Princess."

"I was a lowly snowflake." A quiver shook her voice. "He wouldn't come to the show, saying that he was going to wait until I became the Snow Princess because that would mean I was the best."

"That's lousy, really lousy."

"He told Mother that it would inspire me to set goals, and in his own way, he meant well." She smacked away a tear that had slipped from her eye. "Oh, this is ridiculous. It was ages ago—I can't believe it still bothers me. Anyway, it's good he didn't come. I stepped on the snow leopard's tail and ripped it off. Father would have died."

Man, the guy is heartless, Jace thought, though he had already drawn that conclusion while hiding in Drakeworth's closet.

Reminding himself of the two men's dirty deeds had been a big help when he returned to sea after the first robbery and guilt troubled his thoughts.

It wasn't regret about Sheffield and Drakeworth, though. No, Jace had a satisfaction about those two, believing they got what they deserved. Nor did he worry about the robbery taking money from innocent depositors. That he could rest easy about, knowing they were taken care of because the FDIC now insured up to five thousand dollars of each person's money, a plan that went in right after the Crash.

What Jace felt bad about, what hovered on the boundaries of still moments, were the scared faces of the people in the bank when he barged in. The faces would have grabbed on like leeches if Jace hadn't had the memory of Sheffield and Drakeworth, two self-crowned kings whose greed sent people down a rougher road in life.

And now, he had more reason to despise the men. He was looking at the reason now, a woman whose soul was as soft as the sand she was settling onto, letting the waves roll over her long legs. He dropped behind her, his knees burrowing into the sand, and rubbed her shoulders while resting his chin on the silky hair piled loosely on top of her head.

To them, she was only the means to an end. To him, she had become everything.

"Jace, tell me the rest," she said as she raked her fingers through the sand, coming up with a small handful of tiny shells, so thin and delicate that they were nearly transparent. "Let me know everything about you."

Jace explained that his next long leave was in 1932, during the early weeks of November when FDR was elected president, his promises of a New Deal crushing Hoover by millions of votes.

His leave began in Ambrose Point, where the late autumn sky hung above the ocean like gray slate and was prone to outbursts of chilling rains. It made the bungalow, so empty without Granddad, the last place Jace wanted to be. Instead, he spent a lot of time with childhood friends, and that was when the chance to buy into the boat business came along. Still serving in the navy, he wouldn't be around much to help with the business, but his partners didn't mind. They were just glad to have another investor.

On the morning Jace left for his second robbery, his friend Marty, who kept the Auburn while Jace was at sea, waved him off. "I started it up once a week," he said. "Kept the engine from getting lazy."

"Thanks," Jace said as he stuffed his duffel bag in the passenger's seat. "See you in a couple of weeks."

"Hope your business goes good."

He gave Marty a wave and rolled up the window then left for his second mission, this time for Antonio Costiano. Before, he had gone south; this time he'd go to the north branch of the People's Standard.

It posed complications from the start. First, it wasn't in a building to itself, but was the heart of one building housing several businesses.

Connected to one side of the bank were an appliance repair store and a hat shop. On the other side was a drug store and a vacant office. The second inconvenience was that the building faced a street that didn't let cars park in front of it. Patrons were routed around the building where they could leave their cars in a parking lot. Jace sat in the Auburn and contemplated the problems.

He would have too far to run, and the parking lot was busy, overrun by people with aches and pains, broken toasters and occasions to wear hats.

Too many people could get in the way. Too many things could go wrong. When he weighed the risks, the scales broke.

There had to be another way. His eyes ran the length of the long building, the ground-level windows telling him that there was a basement. Using judgment to measure the windows, he determined that a slender man could slip through them but knew his own shoulders were too broad to pass and would be reduced to bloody shreds if he tried to force the issue.

Still, he wanted to have a look around . . .

He was browsing the drugstore when a crowd of high schoolers burst in, distracting the soda jerk and sales clerk with candy sales and ice cream orders. Jace slipped to the stairwell and hurried to the damp basement.

There was a lead pipe running across the ceiling and a wall vent about seven feet up, its grate mounted with a top spring latch instead of screws. Steadying himself on an old stool with yellow foam sprouting from cracks in its red vinyl cover, Jace was able to raise the grate, seeing a short, dust-coated tunnel.

He got his head and chest inside the tunnel, then pushed off from the stool. The push sent him in as far as his waist, but the tunnel was an empty cylinder with nothing to grab for leverage. He rose on his elbows and began to army crawl, relying on the strength of his arms to drag his legs in with the rest of him.

He crawled to another grate, this one opening to the basement of the vacant office. He pushed it open and rolled onto his back. Grabbing a lead pipe that was mounted a few inches beneath the ceiling, he pulled himself from the vent and dropped to the floor.

If anyone had ever occupied this office, they moved out every last scrap of evidence. The space was completely empty. Jace removed his coat, a three-quarters-length trench that the salesman insisted was second to none. Jace tested the claim, threading the coat through the small space between the pipes and the ceiling. When both ends of the coat dangled across the pipes, he grabbed them like ropes and began to climb the wall. He inched his feet toward the vent, his stomach muscles on fire and his upper arms trembling under the intense strain of the maneuver. Military training had taught him to walk walls, but it still hurt like crazy.

Feet first, he fed himself into the vent and scooted to the next grate. Beyond it was another basement, this one much larger and belonging to the People's Standard.

The place was a maze of broken office furniture, boxes, and piles of dusty ledgers. Jace stepped through the clutter and to a self-locking door that opened to a dark hallway. Propping it with a book, he moved cautiously into the darkness, pressing his back to the wall as he edged along, heading for another hall that criss-crossed this one like an intersection. The one he was approaching was well lit, and he suspected it led to the bank's vault.

When he reached the next hall, he paused to look from left to right. On one end was a flight of stairs; on the other end was a heavy door protected by a combination lock.

Jace glanced at his watch. Almost five-thirty. Nearly a half-hour since the bank closed for the day. Someone should be coming down the steps any minute now . . .

He returned to the storage room and waited for footsteps to

descend on the stairs. When they came, he opened the door a crack and peered down the hallway toward the lighted section, seeing a guard pass by with another man, probably the branch manager. His hands secured money from the day's business, all counted and categorized by denomination.

Satisfied, Jace let the door slip shut then smiled to himself. He knew exactly how he was going to pull this off.

The next evening, Jace stepped into the lighted hallway and met the guard and the manager at the bottom of the stairs, his sudden appearance causing both men to go rigid and the money to fall from the manager's hands.

At first, Jace was most interested in the guard.

"Please hand over your gun," he instructed from behind his black mask.

The guard, staring at the revolver in Jace's gloved hands, quickly complied.

"And your keys."

Again, the guard cooperated, handing over a metal ring that was heavy with an assortment of keys. It likely contained a key to every room in the bank, but Jace only cared about the one that unlocked the door to the storage area. That door was the first punch on his ticket to escape, but he didn't stand a chance if the guard could access the room quickly. Jace knew the guard could hand the cops another set of keys but was hopeful that the glue he had filled the keyhole with was now as hard as cement. That should hold them up awhile.

Next, Jace turned his attention to the manager, whose perspiring bald head glistened like ice on a frozen lake.

"Gather up the money," Jace said as he thrust a duffel at the manager, "and put it in this bag. Please."

The manager stooped and gathered the money that littered the stairs. When the bag was full, his shaking hands presented it to Jace.

"Thanks," Jace said as he began backing down the hallway, toward the storage room. "Once again, I've found the service of the People's Standard to be second to none."

He slipped into the storage room and kicked away the book serving as a doorjamb. After tossing the guard's gun and key ring onto a battered desk, he grabbed a stepladder, ran to the window, and rammed it through the glass. Next, he ripped off his black shirt and raked it against the jagged edges of the window frame, leaving shards of material impaled on the glass. It was only a diversion, one he hoped would send his pursuers on a search through the parking lot.

He placed the step ladder under the vent and shot up it, pushing it away from the wall before he disappeared into the tunnel. Adrenaline burning his veins, he shimmied through the vent and back to the basement of the vacant office. There he had a change of clothes—tan pleated trousers, a Shetland sweater, and his trench coat with its zip-in lining.

Nice feature, Jace thought as he grabbed smooth, flat stacks of money from the duffle and shoved them inside the coat's lining.

He zipped up the lining, tossed the coat over one arm, and went upstairs, letting himself out the office the same way he had come in—right through the front door. That was how he had stolen away the night before, leaving it unlocked for his return.

An awning shadowed the door stoop, and two tall evergreens were on either side of it. Jace stood in the darkness for a minute, watching the flashing lights on the police cars that had overruled the no-traffic laws of this street and were parked in front of the bank.

A crowd had gathered, mostly kids from the drugstore and people on their way to a nearby movie theater. A group burst from the drugstore, hypnotized by the police lights, and rushed by the stoop without noticing Jace. He fell in behind them and joined the spectators in front of the bank.

"Break it up, folks, let's move on," a cop ordered as he moved through the crowd. "Unless you've got information, we need you to clear the area."

The onlookers dispersed, most of them walking toward the theater. Jace followed along, spending the rest of the evening watching I Am a Fugitive from a Chain Gang.

Again, he read about it in the next day's newspaper. This time, he'd been given an official title.

The People's Bandit.

He liked it.

Jace stopped, concern suddenly pulling him from the story. "Did Leyton fire that guard?" he asked, snapping a twig and tossing it, his eyes following its journey as the tide swept it across the sand and tossed it to the waves.

"The branch manager, too."

Jace shook his head. "Too bad your father didn't know about the third robbery—maybe he would've fired Leyton."

"Didn't know?" She gave him a questioning look. "Father knew about the third robbery. It was at headquarters, right after you and I met."

"Not exactly."

"I don't understand," she protested, confused. "You robbed us three times."

"Four times," he corrected, thinking how beautiful her eyes looked beside the ocean.

"When I hit the headquarters in June, that was actually the fourth robbery."

"When was the third one?" she asked. "I didn't know a thing about it."

"Your father didn't either." He took a deep breath, realizing the tremendous risk he had taken nearly a year ago. "But Leyton did."

》 《

It was September 1933, and he'd returned to make his third robbery, this one for Jared Adams.

Jace drove to the Waggoner Street branch of the People's Standard, planning to study its comings and goings. What he found was an empty building, cleaned out except for cobwebs.

The bank was gone.

He wondered if Sheffield had felt the bite of hard times and been forced to shut down this branch. While the possibility amused Jace, it also raised a problem, leaving him with only one Sheffield bank left to rob—the headquarters in the heart of downtown. The biggest and the best, the one he wanted to save for last.

Not that it really mattered, but Jace wanted to take something from each of Sheffield's banks, just as and he and Drakeworth had taken something from each of Jace's clients. It was the poetic justice that Jace liked, but he guessed it was small in the grand scheme, as long as the end result was the same. He'd just have to decide which bank would see lightning strike twice.

He drove to the headquarters and parked across the street, where the first thing he noticed was the red Duesenberg parked out front. Gleaming like a polished ruby, it seemed to flaunt itself among the less-spectacular cars lining the curb.

Jace wasn't sure if he wanted to rob the headquarters or revisit the north or south branch. The only thing he was sure of was that he was starving, his stomach alternating between growls and queasy waves. He got out of the Auburn and crossed the street then went to Miller's Diner on the corner.

At three in the afternoon, the place was empty, quiet in the lull between lunch and dinner. Even the person who worked behind the counter was nowhere in sight.

Jace slid onto a stool and glanced through a newspaper someone had left on the counter. He rustled through the pages until he found the sports section. Next he turned to the comics for his daily follow-up on Dick Tracy.

"You're not a regular."

Jace looked up into the kindly narrow face of a silver-haired man, standing behind the counter and wiping his hands on a rag. "Sorry, I was in the back. How 'bout my famous BLT?"

"Sounds good," Jace said, noticing that the man's blue eyes were vacant as they looked towards him but not at him, gazing over his left shoulder instead. He realized that he was blind. "How'd you know I'm not a regular?"

The man grinned as he slapped a thick slice of tomato on a bed of lettuce. "I know a newcomer by the time of day they come in. All my customers are regulars during lunch and dinner, so anybody in between must be a first-timer."

"You own this place?" Jace asked.

"For now. " The man laid aside his knife. "I still get a decent lunch crowd, mostly people from the bank down the street, but business isn't what it used to be."

Jace thought of the defunct branch of the People's Standard. "Speaking of the bank, what happened to their branch on Waggoner Street?"

The man set Jace's sandwich in front of him. "Merged with the north branch."

Jace tore into his sandwich and chased it with a swig from the bottled Coke he hadn't ordered but the man had given him anyway. "Why'd they merge?"

"I hear it's because they didn't like the kind of people who were settling in the Waggoner Street area. Negroes, poor whites." He pulled up a stool and sat down across from Jace. "Didn't think that kind of clientele was good enough to walk through their fancy doors. By the way, are you finished?"

Jace polished off the last bite. "It was great, thanks."

"Anyway, I'm talking too much," the man said as he cleared away Jace's plate. "But I'm mad at the bank right now." He tossed the plate into the sink, where it clattered against utensils and cups. "I've been a good customer for a long time, but this past July was hard and I couldn't make my diner payment on time. I scrounged it up a few weeks later, but they weren't too nice about it." He ran a damp rag across the counter and frowned. "They said I should've been able to make the payment on time—that they had enough employees who ate lunch here to cover the debt. Can you believe that?"

Jace could. Easily.

"I thought it was ugly, not the way you should treat a customer, especially one who's been around awhile."

"Some people just care about the bottom dollar," Jace said flatly. "Past performance means nothing."

"Well, it should," the man grunted.

They talked a while longer then Jace paid his bill and left. As he stepped outside, he didn't know that the blind man would have his little diner seized by the bank in less than a year, and that it would ignite a fight between a certain young woman and her fiancé.

Walking back to his car, his mind rehashed everything the man had told him, especially about the bank not liking the clientele around Waggoner Street. That kind of snobbery didn't shock Jace, especially in regard to Drakeworth. Jace recalled the arrogance of Drakeworth, the way he had reigned over Southern Gold like a sultan of finance, making assumptions about the lives of people he knew nothing about.

After all, when the barber down the street loses his piddling of a savings, it's not a devastating event at large . . .

Jace bristled, remembering the pretentious comment. Suddenly, he was wondering how Drakeworth was holding up these days. Curiosity sent him to a phone booth on the corner. The phone book inside the booth directed him to River Drive, a neighborhood that was well settled, its front yards black from the shade of towering magnolias and weeping willows. On one side of the street, the backyards met up with the banks of the Holiday River. Drakeworth's house was on the water, a two-story brown brick that was Cape Cod in design with a thatched roof that sloped over the front porch. It was positioned on a hill with a stone retaining wall that bordered the front yard and a long flight of steps leading to a walkway.

He turned onto another block and slid the Auburn against the curb, where he cut the engine and sat for a minute while considering a new idea.

Maybe I should hit Drakeworth instead of the bank, he thought with a smile. Something in that house had to be worth big bucks.

He strolled to River Drive, eyes admiring the stately homes lining the street. Several of the houses belonged to doctors or dentists who had their offices inside, and Jace was glad to see their suspended signs. At least if someone spotted him on the street, they might assume he was a patient, rather than a man casing a neighbor's house.

The mountain of steps leading to Drakeworth's yard didn't concern Jace. After years of climbing the lighthouse steps, these were a breeze. He took them in no time and was quickly encased by the trees that monopolized the front grounds.

Today wasn't the day he planned to rob Drakeworth. He only wanted to look around and set the course, figuring out how he would get inside the house. He'd watch Drakeworth for a few days and learn his schedule then strike after sunset, preferably when the snake had slithered out for an evening. That was the plan so far, but then . . .

Nature revolted as a car roared into the driveway, spewing dirt and stones in all directions. Squirrels sprang into a chattering frenzy as they scurried up tree trunks and birds fled through the high limbs, wings flapping like wet sheets in the wind as they sought safety in the clear sky.

Jace tensed like he had in Drakeworth's office. What was it with the jerk and his timing?

He dove for cover beneath a weeping willow. Its limbs were heavy, drooping to the ground and shielding Jace like an umbrella made for a giant. He backed up to its trunk and waited for Drakeworth to do something.

Keys jangling, Leyton strutted along the walkway and bolted up the steps. He opened the screen door and unlocked the wooden one it protected, then stepped inside and tried closing the wooden door with the back of his heel. It stopped one-fourth of the way short.

Jace moved from the tree trunk and pulled back some of its long, dangly limbs. Peering out, he saw the Duesenberg parked in the drive. It was the same one he had seen in front of the bank.

Should have known.

He stepped from under the tree, nervously amazed by what he was about to do. He walked up the steps and onto Drakeworth's porch then stood outside the screen door. Ready to pass himself off as a salesman or someone asking for directions should Drakeworth spot him, he looked into the house and saw the devil himself sitting on a sofa, his back to Jace.

Drakeworth was leaning forward, toward the coffee table, where he had placed his briefcase. He snapped it open, showing Jace neat stacks of money, so many stacks that Jace puckered his lips as if to whistle, though he dared not utter a sound.

He's either paying someone off or trying to leave the country.

Leyton rose and crossed the room, going to a roll top desk and retrieving a large manila envelope. He returned to his seat and began stuffing the money into the envelope, his terse, angry movements telling Jace that this money was going into someone else's pocket, not Drakeworth's. He watched him place the envelope inside the briefcase and close it up, wondering if he was being blackmailed, buying someone's silence.

Leyton stood and tore off his suit coat, flinging it across his shoulder. Loosening his tie, he crossed the room and started up the stairs, disappearing behind a wall and leaving Jace and the briefcase with nothing but a screen door between them.

There was no time to think about it, really. No time to do anything but seize it as one of those rare opportunities to make a move.

He eased open the screen door and darted toward the coffee table. His fingers gripped the handle of the briefcase, and he lifted it off the table, careful not to disturb the two brass candleholders that sat in adornment.

Heart thundering, he slipped back out the door and ran through the trees and down the steps to the sidewalk. He began walking away from the house, his steps quick but not hurried enough to arouse suspicion among the neighbors.

Even after pulling off the one-man robberies of two banks, Jace felt stunned by the brazen move he had just made. Heading for the Auburn, his palms sweated and his footsteps pounded in his ears as a slew of words crossed his mind. Crazy . . . death wish . . .

Yet, it had been quick and easy, and as he started the Auburn and pulled away from the curb, his only regret was that he hadn't been able to see Drakeworth's face when he discovered his payback money was gone.

Over the next few days, Jace read the paper as usual, but it was only to keep up with the World Series and Dick Tracy. There was no mention of a robbery at the home of Leyton Drakeworth.

Just as Jace suspected it would, the theft went unreported.

"I can't think who he would be paying off, or why," Julianna said. She was sure, though, that he had made enemies over the years. It was comforting to think he didn't have the upper hand over everyone and was not completely all-powerful in his quest for gold.

"If Leyton took that money from the People's Standard then he's a bank robber, too," Jace said. "Like me."

"No, not like you." Julianna waded into the surf. It was warm, heated by the sun. "You're much more human than he is. At least you do good things with the money you take, and you don't steal it from someone who has put their trust in you."

"Well, the way you put it at least sounds better." Jace followed her into the ocean. It was graduating shades of blue today, growing darker in color the farther it stretched.

"After the third robbery, did you go back to sea?"

"For one more year."

"And your last robbery—the fourth robbery—was at the headquarters? The one that happened—"

"A couple of weeks after the night we met," he finished for her.

The night we met, Julianna thought, the six-week-old memory as vivid as it had been the next day, when she had found herself enthralled by his eyes and weak-kneed by the long kiss atop the star-washed roof of the Downtown Panache.

The beginning of the end of life as she knew it. The night that changed everything.

"I guess that robbery was for Robert Willows," she said, turning to him in the water, the waves lapping at their legs and soaking the skirt of her sundress. "How did you pay those people back, Jace? Did you just show up at their doors?"

"No, it wasn't that obvious," he said, looking past her toward the lighthouse.

"How, then?"

He smiled uncomfortably, still not meeting her eyes. "I just did. Let's leave it there."

She was touched by his discomfort. "You're bold when you talk about jumping trains and making escapes, but you turn bashful when it comes to the better side of your bank robbing."

"I just made some paybacks, Julianna, but I'm no hero."

"You certainly had your reasons for doing what you did."

"Yeah, but my reasons only explain why I robbed the banks. They don't excuse it," he said honestly. "I've never tried to convince myself that they did."

"So you don't liken yourself to Robin Hood?"

"A guy in green tights? No, never." He looked back at her and playfully rustled the top of her head then started out of the water, pulling her with him.

"Jace, why didn't you go back to sea after the last robbery?" she asked as she splashed behind him.

"I didn't re-enlist," he said over his shoulder, "because I went looking for you."

She was smiling when they reached the shore, smiling when he drew her into his arms.

"I need you to know how I paid my clients back. Paybacks were the whole point of the robberies."

"Okay," she said, her curiosity burning in her eyes.

Jace nodded toward the bungalow. "Come on. I'll show you."

She went back to the bungalow with him, eagerly watching as he went to a desk in the front room and dug some receipts from the bottom drawer.

"These will tell you everything," he said as they went onto the porch. The house still felt like an oven. She leaned back in a white Adirondack chair and looked carefully at each receipt, her eyes welling with tears as she read.

September 1931—house restorations for Sally Jackson. November 1932—tuition paid for Antonio Costiano's son. October 1933—bicycles, BB guns, dolls, clothing, shoes delivered to Jared Adams. June 1934—medical bills paid for Robert Willows.

She couldn't speak but reached for Jace's hand as he sat quietly in a chair beside her.

"I hid those receipts," he said, "because they help sometimes when the guilt hits me. I take them out and look at them, you know?"

She nodded that she did and looked through the receipts again. When she felt she could talk without crying, she said, "You did everything anonymously, Jace."

He said nothing but shifted uncomfortably in his chair.

"What kind of medical bills did Robert Willows have?"

He got up and went to one of the pillars supporting the roof of the porch. Eyes on the water, he said, "His kid had polio." He uneasily smacked the pillar. "Any more questions, Julianna? I'm really ready to change the subject."

"Just one." She went and stood beside him. "You didn't rob the banks for exactly what the work on Sally's house cost, or for exactly the price of all those toys. If there was money left over, what did you do with it?"

"What all bank robbers do," he answered, his tone lighter. "I buried it for a rainy day."

"No, you didn't," she said. "Seriously, what—" She stopped, recalling her last night at the shelter, Lilly standing on the porch, thanking Julianna for a gift she knew nothing about. It was the same night Jace had come for her, saying that he had been following her since she'd left Dreamland earlier in the day. It was easy to watch the comings and goings of the shelter and know what its purpose was, and that it wasn't a self-funded facility.

"Never mind, I know the answer," she told him. "You gave it away."

"You're sure about that?"

"Positive." She pressed herself to him and rested her face on his chest.

He shrugged. "I couldn't think of anything I wanted to buy, so . . ."

"You're a humble man, Jace, and your heart is better than you probably know."

CHAPTER
ELEVEN

Before leaving town, Leyton had one person to do business with.

His name was Tommy Lipton, better known as Lightfoot even though he was big and thick with a belly of mush that had seen too many dumplings. Yet, when it came to dodging cops and jilted women, Tommy slipped away with graceful ease. Thus, the nickname.

Tommy called himself a good ole boy who had done well, but despite his tailored suits and expensive cigars, his flashy rings and fleet of cars, he was just a yellow-haired, ruddy-faced, country-raised thug, a bully who ran a Southland version of the mob and harbored the mean spirit of a striped snake. Here was a man who had broken his brother's nose because he snored during Amos 'n' Andy, a man who beat up a girlfriend because she cut her hair short, a man who would probably deck his mother if Sunday supper was late.

Above all, Tommy was a huge thorn in Leyton's side.

The men had met during the mid-20s when Tommy came to Southern Gold for investment advice. Leyton had been impressed by his moneywad, most of it accumulated from bootlegging. He decided to manage the account himself, making so much profit for Tommy that the man decided he and Leyton needed to be good buddies.

Tommy had owned three big speakeasies, where patrons were admitted after rapping a specific rhythm of knocks on the door then whispering a password into the doorman's ear. Tommy had been ready for police raids, having installed electric switches that could seal the doors shut, and concealed drains where they could quickly pour away their outlawed spirits. As it was, the cops weren't a threat since payoffs and free drinks made it easy to bargain with police chiefs, as well as a few district attorneys and federal agents.

Tommy's long-time boys had overseen the daily operations, and his new best buddy Leyton had managed the money, working after hours and on the sly while maintaining his airs and respectability at Southern Gold and later at the People's Standard. As payment, Tommy allotted Leyton a percentage of the illegal earnings, but Leyton always gave himself a larger cut. The profits were so huge that Tommy stayed happy and unsuspicious. For a long time, anyway.

It wasn't until the Hoover and Roosevelt Presidential race of '32 that Tommy saw the light. With both candidates in favor of repealing Prohibition, Tommy grew depressed, foreseeing the end of his speakeasy riches. One night, blubbering in his drink, he deepened his misery by looking over books from the past, where years of profits were recorded.

Through blurry eyes, he had studied the numbers from 1926 to 1932, growing more sober with every year. He knew the books were doctored to make the businesses look legitimate as strictly food and entertainment establishments, but he didn't care about that. All that interested Tommy was the bottom line. Fact was, the speakeasies should have made more money than the books showed. So where was it?

The next day, sober as a judge, Tommy had called a meeting with his good buddy Leyton, asking him to stop by the house on his way home from work.

Leyton had found Tommy standing in front of his red brick hearth, below his prized deer head and a couple of mounted rainbow trout.

He had greeted Leyton with a broad, gap-toothed smile and a couple of options: fess up and pay back or deny everything as his knees were being nailed to the floor.

Leyton agreed to quarterly payments for five years. That's how long Tommy calculated it would take Leyton to pay back what he'd stolen, plus fifty percent interest.

For the first eighteen months, Leyton had made his payments in person, going to Tommy's house and handing over the cash while Tommy taunted him, flanked by three or four boys sporting lopsided sneers while smacking their knuckles against callused palms.

"Well, Benedict Arnold, I reckon you're meeting these payments by embezzling from Old Man Sheffield," Tommy liked to say. "When he finds out and cans your tail, I won't be able to hold back my wild boys. They love it when someone gets behind in their payments." He would then make a slicing gesture with his finger, drawing it swiftly across his throat.

Lately, the arrangements were being handled differently, with Leyton meeting one of Tommy's men in a predetermined spot and handing over the payment. That's because the man called Lightfoot was doing quite the dance these days, hiding out with various girlfriends until the Feds cooled their search and he could slip out of the country.

Since the end of Prohibition, Tommy had gotten deep into racketeering. Hoover's G-men had breathed down his neck on a daily basis, but never got the ironclad evidence to send the Dixie snake upriver. Until he kidnapped a socialite, the wife of one of Atlanta's favorite sons who ignored a gambling debt to Tommy. Tommy let the high-class broad go once the debt was paid, but he couldn't get rid of the federal kidnapping charges nipping at his heels.

When Leyton had first heard that the heat was high for Tommy, his hopes hit the ceiling, thinking that maybe this would send Tommy into such deep hiding that he'd forget about Leyton's payments. At least for a while, giving Leyton some reprieve.

No such luck. That was when Tommy made the new arrangement, knowing that Leyton wouldn't dare tip off the Feds or let himself be followed to any hiding places. It wasn't that Tommy had returned his trust to Leyton; he just knew the man wasn't stupid enough to mess with ole Lightfoot again.

Now, before leaving for Ambrose Point, Leyton arrived at Nathaniel's Pub to make his payment. He took a seat on a stool, waiting for Tommy's boy to sidle up next to him. Impatient, he drummed his fingers on the bar and stewed about the money he had paid out to these roughnecks. He stewed even harder thinking about the payment that had been due last September. He had come up with that one twice after someone swiped his briefcase. Just walked into his house and helped themselves. What a mad, scrambling panic that had thrown him into, how he had feared for the safety of his knees . . .

A few minutes passed and Tommy's bill collector came in, looking like a wild boar with a vocabulary comprised of growls.

The boar ordered a beer then straddled the barstool next to Leyton. He growled something unintelligible, and Leyton assumed it was a demand for the money since there was nothing else he and this country beast could possibly have to talk about.

Leyton nodded and got up from the bar, wondering if the eyes of federal agents were burning into his back as he walked toward the men's room. Inside, he stepped into a stall and emptied his briefcase of its contents, which was a fat manila envelope, ready to burst from the stacks of bills stuffed inside of it. He propped it on the toilet paper holder then flushed the commode and washed his hands for effect, just in case any agents were hiding in another stall. On his way out the door, he met the stubble-faced errand boy, who deliberately rammed his shoulder into Leyton's before passing by with a snarl.

Leyton returned to the bar and ordered bourbon. In keeping with Tommy's instructions, he lingered until the boar had been gone for fifteen minutes. Once the time was up, he finished his drink, grabbed his briefcase, and left, able to forget about Tommy for another three months.

It was time to clear his agenda for Julianna.

Six hours later, he arrived at the Ambrose Shores Hotel. The Duesenberg roared, grabbing the attention of the valets and bellhops standing out front. The Ambrose Shores was the nicest hotel on the point, ten stories of brilliant white stucco situated amid palms that fanned the immaculate grounds.

Knowing that all eyes were watching him, Leyton hopped gallantly from the Duesenberg and tossed his keys at the red-uniformed valet, smacking the young man squarely on his gold-braided chest. Leyton snapped his fingers at a bellhop and pointed to the trunk of the car. "You'll find my bags in there."

He strode across the hotel's gleaming, white-and-gold flecked lobby, bypassed the line of people waiting to check in, and presented himself at the desk.

"Good evening, sir," the clerk said as he cast an anxious glance at the people who had been waiting in line, now grumbling as they watched Leyton. "The Ambrose Shores welcomes you, but there are a few people ahead of you. If you wouldn't mind—"

"I'll take a suite," Leyton interrupted sharply. "Top floor, ocean front. I hope I'm correct in assuming that your hotel offers room service."

"Absolutely," the clerk assured him, sighing as though he'd decided that it was better to get this man registered and out of the way.

Accompanied to his suite by a college-aged bellhop, Leyton ignored the kid's polite attempts at conversation, preferring to stare straight ahead without comment. When they reached the suite, the bellhop carried Leyton's bags into the master bedroom while Leyton surveyed the large sitting area, his blank expression indicating that he was unimpressed by the décor.

"May I put some things away for you, sir?"

"I expected that such tasks went without asking."

"I always ask, sir," the bellhop explained. "Some guests like to do their own unpacking." He placed Leyton's hanging clothes in the closet and neatly laid his folded items inside the dresser drawers. After arranging the toiletries in the lavatory, he stepped into the sitting area.

"You're all settled, sir," he called to Leyton, who had moved onto the balcony and was looking toward the ocean as it shifted beneath the silvery-white moon. "Is there anything else I can do for you?"

"No."

"You're sure?" the bellhop pressed. "Perhaps you would enjoy a newspaper?"

Leyton scowled, irritated by this kid's attempt to squeeze out a tip. He spun and stomped into the sitting room.

"Does the hotel pay you wages?" he demanded.

"Yes sir," the bellhop said, taking a step back.

"Then let me state that it's not my policy to tip people who are already being compensated." Returning to the balcony, he added over his shoulder, "Pass that on to your friends."

"You have a good evening," the bellhop said as he made a quick exit.

Alone now, Leyton looked up and down the shoreline, its assortment of hotels and homes lighting the coast like candles in the sand. Voices floated by on the wind, tiny bits of conversation and broken laughter lifted from the boardwalk. Farther down was the point, where the lighthouse stood duty, penetrating the night with a yellow beam.

Somewhere, in the midst of this resort, was the one he had come to find.

"Julianna, love," he swore to a passing gust of wind. "We shall meet again."

》《

Several miles down the shore, in the bungalow tucked near the point, Julianna finished reading the last page of Jace's manuscript. She placed it with the pages that had preceded it, stacked neatly beside her on the sofa.

The manuscript had been a surprise, a treasure he had pulled from the same drawer as the receipts. She knew he wanted to write but had no idea he had actually started a book.

"You're a wonderful writer." She spoke with admiration as she looked at him across the room, where he had spent the last couple of hours waiting for her opinion, passing the time by fidgeting with the radio, alphabetizing his jazz records, and dozing restlessly. "You have to finish it, Jace."

"Someday," he said as he sprawled on the sofa, sending the top few pages of his story scattering to the floor. "Did you really like what you read? Were you even able to get the gist of the story?"

"Completely," she assured him. "A sailor runs to sea to forget his great love, only to find that the sea is a daily reminder of this woman. He fights the wrath of nature, the swords of pirates, and even finds himself shipwrecked, but eventually the sea leads him back to the woman he wishes he had never left."

He smiled, impressed. "Sounds like you got it."

"I loved it, right from the opening paragraph." She retrieved the first page from the floor and read what he had written. "She was a temperamental lady, with moods he likened to the sea. A calm paradise that could suddenly be thrown into churning agitation, a stormy gale that would have to run its course. When he went to sea to forget her, it proved a painful journey, as the shifting emotions of the water were a constant reminder of the one he was running away from." She put the page aside. "Jace, it's really, really good."

"You're the only person I've let read it."

She told him that his self-revelations had only drawn her closer, entwining her with him all the more. He rested his head in her lap and raised her left hand then fiddled with the ring on her finger. "What are your dreams, Julianna?"

"You're trying to change the subject," she playfully scolded. "I want to talk about your book."

"No, really." He looked earnestly into her face. "What are your dreams?"

She sighed and laid her head against the back of the sofa. "I don't know," she said quietly. "Father decided my dreams for me and I spent most of my time obliging him." She paused, cringing at the truth. "I never asked myself what I wanted."

"Now you're free to."

"Yes," she said, feeling better. "I am." She re-situated herself on the couch, stretching out beside him, moaning over her tired muscles. He had taken her out on Ambrose Annie today, where she had helped a ten-year-old tourist reel in a huge bass. It had taken her and the boy thirty minutes to haul the fighting fish onto the deck. "I've already ruled out a professional fishing career."

"Not too many women look as good as you did wrestling with a fish."

She smacked him with a throw pillow. "We're going to be happy, aren't we?"

"Going to be?"

"I mean, we're going to stay happy," she said. "That's what I dream about more than anything—staying happy."

CHAPTER

TWELVE

Leyton was up early, drinking Sanka while the radio announcer rambled on about the Midwestern drought and damaged wheat crops. From there he began talking about Roosevelt and his move to form the FCC, hoping to regulate the broadcasting industry and increase telephone service in rural areas.

Who cares? Leyton smirked. The news wouldn't impact his life. So what if the price of Wheaties went up? He could still afford them. And as for phone service on the farm, big deal. There was nobody past the city limits he cared to call.

The only news he wanted was news about Julianna.

He changed from his silk bathrobe into his tennis whites. Shorts, shirt, and blue-trimmed, crested sweater vest.

Leyton anticipated that finding Julianna was going to be easy. The area wasn't that big, and he decided to scour it himself rather than go to the sheriff for assistance. There was still time before the wedding—he could spare a weekend if it meant finding her himself, if it meant the bliss of seeing the petrified look on her face when she realized he had tracked her down . . .

He walked along as the town yawned awake, passing hotels where pool keepers were arranging canvas lounge chairs around ovals of sparkling aqua water. Shop proprietors stuck Open signs in their windows, and other early risers made their way to restaurants serving breakfast. On the boardwalk, gruff arcade operators were setting up the their booths, laying out balls, rings, and imitation rifles rigged to hit nothing. The cotton candy vendor stacked his paper cones while whipping up a batch of his pink goods, and two colored men swept away sand and cups that littered a grandstand.

Watching them work, Leyton was glad to be who he was. His hard work had paid off; he was never meant to belong alongside these laborers. Of course, they were necessary and he didn't resent their existence—he just understood that they were meant to make his existence nicer, cleaner, easier, and more enjoyable.

He left the boardwalk and went to Ambrose Square, feeling more at home as he strolled the newer and cleaner streets, pleased to see expensive shops, obviously a better match for the wealthy tourists who frequented the resort.

He paused in front of Lucinda's Boutique, appreciating the fine ladies clothing presented in the window. This was where he wanted to begin his search for Julianna, certain that she had bought clothes since arriving at Ambrose Point. He recalled Audrey taking inventory of her daughter's closet, realizing with dismay that she had fled with only the dress on her back.

Lucinda herself greeted him. She was sixty-ish, well dressed and heavy set with expertly applied makeup and pearls draping her neck and wrists. Her double chins were set high, and she spoke with a touch of airs.

"A very good morning," she said. "Are we shopping for our wife?"

He flashed what he believed was his most charming smile. At least, it appeared that way to him when he practiced before the mirror. "And a good morning to you. You indeed have an impressive selection of clothing, but I'm actually looking for a young woman who may have visited your shop." He retrieved his wallet and took out a picture of Julianna that had been taken the afternoon of their engagement party.

Before looking at the picture, Lucinda held up her hands. "She isn't in trouble, is she?"

More than she knows, Leyton thought, smiling again at Lucinda and shaking his head. "No, she's my cousin. Her parents are in Europe, so they can't give me the name of her accommodations here in Ambrose Point." He rolled his eyes. "And her parents' servants were of no help, seeing how they misplaced the information."

"Please, say no more," Lucinda said as she joined Leyton in some mutual eye-rolling. "I know all about inadequate servants." She studied the photograph closely before shaking her head. "I wish to help, but the young lady doesn't look familiar. I'm positive I would remember her. She's quite lovely."

Leyton slipped the photograph back into his wallet. "Would you be kind enough to direct me to some other clothing stores in the area? I'm sure none of them meet your caliber, but perhaps my cousin paid them a visit."

"Well, I'm the only shop of this kind on Ambrose Square," Lucinda said in a hoity-toity voice. "But there is a clothing store or two in the old part of town, catering mostly to locals." She said locals as though it were a curse word then proceeded to give Leyton directions. "You simply go south on Route 3 for six miles."

He left the shop and hurried back to the Ambrose Shores, giving his name to the valet who had come on duty that morning. Unaware of Leyton's grand arrival the night before, the valet didn't anticipate the verbal assaults that would follow his eager jump to assist this guest.

"What did you do?" Leyton said through gritted teeth when the valet came around with the Duesenberg. "Stop for brunch?"

"No sir, I—" The valet swallowed hard and checked his watch. "I retrieved your vehicle in the proper amount of time, but I will try to improve in the future."

Leyton walked slowly around the car, scrutinizing it mostly for dents and scratches, though any mark would induce a comment.

"I see some marks on my car," Leyton said as he jerked his thumb toward the trunk.

The valet leaned in for a look, but the smudges were too small to see.

"Sir, I'm not seeing—"

"There," Leyton snapped, "just above the trunk lock."

"Sweet mama," the valet muttered when he finally sighted the two guilty marks. Small fingerprints, probably made when the bellhop retrieved the man's luggage and shut the trunk.

"I'll remove them, sir," the valet said as he yanked a handkerchief from inside his jacket.

"Not with that, you won't," Leyton protested. "I only allow cheesecloth."

The valet straightened and made no attempt to hide his irritation. "Beg your pardon, but I'm fresh out of cheesecloth."

"Never mind," Leyton snarled. "I'm in a hurry." He pushed past the valet and got into the car, throwing it into gear and ripping away from the hotel with a screech.

"Incompetent second-class citizen," he muttered as he swung onto Route 3 and hurled himself south, finding that Lucinda had been accurate in describing the town as old. Leyton supposed that some would call it quaint, but all he saw was a sleepy, sun-faded town, its only sign of life right now being three old geezers propped outside the barbershop. Their crinkled faces perked with interest as he tore down Main Street, churning up cyclones of sand as he went by.

The clothing store minced no words, simply calling itself Ladies Apparel. Comparing it to Lucinda's, Leyton found this store bland, knowing that the dull signage and scant window dressings would deter Audrey like a plaque. Julianna, on the other hand, had probably left home with limited funds, making her more inclined to be frugal. Leyton only hoped that she hadn't bought more of those shirtwaist dresses he so hated, the common kind she wore when helping out at that mission for lazy bums.

He locked the Duesenberg and walked toward the clothing store, passing the curious old men without so much as a quick nod.

"Help you find something?" The offer came from a withered voice that Leyton ignored.

"Guess not," said another, shrugging his feeble shoulders.

Leyton rammed through the door of Ladies Apparel and made a line for the young saleswoman behind the cash register. He measured her up in a split second, admiring her honey-toned hair but dismissing her figure as too average.

She, on the other hand, seemed taken with him, and smoothed her hair as he approached.

Drop ten pounds and maybe you'll warrant some chitchat, he thought, noting her interest. "I'm looking for someone," he said as he thrust Julianna's picture at the woman. "Have you seen her?"

"Hmmm, I'm not sure." She stared hard at the photo. "Oh heck, I'll ask Vivian." She slipped behind a curtain and went into the back of the store, returning a minute later with another salesgirl, presumably Vivian.

Leyton raised his eyebrows, liking the second girl better than the first from the sun-bleached hair to the thin build. Smiling, he turned all of his attention to her.

She took one look at Julianna's picture and said, "Oh, you bet, I've seen her."

"You have?" The other girl's face sank, registering disappointment that she couldn't be the one to help the man.

"Jeepers. Celeste, you must remember her!" Vivian insisted. "She bought that polka-dotted dress we had in the window. She said she was getting married."

For Leyton, the words were like a sudden punch to the stomach. A burst of air escaped him, and his gut twisted as though someone were wringing it out like a rag. The tan on his face faded, edged out by the green pallor of nausea as an acidic bile burned his throat. With the two salesgirls still jabbering to each other, he turned and took long strides out of the store, but found no composure in the heavy humidity. It only magnified his symptoms.

He gripped a lamppost to steady himself and focused his attention on the drugstore across the street, willing his mind away from his churning stomach. Feeling a little more stable, he sprinted for the drugstore and slid onto a stool at its soda counter.

"Sun getting you?" the soda jerk asked with a knowing grin.

Leyton barked, "Give me some water."

"Coming right up." He took a paper cup and packed it full of crushed ice then ran it under the tap.

Leyton downed the water in one gulp then tossed some of the ice in his mouth, swishing the frozen crystals around until they melted. He was beginning to feel like himself again. Except, of course, for one major thing.

Julianna had married someone else. He was truly baffled as to how that had happened, as he was so certain that she was meant to be his wife.

Now the most important question was, who? Who had stolen her away from him? And along with her, all that he stood to gain by way of her family's money and her own personal trust fund? Was it so terrible that he desired those things as well? No, there was nothing wrong with a man wanting wealth, its security and the comforts it could buy. There was, however, something wrong with another man intercepting his Julianna for it.

The thought enraged him, and in the space of a few seconds,

Leyton's future darkened as though a storm cloud had suddenly hovered over him. He had to find Julianna, and he realized that it started with finding the man who had intruded into their present and intended to steal their future. He wouldn't stand for that, he absolutely wouldn't. Where to start? There had to be paperwork, a record of a marriage license, something that would tell the tale . . .

"Hey," Leyton snapped his fingers at the soda jerk.

The jerk was leaning against the sink, absorbed in a Perry Mason novel.

"Hey." Leyton spoke louder.

"Sir?" the jerk said pleasantly, putting aside The Case of the Sulky Girl.

"Where is this town's courthouse?"

The Ambrose County Courthouse was a perfect square. Small and compact, its exterior was weathered beige stucco, scored to look as smooth as stone. It sat a couple of blocks off Main Street, the only building on a shade-splattered lot.

For Leyton, the newest information in Public Records was a bittersweet revelation. Bitter because it confirmed Julianna's marriage; sweet because it identified the new groom. Now all Leyton had to do was track down the newlyweds. He had a few wishes to extend.

He returned to Main, seeing that the old men were still sitting their ground in front of the barbershop. Looking all business, he approached them.

"Do any of you know Jace McAllister?"

"All the locals know Jace," replied one man. His blue eyes were watery, the sockets sunken in his face like wrinkled craters. Despite the ravages of age, they still surveyed Leyton up and down suspiciously. "Why you wantin' to know?"

Leyton relaxed his stern posture and smiled, trying to soften his edge and look less threatening. "I'm an old friend," he lied. "But I haven't seen Jace in a while."

"He's been at sea," explained the feeblest of the men, who sat hunched over in between the other two. "But I hear he's back now."

"I've been at sea, too," Leyton said. "That's how McAllister and I lost touch."

"Happens," said Old Suspicious Eyes.

"He told me to look him up if I was ever in Ambrose Point." He smiled more broadly at the trio. "Well, here I am. Do any of you gents know where to find him?"

"I s'pose he's down by the lighthouse, in the house he and his granddad lived in," said the third old man, this one tall and bony with a long face and round wire-framed glasses. For a moment, Leyton wondered if he was looking at the inspiration of the farmer in American Gothic.

"His granddad passed on a while back," the farmer-look-alike continued. He leaned back in his chair, face pleasant and eyes gazing, looking like he was about to launch into a long story. "Now, there was a good man . . ."

Leyton said a quick thanks and bolted from the old-timers, not about to be bored to insanity by listening to one of them ramble about a fellow elder. The storyteller of the group, unmoved by Leyton's departure, turned to the man on his right and continued talking.

Back inside the Duesenberg, Leyton's smile vanished, and his eyes narrowed to angry slits.

So, this sailor thinks he can cash in on my security, Leyton seethed as he threw the car into reverse and backed out of the parking space. He hit the gas full force and tore away from Main Street and careened onto Route 3.

I'll find a way to undo this, McAllister, he swore to his never-seen rival. This isn't about the best man winning—it's about the only man winning, and that man is me.

Leyton could see the point jutting into the Atlantic. He slowed to look for the house the oldster had spoken of and saw what he thought might be it, a bungalow that was the only structure between a sagging dock and the lighthouse.

"You gave up Daddy's mansion for this, Julianna?" He shook his head in disgust. Then, hoping that Julianna would soon be answering that question to his face, he pulled up to the top of the driveway and cut the Duesenberg's engine. After shifting into neutral, he let the car coast to the bottom of the drive, not feeling the least apologetic for dropping in unannounced on newlyweds.

Problem was, he didn't know what, exactly, he was going to say to his wayward fiancée and the new man in her life. While driving to Ambrose Point, he had rehearsed various speeches in his head, deciding to approach Julianna as the suitor who had seen the error of his ways, waxing poetic with promises to make amends. It was a hearts-and-flowers façade he could maintain until the wedding march was over, and then . . . oh yes, then she would learn the real rules of living with Leyton Drakeworth. He knew what it was like to live without order, around people who could not be depended upon for even the most basic things. He knew, but he would never know again, because his household would run on a very different track.

But that was before Julianna married someone else. It was before this stranger named McAllister threatened to make a fool of him—a fool with less money. And it was before the personality of his anger had taken on a new characteristic, going beyond pride and control, humiliation and a severely bruised ego. Now he felt the early beginnings of desperation slowly gnawing around the edges of his anger and urging him to do something, anything, just as long as it was some kind of a move.

Let nature take its course, he thought as he got out of the Duesenberg and went to the door. He drew back his fist and banged a rapid succession of knocks. No answer. He knocked again, louder and longer.

Again, no signs or sounds of stirring about inside. This time, his rap on the door was furious, causing tiny needles to sting his fist as he pounded. He worried suddenly that the happy couple had moved on, that he could knock from now to eternity and never see it open.

Calm yourself, old boy. Maybe they just stepped out.

He peered in the parlor window, reassured to see that the room was furnished, though with nothing he'd use in his own home. He went to the back of the house and looked in another window, this one showing him bedroom quarters. As he was turning away, he saw something distastefully familiar on the bed, recognizing it as one of Julianna's shirtwaist dresses.

He returned to the front of the house, gently chiding himself for the earlier touch of panic, and priding himself on how smoothly his detective work was going. In a matter of hours, he had learned much of what he needed to know, unpleasant as it was.

Still, his good luck would prevail. Where Julianna was concerned, it always did. He needed only to look into the past, to review their life together so far. From there he could draw on the sustaining comfort that he had the undying devotion of Richard, and from that came the upper hand over Julianna . . . and the final word in every facet of her life.

He stared at the ocean and laughed into the wind, as if to defy the power of all that was bigger than man. Of course this was going to work out in his favor.

Confident, he swaggered back to the Duesenberg and fired up its engine.

CHAPTER

THIRTEEN

Jace and Julianna had set out earlier that morning for the county fair a few hours outside of Ambrose Point. Julianna wasn't sure if they'd ever make it to the fair, but she wasn't concerned. They were having too much fun along the way stopping at roadside vendors, buying peaches from the back of a truck and boiled peanuts that proved too awful to eat. They tossed them out the window for the birds to gather.

They began seeing a parade of signs for the fair, each one trying to entice motorists to turn left at Walker's Farm and come for the fun.

Lumberjack Shows! Pie Eating Contest! Fairest of the Fair! But the real clincher, Jace insisted, was the sign that boasted: See Snortles—World's Biggest Hog!

"I'd hate to be on my deathbed and know I missed Snortles," Jace said.

Julianna laughed. "Then by all means, turn left at Walker's Farm."

They parked in a field across from the fairgrounds, which was nothing more than a field itself, though it had been mowed for what was apparently a big event in this county. It looked as though everyone in town was there, many of them showing off their livelihood or pastime, whether it was doll-making or tomato-growing, piecing together quilts or nurturing cucumbers into pickles. There were people making music, some by tapping spoons or blowing into brown jugs, while others played harmonicas, strummed banjos, or rapidly seesawed bows across their fiddle strings. Men guessed your weight and guessed your age, while women invited you to sample their pies, made from apples, peaches, and every kind of berry the earth raised.

Jace grabbed Julianna's hand and threaded her through the crowd, stepping quickly until they reached the livestock barn. Inside, the smell rose to high heaven but didn't discourage the big knot of people around one particular pen. Signs were plastered all around it.

Big Boy Snortles! Eight Hundred Pounds! Don't Feed Snortles!

They joined the crowd and gradually worked their way up to the wooden railing, now only a couple of feet from the popular Snortles. He was standing on a bed of hay, oblivious to the crowd as he happily partook from a washtub of slop.

"He's no hog," Jace decided. "That's a hippo."

Julianna gave him a playful smack on the arm. From one corner of her eye, she caught a dirty glance from Snortles's owner, a black-haired farmer in denim overalls, looking bored as he straddled a chair in the pen and took a huge hunk from the side of a green apple.

"Can you die in peace now that you've seen Snortles?" Julianna asked as they stepped back into the sunshine.

"Absolutely." He took her arm and put it through his as they strolled toward a goat corral. "Tell me," Jace said, "in between your ballet recitals and piano lessons, did you ever feed a goat?"

She pretended to think about it then shook her head. "No, tending to farm animals is one activity Mother never encouraged."

They came to the corral, where Julianna filled both hands with broken crackers and held them over the fence. Goats trotted toward her from all directions, rearing onto their back legs when they reached her and placing their front hoofs on the fence, head-butting each other out of the way. One goat leaned across the fence, resting his front hoofs on Julianna's shoulders, and looked eagerly into her eyes as if trying to charm her into a second helping.

"They're sweet," she said as they moved away from the corral,

Jace again linking her arm through his. Languidly, they walked about, pausing from time to time to watch an event or sideshow. The lumberjack who glistened bronze in the sweltering sun, splitting logs so fast that his ax whizzed through the air in a blur. A young boy whose colorful parrot could sing Dixie. And two women who were in a heated contest at the ring toss booth, vying to win a strand of fake pearls as the game operator baited them on, dangling the necklace before them.

The morning quickly slipped into afternoon. Hungry, Jace and Julianna bought some fried chicken, corn on the cob, and two slices of peach pie, which they ate in the shade of an oak.

"I think Snortles was the highlight of the day," she said as she finished her pie.

"I still say he's a hippo." Jace glanced at his watch. "We better head home."

As if in agreement, the cloudy sky suddenly darkened and fat raindrops splashed to the ground. Jace and Julianna ran from the fairgrounds and to the car, diving inside just before the heavens really opened, dousing everything below in a hard, blinding rain.

"Just a summer storm," Jace said. "It'll blow over."

"I love summer storms," Julianna told him as she watched the rain pour down the windshield, covering it like one big clear sheet. "The way they happen on you so suddenly, like they know you've had all the heat you can stand."

Jace relaxed in the driver's seat, letting one hand wander to Julianna's side of the car. He fiddled with her damp hair as he leaned back his head and closed his eyes, listening to the thunderclouds that were rolling across them.

"Jace, it's been a perfect day."

"Hmmm, there'll be more." His voice was sleepy. As tired as he was from walking in the heat, the rain was affecting him like a sedative, lulling him into an afternoon doze.

Julianna leaned her head back and rested, too. The rain showed no signs of stopping and was soon accompanied by wind that rapidly picked up in strength. Julianna opened her eyes to see that it was blowing the rain sideways, while water on the ground was rushing like it had just been released from a dam. "We definitely want to wait this one out," she said. "Look at this, Jace."

He sat up and took in nature's show. Hot dog wrappers, paper cups, newspaper pages, and other pieces of waste swirled by the windshield. Suddenly, the Auburn and other vehicles around it seemed to be under the siege of rocks and gravel. From pings to thuds, they were being pelted over and over.

"It's hail!" Julianna cried as she saw several larger icy chunks strike the ground beside her door. "Some of this is as big as tennis balls!"

Jace ducked low in the driver's seat and craned his neck toward the windshield, straining to see through the rain and into the sky.

"What's causing it?" Julianna asked.

Jace saw the answer before Julianna finished asking the question, saw it in the form of a vicious greenish-black cloud descending to the ground, its swirling funnel in search of things to inhale and chew to bits. His mind raced, thoughts tripping over themselves as he tried to guess the odds of being this close to nature's fury twice in his life. The first evil had taken his mother; was this one intent on . . .

"Get on the floorboard!" Jace shouted over the tornado's roar.

There was no time to seek lower shelter; there was only a second to pray before the monster touched down, spewing debris as it charged forward like a freight train that had jumped the track.

"The floorboard!" Jace repeated.

But Julianna couldn't move; she seemed paralyzed with horror as she watched a huge tree, roots and all, sail past the windshield. The tornado tossed it as if it were nothing more than a newspaper.

The Auburn strained to hold its ground, shaking violently as the wind whirled around it. Jace pressed hard on Julianna's shoulders and forced her to the floorboard, then flung himself face down across the seat, using one arm to cover Julianna's head and the other to shield his own.

And then, as quickly as it had descended upon them, the twister left, going airborne and disappearing into the clouds. It left behind the stillness of shock, as those in its path struggled to regain their bearings.

Jace and Julianna stumbled from the Auburn, seeing no signs of serious damage, only pings and dents from where hail had struck the cars. The tree that had narrowly missed them was nowhere in sight.

People began to pour forth, some from the fairgrounds and others from inside cars. Everyone looked toward the sky, shielding their eyes against the sun, which had returned in blazing glory.

"Did you see that?" everyone seemed to be asking. "Did you see that?"

Jace and Julianna had only gotten a partial view of the storm, the hood of the car limiting how much they could see. Eyewitness accounts quickly filled them in.

"Touch and go, she was."

"Swooped down in the woods over there, then it went right back in the sky."

"Sent a tree flying like it had wings."

Jace put his arm around Julianna's waist. "You okay?"

She nodded that she was, even though her face was ghostly pale and she was resting a shaky hand on her chest.

"Ready to go home?"

"The sooner the better."

As they walked back to the Auburn, Julianna scanned the sky, seeing only the serenity of cottony clouds against a dome of vivid blue.

They didn't get far from the fairgrounds before they came upon the formerly flying tree, now grounded.

Flustered travelers milled about the road, wondering how to cross a bridge that now held a tree, and a big one at that.

"This is the only road in or out of Ambrose Point," Jace said, getting out of the car for a closer look.

He joined a group of men who were trying to move the tree. Sweating profusely beneath the sun, they couldn't budge it. It must have weighed tons, and its trunk was too thick for a man to wrap his arms around it.

One man wiped his brow with his sleeve. "Unless we can get someone out here with a crane, ain't nobody going anywhere for a while."

As it turned out, it would be the next day before anyone could move the tree. That was the announcement made by a local deputy.

Everyone in earshot groaned but resigned themselves to a night away from home.

"Do you want to find a motel or sleep in the car?" Jace asked Julianna as they turned around in the road and drove away from the impassable bridge.

"The car sounds kind of cozy," she told him.

They returned to the fairgrounds, as did most travelers. The parking area was nearly full, with people reclining on hoods and lounging in truck beds, children playing and radios crooning. All in all, it wasn't a bad place to camp. Food was plenty and outhouses were available.

Leyton was placing a phone call.

"I can only talk a moment, sir," he said to Richard. "The hotel informs me that there's a problem with the telephone lines." In reality, the lines were operating fine. Leyton simply didn't want to answer a lot of questions.

"What did you find out?"

"I've tracked down our runaway girl," Leyton said. "I went by her accommodations this morning, but she wasn't in, so I plan to return later and see if we can chat."

"What kind of accommodations?" Richard wanted to know.

Leyton held a sheet of paper beside the phone receiver and began to wad it up. Through the crackle, he shouted, "Sir? I can barely hear you!"

"I can hear you pretty clearly," Richard said. "There's a bit of noise, but otherwise—"

"What?" Leyton said, balling up another sheet of paper.

Richard raised his voice. "I said I can hear—"

"Sir, I'm terribly sorry for this distraction."

"It's not your fault, son. Tell the hotel you'll not pay for this call."

Leyton stopped wadding up the paper. "That's better."

"Did you have to enlist the sheriff's help?"

"Happily, no," Leyton said. "I would have done so had I not located Julianna right away. Her safety is my top concern, but I must admit relief over not having to humiliate her in such a way. And too, sir, there was the chance that a police search would lead to a family scandal."

Having revealed all he wanted to for now, Leyton crumpled up another sheet of paper. "Here we go again, sir," he laughed. "I'll hang up now but will touch base shortly."

He returned the phone receiver to its cradle, satisfied with the conversation.

And now it's time for a drink, Leyton smiled.

Inside the Seafarer's Tavern at the Ambrose Shores, Leyton downed his drink quickly and ordered another, throwing back his head and finishing it in one hearty gulp.

"One more for the road," he told the bartender.

His third drink gone, he left the hotel and drove back to the house.

Seeing that Julianna had not returned, he pounded the steering wheel and pressed the accelerator.

Returning to the hotel, Leyton ate dinner by the water, his table beside a window that faced the swimming pool of Ambrose Shores. His stomach tingled with light anxiety, but he still savored every bite of his meal and languished at his table until shadows spilled across the patio.

It was time to try the house again—surely by now the couple would be back home. Leyton left the hotel with renewed purpose, pleased by the idea of dropping in on Julianna.

Perhaps she'll invite me in for an after-dinner drink. He laughed at the thought, knowing it was more likely she'd slam the door in his face. Not to worry. Doors could be kicked down.

He amused himself greatly, but the laughter didn't last long. He stopped abruptly when he saw not one patch of light filling any of the house's windows.

Jace took a blanket from the Auburn's trunk and draped it around Julianna's shoulders.

"That man's snoring was killing me," she said as they walked away from the parking lot. The Auburn was parked beside a truck where the owner lay sprawled in the bed, his snores rivaling a loose chainsaw. On the other side of them was a couple who erupted into a spat every twenty minutes or so. She and Jace tried rolling up the Auburn's windows, but the humidity was suffocating.

They made their way beyond the lot and into a pasture of cool grass. They walked to the top of a gently sloped hill where Julianna spread the blanket.

Jace dropped to it and stretched out.

"Look at all the stars," Julianna said as she joined him on the ground and rested on her back. "There must be a million of them."

Jace pointed to one that was exceptionally bright. "That's Venus."

"If you could live on any planet besides Earth, which would it be?" she asked.

He thought a few seconds and then said, "Pluto. The cops aren't looking for me there."

"What would you do on Pluto?"

"Be king," he said. "King of the Pluton People."

"You'd freeze on Pluto."

He rolled over and covered her upper body with his. "Not with you there, Queen of the Plutons." His mouth began to nuzzle her neck.

"What are you doing?" she teased.

Words muffled, he said, "You know what I'm doing."

She couldn't stop a giggle. "What if someone walks up here and sees us?"

"I'm guessing they'll turn around and leave." His hands caressed her shoulders and her sides . . .

She laughed again, but this time he caught her mouth with his. As she responded to the kiss, his hands began to move with more ardor.

As her eyes slowly closed, the last thing she saw were silver stars in a navy sky. She clung to him as he lifted her toward them, and together they soared through the galaxies.

Back in Ambrose Point, Leyton saw stars too as his head dropped forward and hit the bar in the Seafarer's Tavern. His eyes popped open and he sprang back up, snapping his fingers for the bartender.

"One more bourbon," he ordered. "On the rocks."

The bartender complied and Leyton downed it quickly. How many did this one make? Eight . . . nine. He couldn't remember.

CHAPTER

FOURTEEN

On his second morning in Ambrose Point, Leyton slept off last night's liquor. He stirred once and glared through the gray light of his curtain-drawn room, ordering the maid to leave.

It was mid-afternoon before he put his feet on the floor and staggered to the bathroom. After splashing cold water on his blurry eyes and brushing his coated teeth, he began to revive and focus on his reason for being here.

He presented himself at the bungalow, its stillness telling him it was empty before he got out of the car. He tried to pay a call anyway and his rising desperation could be heard in the way he pounded on the door, like a minuteman coming to warn them of British invasion.

Finally, he gave up and stormed toward the car. On the way, he saw blue wildflowers growing beside the house, swaying in the wind skipping off the ocean. He yanked the flowers, tearing them from their source of life and flinging them to the sand.

The morning's early disappointment hovered over Leyton like a dark cloud, following him wherever he went. He decided to try the boardwalk next, but even its cheery atmosphere annoyed him. And being accosted by an organ-grinder whose monkey had a short fuse only made matters worse. When the dancing, green-vested monkey tugged on Leyton's pant leg, Leyton answered with a hiss that caused the animal to screech and spring upward, attaching itself to the open collar of Leyton's shirt.

"You filthy—" Leyton grunted as he pried the monkey loose and threw him to the boardwalk.

"Don't hurt my monkey!" the organ-grinder shouted as he whipped off his hat and went for Leyton's back, beating it as though trying to kill a fire. "Apologize!"

"Forget it," Leyton said as he broke away and pushed through the highly amused crowd who had gathered to watch the sideshow. "If you call that entertainment, then you're sorely sheltered!" he shouted when he made his way past the onlookers. He hurried away with his head high, went further down the boardwalk, and took a seat on a bench. Now maybe he could do what he came here to do, which was watch for Julianna.

Could it be? He smirked after a while, thinking that he might have spotted her. From the back, the woman appeared to be Julianna, standing just as tall and walking the same walk, and her shoulder-length brown hair waved as the breeze directed it away from her face. What's more, she was in the company of a sailor.

He pursued the couple, darting in and out of browsing tourists. By the time they reached the amusement rides, Leyton was close enough to reach out a halting hand . . .

The sailor spun around, glowing red as he faced Leyton. The woman turned, too, showing Leyton that she wasn't even close to being Julianna.

"Why are you following us?" she demanded.

"Sorry," Leyton grumbled. "I mistook you for someone else."

The sailor stepped forward, placing himself between Leyton and the woman. "If you aren't gone by the time I count to three, I'm gonna bust your legs and dump you off the pier." He held up one hand and began counting off his fingers. "One . . . two . . ."

Leyton bolted into the mass of carnival-goers and didn't slow to a normal gait until the tinny music and revolving lights were well behind him. Disgusted, he returned to his hotel room, where he ripped the spread off his bed and wadded it into a mammoth knot that he punched over and over again. Stomping into the bathroom, he raked the bottled toiletries off the vanity, sending them to the floor where they shattered and splashed their contents against the wall.

He'd had enough. Enough. If he didn't get his hands on Julianna soon . . .

He gripped the brass towel bar and tore it from the wall. Minutes later, the phone in his suite rang and he answered with a terse, "What?"

"This is the front desk, Mr. Drakeworth," came a male voice. "Is there a problem, sir? The guests in the suite next to you reported a disturbance."

"There isn't any disturbance," he said, greatly annoyed. "The towel bar in my bathroom fell. Send someone to repair it."

He didn't wait for a reply before slamming the receiver back into its cradle. He then hurried from his suite and to the lobby, where he clapped his hands at a valet.

"Get my car."

When it was brought around, he practically yanked the valet from the driver's seat and jumped inside. His destination, of course, was Jace McAllister's bungalow.

You had better be back, Julianna . . . we have much to settle.

She wasn't back. Leyton glared at the house, as though getting angry would miraculously cause Julianna and her new husband to appear in the sand.

He roared away and began driving up and down Route 3, passing the house dozens of times. After a while, it seemed to mock him with its emptiness.

Returning to the Ambrose Shores, he took his usual seat at the tavern's bar. Without waiting to be asked, the bartender brought him a bourbon on the rocks.

"We've gotten to know your face quite well, Mr. Drakeworth."

"Just keep them coming."

Agitated, he rocked slightly on his barstool while destroying a stack of cocktail napkins, reducing each one to a pile of tiny pieces.

Where could she be?

Three drinks and ten napkins later, he was back in the car and heading to the house. In the black night, he almost passed it, as there were no lights to mark its spot.

As he idled in the Duesenberg, Leyton's throat ached with frustration. He actually felt like crying, but after overcoming the shame of his childhood, he had vowed that he would never cry again.

He had a few more bourbons in the tavern and a few more runs by the house. Finally, he went back to his suite, where he took five messages from Richard and dropped them in the trash.

Then he began to pace. Time was running out.

It was hours before Ratchett's Tree Removal meandered to the bridge earlier that morning at the fair grounds, and another couple of hours before they cleared away the tree.

Traffic going toward Ambrose Point was heavy and moving painfully slow.

"It'll be next week before we get home," Jace complained. To make matters worse, the temperature had hit a record high.

The first town they came to was named Graybell, and it had a bowling alley.

"I'm a pretty good bowler, you know," Julianna said.

"Yeah?" he answered, pulling into the parking lot. "Let's see what you're made of."

The bowling alley was cool and dim, decorated like an old Western saloon. They played three games, giving traffic a chance to thin out.

Eventually they did make it back to Ambrose Point, and despite the fun of their detour, Julianna was glad to be back in the bungalow that had in such a short time begun to feel like home. She and Jace fell exhausted into bed late that night.

The next morning, Juliana was nudged from sleep by the waves. She looked at Jace sleeping beside her, his arms embracing his pillow. Her fingers lightly tousled his hair, but she didn't want to wake him after their late night.

Julianna yawned and stretched happily beneath the white cotton sheets, relishing their early morning coolness against her skin. It would be easy to languish here all day, but she remembered the icebox and cupboards were nearing empty.

She bathed and dressed then made a quick list of groceries to buy at Johnston's market. That done, she tucked the list inside her purse and picked up the car keys from the kitchen table then set out for the short drive up Route 3. Fondly, she thought of Cassie and her beloved Piggly Wiggly, a Mecca compared to this little market by the sea.

Stepping through its door, she anticipated nothing more than a morning shopping trip.

Deputy Joey Sparrs jerked from his slouched position in the patrol car, the sudden movement causing him to slosh his coffee down the front of his shirt.

Nice, he thought as he watched Julianna go inside the market. Pretty girl, McAllister.

It was pitiful, though, that Jace McAllister getting hitched was the most interesting story this town had heard in many moons. If anyone asked Joey, he'd say the seaside town was like a drab postcard. He'd been stuck here all of his twenty-four years, had worked for the quiet sheriff's department for the last two. Sometimes, while driving the uneventful roads of Ambrose Point, he fantasized about being one of Hoover's G-Men, of chasing down something besides a wandering herd of cows.

Joey grunted and took a bite of his blueberry muffin. Good and fresh, hot from the oven in Johnston's kitchen. Pete Johnston whipped up a batch every morning and put them on the counter, cheap for most folks and free for law men. Joey never missed his free muffin.

Today's muffin was just the way he liked it, but Joey was in bad sorts after having heard on the radio that some country bumpkin had been given reward money for helping the FBI catch a criminal. What had she done to help serve justice? Nothing except be in the right place at the right time, hanging her husband's drawers on the clothesline just about the time the criminal darted from her henhouse, the lady's number one rooster struggling beneath his arm.

In an instant, the lady's life was different. A little sweeter just because an opportunity happened along.

Scowling, Joey popped the last bit of muffin into his mouth. It was time for him to make his usual boring rounds.

Julianna used her back to push open the door, her arms occupied with two heavy sacks of groceries. She peered into one bag and smiled, seeing the Mr. Goodbar for Jace resting on top.

As she walked to the car, her step was light even if her arms weren't. Her steps were reflective of her heart and its first experience of freedom. It was good not to be weighted with burden or worry, good to be relieved of dread. For once, she knew the spirit of hope and the inner calm of happiness. Her life was exactly as she wanted it to be.

Jace had changed her world and risked his freedom to do it. Because of him, courage bolstered her heart, empowered her to resist what she hated and reach for what she loved. Away from her life of propriety and social format, she had found a treasure chest of simple pleasures and draped herself in the riches of easy fun and the bonding of hearts trusting their deepest secrets to one another.

She was more than her father's pawn, more than Leyton's spinner of gold; she was a diamond with many facets, and she was eager to polish them all. Jace spoke to her like a respected partner, trusted her like a lifelong friend. He protected her like a precious gem, and when he touched her as a husband, he drew from her a passion as consuming as fire to a forest.

Thinking of him, she smiled, felt thankful, and blushed all at once.

She longed to talk to Virginia, to tell her best friend how happy she was. She spied a phone booth across the parking lot. On a whim, she set her groceries inside the car, found some change in her purse, and went to call her friend.

She stepped into the booth and lifted the phone receiver. There was no dial tone, and after pressing the button a few times, she knew it was out of order. She leaned against the booth, eyes wandering about her surroundings as she considered what to do next.

Suddenly, her body chilled.

Icicles seemed to encrust every hair on her arms and back, and her eyes widened as if she were a trapped animal. Leyton's Duesenberg had just swung around a curve and was slithering past the phone booth like a snake.

She watched it come to a stop, its quick halt in the road causing her heart to do the same inside her chest. As the car began to back up toward the phone booth, she knew that Leyton had seen her.

Her chill vanished, overtaken by panicky perspiration. She crumpled against the phone booth and ran a hand through her hair, now limp and separated into thick wavy strands clinging to the back of her neck. A tear dropped from one eye, making a lazy trickle down her cheek.

It can't be over . . .

It was a pleading thought, one she was not ready to accept. She shook her head, fast and fierce, trying to destroy the dark sense that happiness was going to leave her.

Leyton hopped from the idling car and sauntered to the phone booth, hands jammed into the pockets of his trousers. He was dapper as always, well dressed and groomed to movie star perfection, but she knew he hadn't come to dazzle. If the eyes truly mirrored the soul, then Julianna saw a jolting reflection of hate directed at her through Leyton's narrow eyes, dark and glassy with a smoldering rage.

Like a volcano, she thought, fear constricting her throat.

Looking quietly crazed but ever calculating, he stood before her.

She swallowed hard and glanced at Jace's car across the parking lot, wondering if she should make a run for it.

Yes . . . no . . . maybe . . .

She thought of Jace sleeping in the house, unaware that Leyton had materialized into a flesh-and-blood threat that was staring their future in the face. Still, despite Leyton's seething presence, it took only the thought of Jace to empower Julianna, shaking her from the fearful stupor that Leyton had cast upon her. A surge of strength burned through her, powered by the love she and Jace had found in such a short time. She drew upon it now, the way she drew life from the air she breathed.

Fight for what you have!

Through the phone booth, Julianna forced herself to stare hard at Leyton, locking into the hot steel of his eyes. Reaching for the door, her hand trembled slightly, but she knew that cowering in the phone booth would be like handing him a sword, giving him the upper hand right from the start.

She stepped from the booth, and Leyton moved forward and stood before her, hands inside his pockets.

"Francine Marst says hi."

His tone and movements were disturbingly smooth, like an animal watching its prey in calm reserve, while plotting how to take it by surprise. "Do you have anything to say, love?"

She kept her voice steady. "Except for good-bye, we have nothing to say."

"Ah, but we do. You owe me quite an explanation."

She shook her head, staring squarely at his forehead instead of into his eyes. They were icy oceans that sent her insides shivering. She hoped her voice wouldn't give away her fear. "You don't need an explanation. You know why things stand as they do."

"So, that's it?" he asked. "You have a change of heart and we just . . . walk away?"

"That's it." She stepped around him and walked briskly toward the market, assuring herself that Leyton was too self-protective to harm her in the presence of witnesses.

The market was dark, cooler than the outside air, and greeted Julianna like a refreshing pool. Her shoulders drooped in relief as she stood above the soda cooler, its frosty air reviving her flushed face. She dug out a bottle of Nehi Grape, choosing one from the ice-cold bottom of the pile, then popped off its cap on the opener that was built into the cooler. Her throat was so parched she ignored good manners by making her first drink a long swig.

She pretended to browse about the front of the market, all the while keeping watch on Leyton through the window. He was leaning against the Duesenberg, his frustration obvious by the creases on his forehead and the way his lips were tightly pinched.

After a few minutes, he yanked open the car door and plunged into the driver's seat. When the engine roared to life, he made a quick turnaround in the road, the car's movements jerky and terse as though it, too, bristled with rage. When he drove away, it was in the opposite direction of the bungalow.

Julianna allowed ten minutes to pass before she paid for the soda and returned to the steamy morning. Hurrying to the Auburn, she only wanted to reach Jace, to tell him what her trip to the market had panned out to be. Together, they would decide what to do about Leyton.

She was barely beyond the market, guiding the Auburn around the curves in the road, when the Duesenberg suddenly filled her rearview mirror.

Julianna's hand flew to her heart, but she was quick to assure herself that Leyton loved his Duesenberg. He won't hit me. He'd never hurt that car.

But Leyton didn't seem concerned about his beloved car at the moment. Julianna's breath caught at how fast the car bore down on her, squashing the distance between them at a speed only a thrill-seeker would have the courage to drive.

Leg's shaking, she debated over maintaining her moderate speed or mashing the accelerator. Her eyes darted from the road to the mirror, back and forth again and again. She despaired more with each glance as the nose of the Duesenberg drew closer to her back bumper. Outrunning Leyton was impossible, his high-performance car and do-or-die airs making him capable of exceeding any speed she might reach. And even if he didn't manage to run her off the road, the curves in the road would surely send her careening out of control.

What was it Jace had told her? Sand and gravel could be like ice.

It was better to keep her foot steady on the accelerator, safer to focus on keeping the car under control. She was starting into a curve, fingers wrapped tightly around the steering wheel, when the Duesenberg suddenly pulled around and cut her off, its bumper only inches from hers.

Julianna's foot went to the brake, a blinding cloud of sand and gravel rising as the tires slipped in protest and sent the car zigzagging about the road. Hanging on with white knuckles, she fought for control of the car, her stomach swooning each time it wavered between the center of the road and the left edge, which bordered a dense coastal forest of pines and oaks.

She came off the curve, returning to a straight stretch of road that restored her hope of escaping. To her right were the beach and the sagging dock. A short distance ahead was the bungalow, her oasis in the sand, but she wasn't about to lead Leyton to it. She'd drive into town to the sheriff's office.

But the Auburn had other ideas. There was a loud popping sound as one of the tires gave out, and then the car careened on a sloppy course toward the beach. She screamed as it lunged from the road and jumped a grassy ditch, coming down on the small sand dunes with a hard thud. The impact killed the engine, threw her to the passenger's seat, and slammed her against the door.

She sat dazed, but only for a second before she shoved open the door and staggered onto the beach. Leyton had brought the Duesenberg to a halt and was hurrying across the ditch, shouting obscenities she couldn't make out, each string of curses snatched by the wind and broken apart. His anger was evident, though, bulging eyes and bared teeth suggesting that he was beyond reasoning.

Julianna ran, her feet like slow plows as they tried to carry her across piles of sand, thick and slippery soft as their sparkling grains cooked beneath the sun. She pushed toward the surf, knowing it had pounded the shore into a hard, flat surface where she could break into a faster run.

When she reached the solid shore, though, Leyton was only an arm's length behind, undaunted by their twelve-year age difference. Pure rage was his driving force, lifting him to peak performance, putting him close enough to reach out and shove her toward the high tide.

She stumbled, falling face-first into the salty, frothy foam of a breaking wave.

Leyton grabbed Julianna by the elbow and dragged her a couple of feet, to where the water was knee high. He plunged her back into the surf, where she stumbled and fell. Her head went under, and she came up coughing and eyes stinging from the salt.

This seemed to add fuel to Leyton's rage, and he pushed her back down as she struggled to get her footing. He held her there for a few terrifying seconds before pulling her to her knees.

"Shall I make a widower out of your new husband?" he sneered. "I'm more than tempted, love. Now get up."

She swallowed the air, the precious air, taking long gulps that tasted as sweet as nectar.

Leyton's teeth clenched. "I said, get up."

She struggled to get free, fearing he would shove her beneath the waves again. Looking at him now, hovering above her with his chest pumping furiously against his wet shirt, she assumed he was capable of following through with his threat to make Jace a widower.

He gripped her wrist and twisted, his fingers turning so hard that she felt like the skin was tearing loose from the bone.

"Let go!" she cried as she tried to pull away from him.

"So you can run again?" He shook his head. "From now on, think of these fingers as handcuffs."

"Why can't you just go away?" She winced. "My father already thinks of you as a son. You don't need me to close the deal."

He raised his eyebrows. "You would have me go home and be made a fool of? Abandoned at the alter? Have people call me the poor jilted almost-son-in-law who Richard Sheffield kept around out of pity?" A nasty sneer took over his face. "Not likely, love."

"I'm married to someone else!" As the words left her, she saw Jace charging down the beach with his eyes pinned on Leyton. She had never felt such relief.

Jace must have witnessed the attack, seen the man pushing Julianna into the water and yanking her around like a caveman who'd wandered from his place in history. She could see his fury as he sprinted along the shore, his open shirt flying out behind him. The closer he got to Julianna, the tighter his hands clenched, knuckles white, his fierce resolve to protect her written on his face.

He was on Leyton like a cloudburst, knocking him away from Julianna and causing him to lose his balance and fall in the water just behind them. It took Leyton a minute to recover, but he got to his feet and sloshed towards Jace as he led Julianna out of the knee-deep water and into the tide that washed the shore.

Snorting like a bull taunted by red, Leyton flung himself on Jace's back but was unable to dislodge Jace's footing, though the sand beneath Jace's feet was slipping away with the pull of the tide. Jace held his balance and tossed Leyton off his back, sending him hard onto the wet sand.

"Go, Julianna!" Jace yelled. "Run back to the house!"

Julianna, standing only a few feet away from the men, broke into run, but she had expected Jace to follow. A glance over her shoulder told her that he intended to fight to the finish.

She saw Leyton pick himself up and go at Jace again, this time trying to shove him in the chest. Jace grabbed his arms, and the men struggled as the tide circled at their feet, both tight-jawed in what appeared to be a quest not to be the first to go down on the shore or back into the water.

Horrified, Julianna turned and ran back to the men and began pounding hard on Leyton's back, realizing with dismay that she was making no difference at all. Occupied with Jace, Leyton appeared numb to her rapid beating.

"Julianna, get out of here!" Jace yelled. "This is my fight!"

"It's our fight!" she screamed back, frustrated that her attempt to help had been useless, and worse, a distraction for Jace. As she backed away, she glanced towards the dry sand and saw a deputy making his way across it, occasionally slipping in its soft and uneven mounds. She hurried towards him, meeting him just before he reached the wet shore.

"Officer Joey Sparrs here," he said, slightly out-of-breath.   "I happened upon the cars . . .

"Oh, thank God," Julianna gasped, then turned and pointed at Jace and Leyton. "The blond one—he's the troublemaker!"

Joey made his way towards the men in the tide, pointing to his badge as he tried to shout above the wind. "Break it up! This is the law talking!"

But the law had lost something, and Julianna saw it before the officer even knew it was missing. There it was, its silver exterior gleaming in the sunlight as it rested in the hot, silky sand.

Officer Sparrs's revolver.

However the gun made it from the holster to the sand, Julianna only knew she wanted it gone, perhaps tossed into the water where it would sink. Seeing it on the beach, near two angry men, she felt her heart clamp with fear.

She had never held a gun before, never even touched one with a reserved fingertip. Now, she lifted the weapon from its resting spot, wanting only to keep someone from getting hurt. Her movements were slow and careful, but she couldn't stop the trembling in her fingers.

A single gunshot cracked the air.

For Julianna, a dreamlike disbelief followed, the roaring of the ocean fading away, drowned out by the thunder of her own heart.

The men were like statues, all staring at her in shock. Even the officer, who should have rushed from the tide and grabbed the gun, was too stunned to move. Of the three men, he gaped the most. Julianna, in turn, gaped at the gun she held in her hands.

A day and night seemed to pass before anyone spoke, though it had only been a few seconds since the gunshot erupted. It was Leyton who broke the trance that seemed to have taken hold of the group.

"She tried to kill me!"

His voice was explosive, weighted with accusation. One hand

was pressed hard against his cheek, where the bullet had torpedoed past. He had felt its rush but was not hit.

"It was an accident!" Julianna screamed as she cast the gun behind her and back into the sand. "I . . . I don't know why it went off."

He removed his hand from his cheek and pointed, his finger firm and accusing. "You aimed for my head!"

"No, she didn't!" Jace defended over the wind as he began making his way towards her. "She knows you're not worth going to jail for!"

When Jace reached her, she looked at him with desperate eyes, begging him to believe her. "Jace, I did not try to kill him."

"I know, I know," he said softly as he pulled her to him and stroked her hair. The water had turned it into ringlets, plastering them against her face and shoulders.

"Leyton knows it was an accident, but he'll use this against me," she insisted, a deep shiver radiating along her spine. "He'll blackmail us, Jace—"

"We'll figure something out," Jace assured her. But even as he said the words, a gray fog seemed to be closing in on both of them, heavy with the sense that tomorrow wouldn't be as nice as yesterday.

Julianna leaned against him, one side of her face resting on his soaking shirt. Terrified, she watched Leyton and Joey talk, heads lowered. Minutes later, or maybe what felt like an eternity, the deputy began walking their way.

"Don't do this, Joey," Jace said when he reached them. He held up a hand. "Whatever he said, it's not right."

Joey's mind raced from the words that had passed between him and the other man, the one barely missed by the bullet.

She pointed that gun right at me and pulled the trigger! Did you see that?

Actually, my back was turned away from her . . .

No, you're my witness. You'll know its true when you hear the story behind it . . .

What story?

The trial will make headlines . . .

Headlines?

Big ones. And a name for you. Get you off this hillbilly beach . . .

"C'mon, man," Jace pleaded to Joey. "Don't let him make a bad man out of you."

Joey ignored him, placing all his attention on Julianna. Without hesitation, he jerked her wrists together and bound them with one hand while using his other hand to retrieve the handcuffs in his pocket.

When he spoke, his voice was loud with forced conviction. If he talked loud enough, sounded firm enough . . . maybe, just maybe, he'd convince himself that he hadn't made a deal with the devil.

"You're under arrest," he clicked the handcuffs into place, "for attempted murder."

CHAPTER

FIFTEEN

Sheriff Tucker Moll was not used to accommodating lady prisoners. Fact was, he couldn't recall a female ever being arrested in Ambrose Point.

First time for everything, he thought. Wouldn't you know, it had to happen the day before I was supposed to come back from vacation?

All he had planned for today was stretching his bear of a body out in his hammock and thinking about the mess of vermilion snapper he'd caught during his week off. Instead, he dressed for duty, having been wakened by Sparrs all hyped up about making an arrest.

Julianna Sheffield McAllister. She was the wife of Jace McAllister but stood accused of trying to kill her . . . fiancé? Hearing that, Tucker had scratched his snow-white head, wondering what kind of radio soap opera was behind this arrest.

When he got to his desk at the sheriff's office, the sneer-faced, high horse of a fiancé explained the situation better, then he and Joey gave statements about the events on the beach. In Tucker's mind, it still sounded like a daytime serial, and he hated that Jace McAllister was involved. Tucker liked Jace. Always had, having known him since he was a kid.

Tucker had been especially fond of Jace's mother, Meredith, and found reasons to go on the point to check on the family. They were always fine, just as Tucker knew they would be, but his real motive for going was to see Meredith, to watch her try to tame her dark hair as the ocean gales scattered it around her face, to hear her windchiming laughter as she responded to his jokes, even the ones he knew weren't funny. He had fancied the idea of trying to court the young widow, but it never became more than a thought. Everyone knew that Meredith had given her heart to one man, and that he'd taken it with him when his ship sank near Hatteras. Probably explained that sad look she sometimes got, the one that came upon her whenever she gazed at the ocean.

Nobody except God knew it, but Tucker put flowers on Meredith's grave every week. Just a handful of wildflowers that he picked himself. He remembered her once saying she'd take a handful of wildflowers over a roomful of roses. Yeah, that's what she had said . . .

Tucker pulled his thoughts from Meredith, always finding it too sad to linger there for long. He had to think about this other woman now, this Julianna who had become the first female arrested in Ambrose Point.

Where to put her? That had been Tucker's first dilemma, knowing those of the female persuasion needed more privacy than men. Tucker thought about having a couple of deputies tack sheets all around the cell, but no—too much trouble. Instead, Tucker had Joey take her to the house of Jean Mixton. Jean was Tucker's older sister, who was forever reminding him that she weighed more than most men, could haul twice as much as any ox, and would be obliged to have him swear her in as a deputy should he ever see the need. Well, he was seeing the need now, and he promised her a badge if she would allow a back bedroom in her house to temporarily serve as a lady's jail cell. A deputy was posted outside the bedroom window in case the woman tried to climb out and escape, and Jean was keeping watch from inside the house.

It was time Tucker met the prisoner for himself.

The bedroom was stuffy and crammed with furniture, mismatched pieces that were ancient and scarred, with knobless drawers and splintered edges. Clearly, the room was used more for storage than housing jailbirds.

Julianna paid it no mind. Head in hands and elbows resting on her knees, she sat slumped on the bed's sagging mattress.

Some trip to the market.

Her feelings couldn't be pinned down to just one. Each time she replayed the morning's events, she ended up in a different state of emotion—there was a searing rage at Leyton for being the root of all this trouble, a fierce self-reproach for going anywhere near the officer's gun, a heart-wrenching despair that she had destroyed the future for her and Jace, and a sheer clammy terror over the hideous crime she now stood wrongly accused of. Only one thing was consistent, and that was the mist of disbelief that surrounded her thoughts.

A light rap on the door alerted her attention. Nervously, she jumped to her feet and smoothed out her dress. It was an old faded yellow housedress Jean had given her to replace the wet one she wore when she'd arrived. It hung on Julianna like a tent, but at least it was dry.

Jean poked her head in the room. "Sheriff's here." Her tone was non-judgmental, as if she neither believed nor disbelieved Julianna's innocence. Julianna thought maybe the woman was waiting for all the cards to be laid out before making up her mind.

Julianna swallowed hard and nodded. Her eyes grew wide when Sheriff Tucker Moll stepped inside the room. The man was huge, his head nearly scraping the top of the doorframe and shoulders as broad as the door's width. He was square jawed and had a full head of hair, as white as winter that stood out starkly against the deep tan on his face. He was rugged, his face lined from years in the out-of-doors, his love for deep-sea fishing making him look older than his fifty-four years.

"Ma'am," he said gently. "Some call me Sheriff Moll, some like my first name better and call me Sheriff Tucker. Then some just call me plain sheriff or plain Tucker. Pick what suits you."

"Sheriff Tucker, how—how's Jace?" she asked, nervously twisting her fingers.

"Fine, as far as I know," the sheriff said.

"He had nothing to do with the claims Leyton Drakeworth is making against me." She tried to make him see the truth by the sincerity in her eyes. "When they were fighting in the ocean, Jace was only trying to help me."

He seemed to ignore the statement, saying only, "He can visit you later."

Then Sheriff Tucker fished a couple of hard candies from his pants pocket. "Peppermint or butterscotch? What's your poison?"

"Butterscotch," she said, relaxing a bit at this show of kindness.

The sheriff popped the red-and-white peppermint into his mouth and rubbed the cellophane wrapper into a tiny ball. Quietly, he said, "Do you have a lawyer?"

"No."

"I'm sure Jace will find you a good one." He settled himself on the corner of an old dresser and rested his hands on his thighs. "You don't have to talk without one present, but if you're comfortable, I'd like to know how you landed in this pickle. What happened between you and this Hastings or Crayton—what's his name?"

Satan, she wanted to say, but she bit her tongue. "Leyton Drakeworth."

"What's the story between you two?"

She knew her story sounded like a melodrama and she poured it out sadly. When finished, she searched his face, looking for reassurance.

He gave her a sympathetic look, but his expression was empty of optimism.

"It sounds bad, doesn't it?" she asked, voice hovering at a whisper. "When you hear about my history with Leyton, it sounds like I had a motive for shooting him."

Sheriff Tucker hoisted himself from the dresser and patted Julianna's shoulder. "I'm going to go see Jace," he told her. "I can steer him toward a good lawyer."

Jace recognized Sheriff Tucker's car before he saw the big man emerge and walk up toward him on the porch.

Tucker helped himself to a chair. Not one to mince words, he said, "She needs a lawyer."

Jace sat and leaned his head against the house. "Is she okay?"

"As okay as you'd expect." Tucker dug some candy from his pocket. "She might get off on self-defense, what with this Creyton, Deyton—what's his name?"

"Satan," Jace said.

"Yeah, so she might get off on self-defense what with him chasing her and dunking her, but it would probably be a long shot—no pun intended." Tucker turned to Jace. "The problem with self-defense is that the gun didn't fire until after help had arrived. "

"You keep talking about self-defense," Jace said. "Are you saying she doesn't stand a chance if she sticks to the truth—the truth being that the shooting was an accident?"

"I'm saying it's a risky defense, on account of her history with what's-his-name." Tucker said as he unwrapped his candy. "The prosecutor will have a field day."

Jace could imagine the possible scenarios drawn for the jury. Julianna Sheffield, spoiled rich girl who ditched her devoted fiancé, left him pining while she ran away and married someone else, then tried to shoot him when he came looking for a reconciliation. Or maybe he would tell the jury that Leyton was a jerk. Did that give Julianna a right to try to kill him? No. A motive? Yes, most definitely yes.

"It's bad, Tucker," Jace said with solemn conviction. "Drakeworth's future was riding on marrying Julianna. Now that it's gone, he has nothing to lose."

Tucker sucked on his candy. "When a man's got nothing to lose, he's capable of anything."

"Yeah, the worst kind of revenge." It scared Jace to think about it, but he couldn't not think about it. This nightmare wasn't confined to sleep but was unfolding before his eyes. Leyton wasn't going to drop the charges and go away, and that meant Julianna might really face prison. The possibility made him sick, as he doubted Julianna's resilience when it came to the daily world of a women's penitentiary. She had spirit and strength, but was worlds away from the tough broads, street-smart and jaded. No, a girl like Julianna didn't belong there.

And what's more, she shouldn't have to be there. Julianna was innocent of Leyton's charges, innocent of Joey's collaborations. Jace knew it like he knew his name, not that he would love her any less if she stood guilty as sin. It couldn't change the heart that beat tenderly toward him, the eyes that smiled whenever he walked into the room. It would never close the door he had opened when he showed her the secrets of his heart, or darken the light she had brought into his world, giving him a reason to care about tomorrow. Even guilty, Julianna would be the great and only love of his life. She was where it began; she was where it ended.

And she was innocent. He had to get her out of this mess.

"Where would Drakeworth stand without Joey's testimony?" he asked Tucker, hope in his voice. He already knew the answer, but wanted to hear it from the sheriff.

The sheriff chuckled. "He'd be standing in quicksand. Dang bullet didn't even nick him, and without an eyewitness to the shooting, Julianna coulda fired in the air for all anyone knows. You coulda fired, I coulda fired, a blasted jellyfish coulda jumped from the water and fired."

"So, Drakeworth has no case without an eyewitness." Jace smiled for the first time all day. "That's what I thought."

"Nah, he could try to press charges, but Judge Smith would throw it out as sure as the sun rises in the east." His face darkened. "But Jace, I've taken Joey's statement. He's ready to swear on a stack of Bibles that he saw your wife go for the man's head."

"Can you break him?"

"I'll try." Tucker pushed himself from the chair and placed his big hands on his wide hips. "But if he sticks to his story, Julianna's lawyer is gonna have to crack him." He started for the steps, motioning for Jace to follow. "C'mon, I'll take you to see her, what with your car being in the shop and all."

"Thanks, but one of my tourist-robbing partners is letting me borrow his wife's car while she's out of town."

"Good," Tucker said, pausing on the top step. "I had Deputy Rogers call the service station for you—he just told 'em that you'd blown a tire and run off the road."

"I appreciate it," Jace said as he lowered his head and massaged his temples. Then looking tired, he lifted his eyes. "By the way, how many people know about this?"

"Just the immediate parties, plus Jean and a couple of other deputies," Tucker said. "Don't worry—I've got rules about waggin' tongues, punishment being that I yank them out. Nothing's official until I say it's official." He stepped back on the porch and gave Jace a couple of quick pats on the shoulder. "Until I've had plenty of tries at breaking Joey, I'm not even letting the newspaper know that today was anything other than the normal, boring stuff."

"Thanks."

"No thanks needed," the big man said as he attempted again to leave. He paused on the edge of the porch, a red blush glowing through his tanned face. "I'll help you all I can, Jace," he said, "what with, you know, having admired your mother and all."

He hopped off the porch and took long strides toward his patrol car. As Jace watched Tucker's departing back, he thought about something his mother once said about the man, something Jace would have to remember to tell him.

Above all else, Jace wanted to see Julianna. She needed him, and he wanted to be by her side, to make the morning, the charges, the ex-fiancé all go away.

He'd turn back the clock if he could. What happened this morning would always be a part of them, would always cause a quick shiver when they thought back to it. Maybe, though, he could halt the nightmare before it went any further, change the course it was starting to take. For that reason, he didn't go see her at Jean's right away.

Instead, he went to the Ambrose Shores Hotel. He banged on Leyton's door for several minutes before it opened, slowly guided by the smug demon himself. He was wearing a white knee-length robe of thick terrycloth, belted at the waist and covering his swimming trunks. In his hand was a drink, and on his face was a smirk, his chin tilted in triumph.

"At last, Lancelot on his white horse," he said. "I've been expecting you."

Jace entered the spacious suite and took stance in the middle of the room, his arms tight across his chest. His eyes were browner than usual, darkened by his dislike of the self-proclaimed King Drakeworth who was strutting from the door to the bar as though wearing a purple robe of royalty. The only thing that marred his blueblood appearance was the bruise under his left eye.

"Nice mouse," Jace told him.

Leyton ignored the jab, but his face turned red. He looked away from the man who put the mouse there in the first place.

"Don't bother sitting down, McAllister," he said as he settled himself on his throne, a stool beside the bar. "Our business will be short."

"And far from sweet," Jace warned.

"I detect that you're unhappy," Leyton said as he lifted his glass to his lips. He savored a drink then set the glass on the bar. "Not that I blame you, McAllister. It must be hard when your new bride becomes an attempted murderess."

"Julianna is guilty of nothing," Jace said as he glared, unblinking, into Drakeworth's eyes.

"Contraire, McAllister, and I have a witness," Leyton reminded him, avoiding the penetrating fire of Jace's eyes by focusing on his drink, rapidly swishing the ice cubes around in his glass.

"Joey didn't see Julianna do anything," Jace said as he took a step forward. "He was watching us, not her."

"What? That chicken fight?" Leyton laughed. "Child's play. Hardly something that would concern anyone except Julianna."

"And you," Jace said with a half laugh. He couldn't contain the barb, having heard Drakeworth yelp more than a few times during their struggle. Jace knew the guy had some battle scars hidden beneath his robe.

Again, Leyton reddened. "What makes you so certain that she's innocent?"

"Because she told me she is," Jace said.

"Your blind devotion is heartwarming, but reality is reality," Leyton said. He finished his drink and slammed his glass on the bar. "Do you think this is easy for me, McAllister?"

"Seems to be." He took another step closer to Drakeworth.

"You've misread me then." Leyton bit his lower lip, fashioning an expression of duress that made Jace roll his eyes. "I love her, too."

"Love?" Jace threw back his head and laughed. Again he approached Drakeworth, this time not stopping until he was at the bar. By then, he was no longer laughing at the man's absurd profession of love. His voice lowered to a smolder. "A man doesn't accuse the woman he loves of a crime she wouldn't commit, no matter what she's done to raise his anger."

Leyton stood and moved behind the bar. "Perhaps I'm not as well schooled as you are in the proper etiquette of true love." He dropped fresh ice into his glass. "But then, I don't know Julianna the way you know her, now do I?"

Jace didn't like where this was going. Clearly, the liquor was kicking in, fueling Leyton's nasty nature and enticing him to cross the line. Jace pinned him with a threatening look.

"Oh, come on, McAllister. Let's have a little man-to-man," Leyton chided. "Some locker room chat, shall we?"

"Change the subject, Drakeworth."

"You've been with Julianna in ways that I haven't, so tell me—"

"Shut up!"

"—how does our little tramp like to be touched?"

That was it. Jace reached across the bar and grabbed Leyton with both hands, gathering him up by the thick cotton of his monogrammed robe. Teeth gritted, he said, "I should have shot you myself."

"Oh really?" Drakeworth sniffed. "I perceive that as a threat, McAllister. Perhaps I should have you thrown in jail, as well. You and Julianna can rot together."

Jace released Drakeworth then, knowing that he could—he would—send the man sailing into the glass liquor cabinet behind him if he waited another second. He had to stop, though, had to avoid assault charges and jail time because he couldn't help Julianna if he was facing his own bars.

Leyton readjusted his robe and dusted himself off, making much production, as if showing Jace that his touch had soiled and offended. When he finally spoke, it was to issue Jace a challenge.

"If you love her . . . save her."

"I plan to," Jace answered. "And I'm sure you've got it all figured out."

"You showed up on my doorstep," Leyton said haughtily. "I assume you came to deal."

"You don't know me, so assume nothing," Jace said.

Leyton studied Jace for a minute. "Where have I seen you before, McAllister?"

"Your worst nightmare?"

Leyton pulled a cigar from the pocket of his robe and ran it underneath his nose, sniffing the rich aroma. "You're vaguely familiar to me," he said. "What are you—a bum from that mission shelter? Some pet project that Julianna hopes to rehabilitate?"

Jace's face showed a blend of suspicion and amusement as he eyed Leyton. "Put your offer on the table, Drakeworth."

Leyton lit his cigar and puffed, the gray smoke rising around him like steam after a rainstorm. "Set her free."

"Free," Jace said flatly, the request coming as no shock. "As in divorce."

"Yes, but there's more to my deal than divorce. You see, McAllister, you could serve Julianna with divorce papers a hundred times, but her mind won't be free if you're able to walk back into her life."

"So . . . you want me to start divorce proceedings and give you my agenda? Will that make it easier for you to have me taken out?"

Leyton puffed again. "Don't think it didn't cross my mind." He stepped out from behind the bar and strode to the double French doors that opened onto the balcony. He stood before them, looking toward the blue-gray water. "Take the rap, McAllister. Make a full confession to the sheriff that you tried to shoot me."

"What about your eyewitness?" Jace called from the bar. "Your sworn statements?"

"I'll say we were confused," Leyton said with a shrug. "There was so much commotion taking place. Julianna tried to cover up, but you're too much of a man to let her continue." He waved his arm, a stream of cigar smoke tagging behind. "Etcetera, etcetera. Dreaming up a convincing story is the least of my concerns, and I'll make it worth Joey's while to stick by me."

Jace crossed the room and placed himself between the doors and Leyton, blocking his view of the Atlantic. Several inches taller, he loomed over Leyton like a dark shadow. "Your offer is crazier than you are."

"Suit yourself," Leyton replied with nonchalance, though he took a cautious step back from Jace. "You'll regret turning it down when you see Julianna harassed on the witness stand, when the jury comes back with a guilty verdict."

"Somehow, I think she'd choose that over being married to you," Jace said. "But your predictions won't come true, Drakeworth—I'll think of a way to end this charade."

Leyton seemed unconcerned, standing before Jace with an eerie smile growing wider on his face. "My deal is her only hope."

Jace shook his head in disgust. "You're a waste of humanity, Drakeworth."

Leyton's hateful smile did not waver. "Since your opinion doesn't count with me, I won't take offense," he said. "But it would behoove you to consider the deal I've presented."

Jace stepped away from the French doors, smiling when the sudden return of sunlight caused Leyton to squint. "The day you stand on that balcony and fly is the day I'll consider it," he said as he walked to the door of Leyton's suite. "No deal. No divorce."

He left then and went to see Julianna, where she likened him to a cool breeze wafting through the stuffy bedroom. Seeing him in the doorway, she sprang from the bed where she had been sitting cross-legged, her antsy fingers braiding the fringe on the musty orange bedspread.

He grabbed her in his arms and pressed her hard against his chest. When they kissed, it was as though they had been separated for years and that each day had been survived by anticipating their reunion.

"Let's sit down," he said, looking around the furniture-filled room. "Shouldn't have trouble finding a seat."

They sat on a dusty loveseat with splintery holes punched randomly through the caneback.

Jace squeezed her hand. "How are you?"

"Holding up," she said. "About as good as this loveseat is. How are you holding up now that I've completely complicated your life?"

"You haven't complicated my life."

"Yes, I have." She lifted a finger to her eye, catching a tear before it slid down her cheek. "I discovered your identity, I intruded into your life—"

"I invited you into my life," he corrected.

"I wrecked your car, I brought Leyton home and," she slapped her hands on her thighs, "now this. Yes, Jace, I'm certain that I've complicated your life."

"I like complicated women," he said, lifting her hand and kissing it. "The more complicated the woman, the more interest she adds to life."

Her shoulders heaved beneath what was a half sob and a half laugh. "Nice try."

"What about the things I've done to your life?" he asked. "If I'd never gone back for you, Julianna, you wouldn't be in this colossal mess. I've complicated your life a lot more."

She cut in sharply. "You saved my life."

If you love her . . . save her.

He pulled her head to his chest and stroked her hair. It was dry now, silky and scented with salt water. "Leyton is sticking to his story and Joey is vouching," he said gently. "Unless . . ."

"Unless what?" She lifted her head so that she could see his eyes.

"Unless I divorce you and take the rap."

She gasped, a hand flying to her mouth as she shot up into a sitting position. "He can't be serious!" But of course he was serious. They were talking about Leyton. "Jace, what did you tell him?"

"I told him no deal, no divorce."

She stood and went to the bed, her fingers tracing the rice carvings on one its four posts. Her voice was dry. "You said 'no divorce,' but you didn't say no to taking the rap, did you?"

He heaved a heavy sigh. "Julianna . . ."

"No!" she cried, racing back to him and dropping to her knees. She grabbed his hands and locked their fingers together then turned her eyes up at his. They pleaded with him, "You can't turn yourself in for something you didn't do."

He eased his fingers loose and placed them on her arms, raising her to her feet and guiding her back to the loveseat. He turned to her, his face as serious as she had ever seen it. "If I turn myself in, Julianna, it won't be for what I didn't do. It will be for what I did do."

She sealed her eyes shut so tightly that white dots floated in the darkness, ricocheting off the corners of her skull and drifting about with no direction, like lost and tormented souls in a black, confined eternity.

The bank robberies . . .

They were the secret of Jace's heart, the secret of her own. They were a burden of guilt they carried together. Hadn't Jace feared that the secret was too big to carry? That it would stir about, like a restless ghost in need of absolution?

"Julianna . . ." He waved his hand before her face, bringing her back from the intensity of her thoughts. "I was telling you that Leyton has no case without Joey's testimony. Maybe I can get Joey to forget Leyton's story in exchange for being the one to give the People's Bandit to the authorities. All he wants is to make a big splash and—" he flashed a playful smile, "no offense, but I'd be more notorious than you." He smiled again. "There's even a reward for my head."

She couldn't laugh with him. She shook her head slowly and her voice cracked with emotion. "If you turn yourself in, it would be to spare me from Leyton's accusations. I—I couldn't live with that, Jace, thinking of you locked away because of me."

"You wouldn't be the only reason."

"I know the robberies are a cloud hanging over us, but there must be another way to pay your debt." Her eyes flickered as abstract ideas rushed through her mind. Only one took on a solid shape. "Sell your book, Jace—we'll use the money to anonymously pay the banks back."

"The book's not finished," he argued. "And it won't get finished while you're sitting on trial facing prison time." He flopped against the loveseat, its weakened back threatening to give way to his weight. Eyes staring ahead, arms tight across his chest, he stewed.

She placed a hand on his shoulder. "I'm sorry. I didn't mean to make you mad."

He pulled her head to his chest. "I'm not mad at you. It's everything, you know?"

"Hmm . . ."

"Julianna, I don't know what to do yet. Nothing is settled, and I need to check something out before we decide anything."

"What?"

"I'm not sure. A person, a house. A person in a house. Whatever it turns out to be, I know it's got something to do with Leyton. When I was watching the bank's headquarters, there was a day when Leyton ran out the front door and jumped in the Duesenberg. He looked . . . agitated. Bugged about something."

"Sounds like he was about to miss his tee time."

Jace laughed, fondly rubbing her arm. "Maybe I'd been sitting in a hot car for too long, but I got this crazy idea and followed him. He ended up at this pub, sitting at the bar, head-to-head with some thug."

"Any idea what they were talking about?"

"I wondered if it had something to do with whoever Leyton was in hock to, back when I skipped out with his briefcase."

She smiled at the thought, imagining the sweaty panic on Leyton's face when he realized the briefcase was gone. "You think he might still be paying them off?"

Jace shrugged. "Can't say, but I got another crazy idea and followed the thug. He led me to this house, nothing special, just a house with a little wrought-iron gate around it. I watched him go to the front door and give some kind of Morse code knock. He went inside, stayed a few minutes, then left."

"I wonder who was in the house." Julianna sat up, curious, and looked at Jace. "Did you find out?"

He shook his head. "It was daylight and there were too many cars around. Figured I'd pressed my luck enough, so I left before anyone got suspicious. The next day, I hit the bank and took the fast way out of town. Forgot all about that little house." He sat quiet for a moment, thoughtful as he stroked her arm.

"You want to go back, don't you? Find out who's inside?"

He nodded. "Yeah, I don't know why, but I get the feeling it's important that we know."

"It sounds dangerous," she fretted, hugging herself to stop the chill that had suddenly attacked her bones. "I'd feel better if you didn't go."

"Julianna, I have to."

"I know. " She quietly resigned, eyes dropping to her lap. "I know."

He looked at his watch. "I have three whole minutes before Jean throws me out." He grinned. "Let's make the most of it."

She went to his arms, sighing deeply as they folded tightly around her. They spent the next three minutes forgetting the concerns of their world as they necked like teenagers in a porch swing.

Jace breathed in the scent of honeysuckle, sweet and heavy in the pre-dawn air. All around him, nature was stirring awake, especially the birds that fluttered amid the glossy magnolia leaves. Two black-and-gray-striped cats were avid spectators but made no move to give chase, preferring instead to watch while languishing beside a flowerbed of pansies.

It could have been the backyard of any ordinary house in America. But Jace doubted the house harbored an ordinary family, and he had driven six hours to satisfy those suspicions. Leaving the night before, he had traveled the dark roads leading back to Julianna's hometown, stopping once to catch a few hours of sleep in the parking lot of a former bank, now failed and empty except for cobwebs.

The house was located on Charlotte Avenue. Jace recognized it immediately by the wrought-iron fence that encased its yard and by the English ivy that had crept up the drain spout to overtake the roof. It looked like an army that had spread out, a deep green mass that was marching to conquer every shingle.

He hid in the backyard, behind a cluster of evergreens growing tall beside the house. He was within earshot of the house, and a kitchen window was open to let in the morning air. Jace waited there while the morning faded from a black canvas to a purple shadow, then brightened up with ribbons of pink swirling through a pale-blue sky.

He wished he knew who he was waiting for. Before Julianna, he would have scoffed at such a hit-or-miss idea, one that's success was dependent on him getting a break. No strategy, no careful planning, but just a good break. He might not have bothered with it, but now he couldn't afford not to take the time. To have a future, he and Julianna needed a break. They needed it today.

Sounds of life drifted from the window. A cupboard closing, high heels hurrying across the linoleum floor. A few minutes later, the kitchen door opened, and a slender woman stepped out onto the patio.

"Kitties?" she called as she set a bowl of food on the patio. The cats bounded through the grass and rubbed against the woman's legs, meowing in harmony as they sashayed back and forth.

Jace put her at about twenty-five and thought her rather cute but rough around the edges.

She was blond, a brassy yellow from lack of upkeep, and her tresses were limp on her shoulders. The face was heart shaped, and again, kind of cute but hard beneath its thick coat of makeup, the most noticeable cosmetic being her lipstick. It was a vivid red that paled the rest of her face and clashed with the dress she was wearing. It was a print dress, a polyester knockoff of the elegant silks and had orange roses against a brown background.

She scooted inside the house then back out again, this time holding a cheap plastic compact in her hand. She flipped it open and studied her face in the daylight.

"Drats," she said as she swiped a pad across the powder then patted the tender area underneath one eye. "Everyone is gonna notice."

A man's voice bellowed from inside. "Polli!"

She jumped and snapped shut the compact. Hurrying inside, she called, "Here, baby!"

"Where's those eggs?"

"I'm getting 'em, baby." She laughed nervously. "Sunnyside up, just like you like 'em."

Jace heard her racing about the kitchen, a skillet being slammed onto the stove, the icebox opening and closing. A chair scraped across the floor, and he wondered if the man had sat down at the table.

"Sorry 'bout the shiner, darlin'," the man said.

"It's okay, baby. You got pressure right now."

"Yeah," he grunted. "Well, I put some money on the hall table. Buy yourself something pretty, or get a new permanent wave."

"Really, Tommy?" She was beaming by the sound of it. "A permanent wave?"

"Yeah, just don't let 'em cut off any hair," he warned. "I told you about that flapper girl a few years back, what I did to her face for chopping off her hair. So don't do it."

"Promise," she said over sizzling eggs. "I wish you weren't leaving."

"Got to."

"Yeah, but why you gotta go clear up to Canada?" she whined.

Jace heard the man slam his fist on the table and the clang of his fork on the floor. "Because I want to get me one of those fancy, doggoned French-Canadian accents!"

"Sorry, baby. I didn't mean—"

"You dingy dame!" he roared. "They ain't lookin' for me in Canada!"

"Okay, baby." Her voice cracked. "I'm just gonna miss ya, that's all."

"I'd be leavin' anyway. That battle-ax aunt of yours is comin' back soon, ain't she?"

"Yeah, her sister's better now. Two months—that's a long time for someone to be sick, ain't it, Tommy?"

"Yeah, long time for me to be hidin' out, too. Dang Feds," he growled. "Thought the heat woulda cooled by now, but that uppity socialite won't quit yappin' for justice."

"The one you kidnapped?"

He slammed his fist on the table again, this time causing a salt shaker to roll. "No, the one who wants me to escort her to the doggoned cotillion!"

"Sorry, baby."

"Sorry, baby," he mimicked. "Yes, the one I kidnapped."

"So you're goin' to Canada, day after tomorrow," she said nervously. "Well, they'll never catch you up there, will they?"

"Nope," he said through a mouthful of food. "And get this, darlin', I'm going first class, just like I've always been accustomed. The boys, they got me all set up on the Silver Star, in the fanciest berth that train's got. Passport, disguise—it's all arranged." He gave a belly laugh. "Ole Lightfoot Lipton's gonna slip by again."

Don't count on it. Jace smiled as he backed out of the evergreens and edged around the corner of the house. He hurried to the sidewalk and down the street to his car.

It was a break, all right. Anyone in the South who could read a paper knew of Lightfoot Lipton. The Feds had watched him for years, never able to gather enough evidence against him until the kidnapping of that Atlanta socialite.

Jace wondered how Drakeworth had gotten tied up with Lightfoot. He had plenty of time to speculate while driving back to Ambrose Point and plenty of time to consider how Lightfoot might play into his own situation.

His first thought was to tip off the Feds to Lightfoot's plans, then make it look like Drakeworth had been the one with loose lips.

Tempting, he grinned, though he knew the long-term repercussions wouldn't be worth the initial laugh. Lightfoot would vow revenge, and that would send Drakeworth on the lam, meaning that Jace couldn't keep up with the whereabouts of his sneering mug.

I have to keep tabs on the man just for Julianna's protection, he reminded himself. It was a fact of his life now. On the run or not, Drakeworth was like a reoccurring rash, and Jace knew he could pop up anytime, trying to wreck his and Julianna's happiness. Forget about that.

Secondly, there was the good chance that Lightfoot's rednecks would catch Drakeworth and have him fitted for a pair of cement boots. No thanks to that, either. Jace had enough on his heart without adding a man's blood to it, even if it was the bad blood of Leyton Drakeworth.

There was only one way Lightfoot Lipton could help Jace and Julianna. He would have to become part of a big picture, and it was starting to take shape in Jace's mind. He would tell Julianna about it tonight.

When he reached Ambrose Point, it was midafternoon. Thunder rumbled in the distance, but to Jace it was a lullaby. He was exhausted, having made this trip inside of eighteen hours with only a cat's nap to sustain him. He fell hard onto the bed, head barely on the pillow before he was submerged in a dreamless sleep.

He awoke four hours later, his hand automatically reaching for Julianna on the other side of the bed. Its emptiness was like a blow to the stomach, and he jerked his hand away from the cruel coldness of the sheets. In such a short time, he had grown accustomed to her presence.

A small part of him wished he had never brought her to this house. If he hadn't, then maybe he wouldn't feel the way he did.

Like he couldn't live without her.

It was going to make it harder . . . so much harder to see her face and then say what he needed to say.

When Jace arrived, Julianna knew immediately that his mind carried a huge weight. His face was tight and his movements tense, telling her that she wouldn't like what he had to say. Part of her was antsy to hear it and have it over with, while the other part wanted to forever avoid the moment of truth.

The whole time Jace had been gone, his words had replayed like a scratched record on the phonograph.

Maybe I can get Joey to forget Leyton's story in exchange for being the one to give the People's Bandit to the authorities.

She knew that Jace was building a plan and that those words made up the foundation. Somehow he was going to clear her name, pay his penance and ensure they had a future together. It was a lovely thought, but she couldn't figure out what he possibly had in mind to make it happen. Frustrated, claustrophobic, and scared, she asked, "How is this all ever going to work out, Jace?

"I can give myself up," he said.

She looked at him, wondering what had happened to the daring bank robber who had eluded capture for nearly four years. The man who outwitted and outran, lunged into boxcars, and crawled through air vents to follow through on a mission.

"Why don't you just break me out of this ridiculous jail and take me someplace where we can be together? Just be together, Jace, no matter the conditions or circumstances? Isn't that what the People's Bandit is supposed to do for the woman he loves?"

She hadn't wanted to speak so harshly, but once the onslaught started, she couldn't seem to stop it. Regret filled her the minute it was over.

She cupped her hand to her mouth. "Jace . . ."

There were tears in her eyes as she looked at the man behind the mask, a man who did not have the heart of an outlaw. He was good, in spite of his actions. Even the worst deeds of his life had been carried out for only the best of reasons.

He crossed the room and kneeled before her, placing his hands gently on her shoulders. Calmly, he said, "Julianna, our life is wrecked right now, but there might be a way to salvage the future. I know you want that."

Head buried in her hands, she nodded.

"I don't want to live on the run," he continued. "And do you know why?" He didn't wait for an answer. "It's because you deserve a better life than that, Julianna." He pulled her hands away from her face. "That's what I do for the woman I love."

"I didn't mean those things," she said through tears. "I'm just . . . I'm scared . . . and I can't sleep . . . This room is driving me crazy!"

"I know," he said, wrapping his arms around her shaking frame and rocking her slowly. "I would have torn it apart by now."

Feeling better, she managed a small laugh. "And I thought the furniture in your living room was bad."

He stood up and leaned against a dresser, studying her face, beautiful even in distress.

"What did you find out?" she asked him.

"You know that briefcase I saw Leyton give to the thug? Well, it ended up in the same house as Lightfoot Lipton. Ever heard of him?"

"Tommy Lipton? His name has been in the news a lot. I wonder how Leyton is involved with him." Suddenly, she brightened. "Jace, have you found a way to blackmail Leyton?"

"Blackmail." He grimaced. "I've corrupted you, Julianna. Before we met, I'll bet that word wasn't part of your vocabulary. But no, I'm not thinking about blackmailing Leyton." He flashed her a grin. "Not that it wouldn't be fun, but I don't know what business he's got with Lightfoot, or if there's even a record of it."

Julianna nodded her agreement. "I'm sure he's covered his tracks."

"Trying to deal with Leyton won't work," Jace said. "He's got too much to lose. Joey is a different story, though. He's got everything to gain, so I think he'll jump at the chance to hand me over to the Feds."

Julianna looked down at her hands and fidgeted with her wedding ring. Voice quivering, she asked, "If you let Joey do that, how . . . how long will you be gone?"

"I think I can work out a sentence of five years tops, shorter with good behavior."

"Five years?" For the empty nights that lay ahead, it seemed like such a long time. But as a punishment for bank robbing, it seemed so short. "How can you get it whittled down to five years, Jace? Will turning yourself in help that much?"

"It'll help some," he told her. "But what will really help is telling the Feds that Lightfoot Lipton is going to board the Silver Star, all fat and happy as he heads for Canada."

Her hand flew to her mouth, but not fast enough to stop a small laugh from getting out. "So that's how Lightfoot fits into the picture." She got up from the bed and went to him, touching his cheek. "Jace, you're brilliant."

"No, I just went on a hunch that seemed to come out of nowhere," he said, looking away.

Her face darkened. "But, Jace, what if the FBI doesn't go for your plan?"

The question didn't seem to concern him. "I don't guess you heard the radio today."

"No, I'm not even sure what day it is."

"July twenty-third, the day after the Feds took out John Dillinger."

"Really?" Her eyes grew wide. "The John Dillinger?"

"Last night in Chicago," Jace said. "A girlfriend tipped them off that he was at a movie. When he came out of the theater, the Feds started to move in. So, Dillinger being Dillinger, he whipped out a gun and shot two agents dead. That's when the others opened fire on him."

"Is he dead?"

"As a doornail. They hit him twenty-some times."

Julianna shuddered. If the Feds had ever caught up with Jace, would they have done that to him? Jace, a bank robber like Dillinger?

No. She shook the thought away. Jace wasn't like Dillinger. He was nothing like Dillinger, who had gunned down so many decent men, not caring that they had wives and children waiting at home, and dreams for a life they never thought would be cut short. Jace? He was a choirboy next to Dillinger, even if they did share the same profession.

"The Feds are riding high today," Jace continued. "And here's a chance to shine some more. First Dillinger, then me, and finally, Lightfoot. Three bad boys inside of a week. I think they'll be willing to talk for a chance like that."

"It sounds hopeful," Julianna admitted, though her face was pensive. "I wonder, though . . . am I really that safe on the outside, with Leyton running around bent on revenge, my father crazed by the way I've disgraced his name, and Lightfoot's cronies trying to even the score? When I think of it that way, prison sounds like a safer alternative."

"I'm asking for more than just a reduced sentence," Jace said. "To begin with, they can't say that I was the one to turn in Lightfoot. To the world, it has to look like an anonymous tip because Lightfoot will put out a contract for whoever ruins his escape. If he couldn't get to me in prison, then he'd go after the person closest to me." He gave her a tender smile. "That would be you. Secondly, I want you relocated to an undisclosed place. Somewhere just you and I—and whomever you trust—can know about until I'm released. That'll keep you safe, just in case Lightfoot does find out who turned him in. Added bonus, of course, is that Leyton won't know where you are."

"That's the best part of all," she said.

"I don't think the Feds will go for giving me the reward money for Lightfoot," he said with a grin. "But there's money I saved from the military and from Granddad, plus you'll get my share from the boat business. You'll have plenty to live on."

She gazed at him, amazed by the depth of his planning, touched that her well-being was the heart and soul of it all. "You've thought of everything."

His brow creased in frustration. "I don't have a foolproof way to protect your name."

"Protect my name." She said the words quietly, shaking her head in awe. "Here you are, getting ready to make this confession, and you're worried about my name?"

"I don't want you hounded or disgraced."

"Oh, Jace." Her voice cracked through the lump that was rising in her throat. "Loving you could never disgrace me."

"Others might not see it that way," he forewarned. "I can ask the Feds that your name not be given out to the newspapers, and they might agree since it would help protect you if Lightfoot learned the truth. There's only a handful of people in Ambrose Point who even know your name—if the sheriff tells them to keep quiet, they will. Leyton, though, could blab your name across the country. I can't control that."

"My father will probably pay him for his silence," she said then added quickly. "Not to protect me, but to avoid scandal to the family name. And even if that's not the case, so what?" Her voice grew defiant. "I want to tell people how good you really are—explain to them why you did what you did."

He smiled but shook his head. "Julianna, you can't talk about that."

"Why?" Frustration edged her voice. "Why can't I help you a little?"

"Because good intentions don't justify my actions," he snapped. "It doesn't matter why I did it. Bottom line is I robbed those banks." He pushed past her and went to the loveseat across the room. Sitting down, he leaned forward and rested his head in his hands. He stayed that way for a few minutes, and when he finally looked up, his hair was mussed and his face looked older than his thirty-two years. "Julianna, I stole from your family. There's no honor in that."

She hurried to his side. Sitting down next to him, she ran a hand through his dark hair. There was a time when his heart pushed him to be a vigilante. Now, that same heart was convicting him. In some ways, she felt like an instigator to his burden of guilt. "Jace, what do you think would have happened if we hadn't met? Would you have confessed?"

He sat back in the loveseat and closed his eyes. Rubbing his temples, he said, "I don't know. Maybe I would've found a way to keep living with it." He opened his eyes and smiled, pulling her to his chest. "But then you came along and made an honest man out of me."

"It's hard to believe this is happening," she said. "Two days ago, life was perfect."

"Yeah, well, Granddad always said your whole life could change in the snap of a finger."

"I wish there was another way."

"There's not."

"Couldn't you give Joey the tip about Lightfoot? Let that be your trading card, instead of exchanging yourself for Leyton?"

"There wouldn't be any glory for Joey," Jace said. "The tip about Lightfoot has to be anonymous. Otherwise—"

"Joey would have to live the rest of his life in hiding," Julianna finished, nodding in realization.

"Letting Joey hand me over to the Feds is what will get his name in the papers." Jace spoke with dry bitterness. "He'll get the fifteen minutes of fame he'd sell out his own mother for. But he only gets it if he stops lying about you trying to kill Leyton. That way, Leyton has no case." He lifted Julianna's head from his chest and looked down into her face. "Tell me again—when did you know you loved me?"

"The first time we met," she said, thinking of how long ago that seemed now, of how much had passed since that star-flooded night.

"Then you didn't know about the bank robbing until it was too late. We'll leave it at that. Otherwise, they might try to nab you for aiding and abetting."

"But I did aid and abet you," she said, "by keeping quiet."

He spoke slowly, his words as firm as his eyes as they stared unblinking into hers. "Julianna, you did not know my secret identity until it was too late. This plan was born to keep you out of jail—we're not going through with it if there's a chance you'll wind up there anyway."

"It just sounds like I'm getting the sweeter deal, that's all I'm say—"

He was shaking his head. "Julianna, I've never taken an upper hand with you, but this . . . this isn't even on the table for discussion."

"Okay," she relented, her eyes growing watery as she wondered what she ever did to deserve a man who could love her this much.

He played with her hair, wrapping the wavy strands around his finger then letting them fall gently back into place. When he spoke, his voice was solemn. "Leyton is a creep, Julianna, but what he tried to pull at least brought things to the forefront. From the time we met, I knew the truth was too big to keep hidden. It was unfair of me to ask you to carry it, too, no matter how you felt about the things your family did, or how hard I tried to pay the money back."

"I made a choice back when I decided not to give you up to the authorities."

"I know, and you're a woman with her own mind, but when I saw you arrested for something you didn't do—and knew that it wouldn't have happened if you'd never met me—that's when all the sins of the past caved in on me. That's when I couldn't keep telling myself that paying the money back would make it all okay." He gave a sad laugh. "Besides, who was I kidding? Even Moses wasn't let off the hook for messing up."

"Moses?" she asked. "How did he come into this?"

He laughed again. "Come on, Julianna, if Moses had to face the music, I'm pretty sure a lesser man like me will have to face the music, too." His laughter vanished. "Sometimes, being sorry is enough. Sometimes it's not. There's got to be some kind of justice for the consequences of my bad actions."

"Yes, I suppose there does," she agreed quietly.

He rested his cheek on the soft crown of her head. "The one right thing I've done in my life is love you. I think you've made me a better man, Julianna. You must have, because I've never before thought of giving myself up. Besides, we both know we can't fully live until the past is really dead and gone."

"I know you're right, I'm grateful you want to spare my freedom, but," a shiver ran through her, "this is scary, Jace."

He drew her closer and his voice dropped to a reassuring whisper. "There'll be brighter days for us, babe, there will."

She nodded as a lone tear slid down her cheek. To everything there is a season, she thought, again recalling Ecclesiastes. A time to dance . . .

"When are you going to do it?" she asked, dreading the answer. "Turn yourself in?"

"Tomorrow," he said, and she knew he hated saying it as much as she hated hearing it.

"Tomorrow," she said sadly, a shudder racking her body. "Tomorrow."

A time to weep . . .

CHAPTER

SIXTEEN

When the sheriff made his way to the bungalow's front porch, he found Jace sitting in the same chair his grandfather had always used when looking out to sea. His eyes were dark and distant, clueing Tucker that he was absorbed in serious thought. Not that Tucker expected anything else. Jace had left word the night before that he needed to see him first thing, and Tucker knew it wasn't because he wanted to know how the fish were biting.

Tucker lowered himself into the empty chair next to Jace and tossed a piece of cinnamon candy into his mouth. "I talked to my sister early this morning," he said. "She says Julianna is holding her own. Eating okay, keeping her composure."

"Gotta hand it to her," Jace said.

"Yep." Tucker crunched his candy into tiny bits. "She's tougher than she looks. It's a shame that Joey is, too. I can't break him, Jace. He's sticking to that story."

Silence settled between the men. Only the waves were vocal as they rolled onto the shore then rushed back to sea. When Jace finally spoke, it was with the solid assurance of stating a well-known fact.

"I can break him."

Tucker was taken off guard by Jace's comment. He cocked his head toward him with a look of friendly challenge. "Can you, now?"

Jace did not return Tucker's look. Instead, he looked at the big man with eyes as sad as the day was long.

A nervous laugh got by Tucker. "What is it?"

"I need your help," Jace told him. He took a deep breath. "There's something you need to know."

Another nervous laugh came from Tucker. "Sounds like you're about to make a confession."

"I am."

"Oh boy." Tucker gave a shaky sigh and began removing the sheriff's badge from his breast pocket. "This is man-to-friend, okay? Not man-to-law. And do me a favor, Jace, don't use your real name when confessing."

"Why's that?"

"Because I want to help you," Tucker said as he stuffed his badge into his pants pocket. "But if I can't help you, I don't want to know what you did." He folded his arms across his beefy chest and stared hard at the ocean. "So don't tell me what Jace McAllister did. Tell me what John Doe did."

"A safety net, huh?" Jace smiled. "You're a good man—Ma always said so."

"Yeah?" Tucker looked at him, always interested in something Meredith had said.

"Yeah, she never could love another man after my father died, but she once told me—"

Tucker sat on the edge of his chair. "What?"

"She told me if she could have loved someone else, you would have been the one."

Tucker turned his eyes back to the sea, too tough to let Jace see them water up over the sentiments of a woman he had loved in silence, a woman who had died years before her time. "Well, you've made my day," he said after a minute or so, when he was able to talk without his voice wavering. "But now I get the feeling you're going to turn around and ruin it."

"Probably." Jace was somber.

"Go ahead, then." Tucker's voice was pained, unable to cover the deep dread he was feeling in his bones. "Get it over with."

Being in the law and sheriffing business as long as he had been, Tucker had heard a doozy of a story before. It was pretty amazing all the ways people could find to get themselves in trouble, but the saga Jace told him was one to sit on a shelf all by itself. If there was a blue ribbon for doing the wrong thing for the right reasons, Jace would win it fair and square.

Tucker had driven around for an hour or so after leaving the bungalow. He needed some time to let it all sink in and get some ideas about what to do next. He'd driven along the coast and out by the lighthouse, but ultimately, he ended up where he always did when he had a lot on his mind and needed to talk to someone.

So here he was, at Meredith's grave.

"I haven't arrested him yet," he said. "I know I should, but—" He paused, the lump in his throat rock-hard. His eyes left the grass and climbed high, where cottony clouds were passing across the brilliant blue sky.

Just how far is eternity? he wondered. Too many miles to count . . . or just a prayer away? Was Meredith even listening, or was he just blabbing to the wind? He wouldn't know until he himself left this world, but for now, he decided to believe she could hear him.

Collecting himself, he squatted down beside the grave and picked a small patch of moss from the base of her headstone. Then he straightened the cone of artificial daisies that had toppled. He looked at the front of the stone and ran his index finger along the inscription.

Meredith Delaney McAllister
May 7, 1886—October 7, 1920
Covered By Grace But Taken Too Soon

She had been thirty-four years and five months old to the day. Just a little older than Jace right now. Had she lived, that would make her only forty-eight right now, and Tucker wondered what her life might be like. Would she have gotten beyond her loss and let herself love again? Really love him, like Jace had said. Ah, but none of that mattered, for they were questions that could never be answered.

"You raised a good son, in spite of how it looks," Tucker assured her. "He took a wrong turn, but he's come back now. Doing the right thing." He readjusted the daisies again. "Takes a big man—a mighty big man—to face up to his mistakes, then pay the piper."

He listened to the stillness. The cemetery always seemed to be under a hush, as though nature was trying not to disturb those at rest. The breeze only tiptoed around the markers and the birds fluttered but didn't sing. Even the ocean had a calmer disposition. Surrounded by it all, Tucker felt a peace deep in his soul, and somehow he knew that Meredith's love for Jace had never carried conditions, that she had loved him through the days of wrong and was proud to see him make things right. She was happy.

Tucker hoisted himself up from the ground. The sun was nearing high noon and he hadn't gotten any work done. He figured things could pan out the way Jace wanted them to, but suspected that timing would have a lot to do with it.

Jace hadn't told Tucker where Tommy Lipton was keeping himself, and Tucker appreciated not knowing. It would put him in a bad position, making it impossible for him to help Jace unless he obstructed justice by withholding information from the Feds. Besides, it was the biggest card Jace had to play, his only real hope of getting the Feds to make the kind of deal he was asking for. He'd be crazy to let go of what he knew before any agreements were made.

Tucker knew Lipton was slick, and that's why he needed to move fast on getting a deal worked out, first with Joey then with the FBI. It was going to be a busy next couple of days.

He knew he needed to go ahead and arrest Jace, but he couldn't bring himself to do it. Not yet. Not till he knew it was going to come together. And if it didn't? If nobody would cooperate? What was he going to do with a confessed bank robber? Well, Tucker wouldn't let himself think that far ahead.

"I'll help him," Tucker promised Meredith. "I'll help him all I can."

Tucker hated to admit it, but in a roundabout way, Joey Sparrs did bring The People's Bandit to justice. Had the young deputy not been so eager for excitement, he never would have corroborated the lies of Leyton Drakeworth. And if he hadn't stood up for the sneer-faced snob, Jace might not have confessed. It was a case of injustice leading to justice, and some would say that the end made up for the means.

In the end, Joey fessed up. He admitted to Tucker that he hadn't seen Julianna take a deliberate shot at Drakeworth. That done, the sheriff was tempted to try and forget all about the Jace's wrongdoings. He felt like canning the deputy, running Drakeworth out of town, and letting Jace and Julianna go about their lives. That's what he felt like doing, but it wasn't realistic. For one thing, Drakeworth would never go quietly, and a desperate Joey might run right back over to his camp. It would be a giant mess, one that would land them all on the witness stand where the truth about Jace McAllister would come out anyway.

And then there was the matter of Jace stealing more than candy from the five-and-dime, and the fact that Tucker's badge was not a plastic toy from the same store. It was real, and he had sworn to uphold it even when the criminal was Jace, someone he could have loved like a son.

He'd been careful when talking to Joey, had made the offer without revealing Jace's guilt. That was information Joey didn't need to know until Tucker had secured his full cooperation.

"You could be a good lawman," Tucker had said. "But you won't get there by persecuting the innocent. Such things come back to haunt you later."

While Joey didn't utter a word, the nervous twitch in his jaw spoke volumes.

"Wanting to make a name for yourself isn't such a bad thing, but do it by bringing in the guilty, not the innocent," Tucker went on. "Forget this malarkey about that girl trying to kill Drakeworth."

"It . . . it's not malarkey. I've told you a hundred—"

"It's malarkey, and I've had it up to here." Tucker drew a line under his chin. "Now do the right thing, Sparrs, and I'll let you arrest a man who really is guilty of something."

And that was when it happened. Deputy Sparrs broke down, literally, as he fell into a chair and started to cry. Not just a whimper, but big alligator tears that raced down his cheeks and splattered on the floor. It had done Tucker's heart good to see the tears, reassuring him that Joey really did care about sending an innocent woman to jail.

When the crying stopped, Tucker saw something besides remorse on the deputy's face. It was relief, like two tons had been lifted from his shoulders. Tucker wasn't surprised. It couldn't have been fun serving the mean likes of Leyton Drakeworth, no matter what kind of goodies he dangled before you.

Like a kid, Joey wiped his nose with his sleeve. "Will . . . will I still have my job here?"

"In case the big FBI job doesn't happen along?" Tucker asked. "In case Mr. J. Edgar Hoover doesn't appoint you to be his successor?"

Joey nodded.

"I should fire you." Tucker was stern. "And maybe I will. Depends on whether or not this near miss makes a man out of you. If it does, I'll be proud to call you a deputy. But if it doesn't," Tucker briskly wiped his hands together, "then boy, you'll be the dust at my feet."

With that out of the way, both men could go about their business. And next on Tucker's agenda was the phone call. Dialing the number, he knew it was the most important call he had ever made in his life, and the most unlikely call to ever leave the humble Ambrose Point Sheriff's Station. Why would a laid-back, deep-sea-fishing, good ole boy of a sheriff ever have cause to ring up the nearest branch office of the FBI?

That seemed to be the same question held by Agent Charlie Mays, the G-Man who was heading up the chase for Lightfoot Lipton.

"What can I do for you, Sheriff?" Agent Mays asked, sounding like he needed a cup of coffee to wake up. "Drunk frat boys smuggling daddy's liquor through your fancier hotels down there?"

"Nah, we've got them under control," Tucker said, knowing he had to play his cards carefully, and that included getting a good rapport going with this agent. "We haven't had any trouble since we got the the Kappa Wappa We're-a Idiots for blowing up a gas can full of gin down on the beach during Prohibition. You'd think those college boys were smart enough to make sure all the gas was emptied out before…but anyway, I've got more important news."

"More important than gas can gin?" Mays sounded bored and Tucker knew it was time to just lay out what he knew.

"I might be able to pass on a tip about Lightfoot Lipton," he told Mays. "Needs to be treated anonymously, though."

"That's no problem," the agent said, suddenly sounding as perked up as man who had just downed a whole pot of coffee. He was listening, and listening with both ears.

"There's something else," Tucker said. "This person with the tip tells me he's got some trouble of his own. Needs a deal."

"We're willing to talk." Mays's voice held the noncommittal tone of a man who was walking a fine line. He couldn't guarantee a deal, but he didn't want to sound discouraging either. On the other end of the line, Tucker smiled sympathetically at the agent's dilemma. He expected as much, knowing it was impossible to promise deals before the whole story was delivered.

"Who's your guy?" Mays asked.

"Claims to be the People's Bandit."

"Do you know his real identity?"

"No," Tucker said, changing ears and frowning as the lie left his usually truthful lips. "He called me—could be a local, a tourist, a drifter. One thing's for sure, though—he's not going to pass on any tips to me unless he gets a deal from you fellas."

"What's he asking for?"

So Tucker laid it all out while Mays listened on the other end of the line, giving no indication as to whether or not Jace's requests could be met. When Tucker finished, all the agent said was "I have to talk to some people.

"Figured that," Tucker said. "Any idea as to when you'll get back to me?"

"Soon" was all the agent agreed to.

"Figured that, too." Tucker chuckled. "Well, I'll be here all night."

"Soon" would prove to be the next morning, but Tucker found the news to be worth the wait, worth sleeping with his head resting on the hard top of his wooden desk. The Feds were going to deal, but they had a couple of their own requests.

"One," Mays said, "make your man give you the tip in person. Two, once the tip is given, you lock him up."

"Then what?"

"Then you wait for us to pick up Lipton," Mays said. "Once that's done, we'll be coming your way. Coming to get your bandit."

CHAPTER

SEVENTEEN

Jace knew about Tommy Lipton's arrest before Tucker showed up to give him the news. The radio had been his early-morning messenger, the announcers broadcasting all they knew about the Feds' latest acquisition from the underworld.

It happened the night before, when agents boarded the elegant Silver Star, delaying her Canadian-bound departure. Inside the sleek and streamlined beauty of her exterior were all the makings of first class luxury—and Tommy Lipton, posing as one Dr. Elliot R. Woodward, could not have been enjoying finer accommodations.

Minutes later, the Silver Star left the train depot, minus one passenger in first class.

"Have you heard?" Tucker asked when he arrived at the bungalow that morning.

Jace nodded. "Two down for the Feds."

"You're next." Tucker sighed as Jace headed for the kitchen to get some coffee.

"You take it black?"

"Like coal," Tucker answered. He took a deep breath. "You know, Jace, if the Feds had their way, you'd already be in jail."

"Thanks for ignoring their orders." Jace set two mugs of coffee on the table. "What's going on with Julianna?" That's all he wanted to know right now. Only when he knew she was safe and squared away was he free to think about everything else.

"I saw Judge Smith this morning," Tucker said. "Her record's wiped clean."

Jace smiled his relief. If nothing else worked out, at least he had that.

"She's still at Jean's house for now," Tucker went on. "I figure she's safer there, what with that Leyton still hanging around. I've been to see him, too."

Jace scowled. "That must have made for a merry morning."

"He's one arrogant cuss." Tucker shook his head. "Legally, I don't have any grounds to run him out of town, but I told him we weren't holding Julianna on anything. Told him that it was best he forgot about her and went on his way."

"He won't do it."

"Nope, probably not today nor tomorrow," Tucker said. "But once the Feds move Julianna out of here, he won't have much use for this town."

Jace went to the window, where the curtains billowed in the coastal breeze. In the windowsill was a small figurine Julianna had bought at the fair, a ceramic sculpture of a bird sitting elegantly upon its perch. Jace picked it up and turned it around in his hands, noting that its stance was graceful, its expression gentle, and its wings contented to rest by its sides, though they were free to lift and take flight if the sky beckoned. Like my Julianna, he thought, a wistful smile crossing his face as he returned the bird to the windowsill.

"You've talked to the Feds." It was a statement, not a question. Tucker wouldn't be here if he hadn't heard anything.

"They'll be here tomorrow," the sheriff said, his voice thick with regret. "First thing."

"Tomorrow," Jace said quietly. "I half expected them to show up today."

"You've got twenty-four hours to call your own, Jace."

Suddenly, there were a million things he wanted to do before committing the next five years to confinement, where the only sun he would see was whatever made it across the stone walls and barbed wire of the prison courtyard. "Is tomorrow just for me or will they be getting Julianna out of here, too?"

"You tomorrow, Julianna the day after," Tucker said as he topped off his coffee. "That Mays agent said he'd send a man back to get her. Said it would actually be safer for her if he did it that way."

Jace nodded, understanding why the agent chose to arrange things in such an order. Better that Julianna slip away quietly than be caught up in the glare of his arrest, and possibly even photographed as the Feds carted him away. His biggest fear, though, was that Leyton would still be hanging around town, and Jace didn't want him to see which direction Julianna left in. It was hardly an exaggeration to say that Leyton would follow her in angry pursuit. "What will you do with her in the meantime?"

"Hide her out in a hotel," Tucker said. His lips hovered above the steam rising from his coffee. "I guess you want to see her."

"It goes without saying," Jace said. "But not at Jean's house or in a hotel." Here was where he wanted to see her. Right here in the house he'd brought her to the night their life together really began. Maybe their love had been born the minute their eyes locked, but it was here that it took root and flourished, here where dreams were told and plans were made. It seemed fitting that his last night of freedom be spent in this house by the water, serene in the sand beneath the beacon of the light, where the melodic waves could soothe the most restless of hearts.

"I know I'm asking a lot," he said. "But you can arrest me first thing in the morning—I'll be ready. And just so you don't feel like you're putting everything on the line, post a deputy outside the house, even though I swear that Julianna and I won't try to skip."

"I'm not worried about you skipping," Tucker said. "You'd have done it by now if that was what you had in mind. Besides, why all the sacrifices for Julianna's freedom if all you planned to do was live the rest of your lives in hiding?" Frustration lined his forehead with deep wrinkles. "What bothers me is Drakeworth still being in town. Don't want him slinking around here tonight, trying to burn the place down. I guess I would need to post a man outside."

Jace smiled. "So, you're saying that you'll let me see her?"

Tucker's face went pensive and Jace wondered if he was thinking back to the day of the tropical storm. He'd come to the point that day, making sure they had all their provisions. He'd stood around a long time, talking to Jace's mother, laughing, sticking a wildflower in her hair. He couldn't have known it would be the last time . . .

"Yeah," he said. "I'll bring her to you."

Why don't you just forget about that woman and go on your way?

Leyton snorted as he recalled the words spoken by that small-time sheriff.

Well, he'd be leaving town, all right, but not without Julianna. He just wasn't sure how he was going to manage the feat, and the absence of an idea was badgering him to no end. That and the fact that his first idea had apparently fallen through.

What happened? he wondered, thinking how tight-lipped the sheriff had been, refusing to explain why the charges against Julianna had been dropped. Did the stupid simpleton of a deputy change his story?

Leyton was not accustomed to failure. After the one slip up that had gotten him in debt to Lightfoot, he'd sworn never to make another costly error. So what had fouled things up with his scheme to get Julianna back into his life? He had to know, and he would know. His pride demanded it.

Joey could dance the dance of avoidance for a while, but Leyton knew he would be on duty tonight. The deputy's mother had told

Leyton that earlier today, aggravated by Leyton's persistent calls to the house.

"I'll just pay young deputy Sparrs a visit," Leyton muttered as he finished off his bourbon. "Let's see if a personal confrontation shakes the truth out of him."

Glancing at his watch, he decided that now would be a good time to go. It was the dinner hour, and Leyton suspected the sheriff was out stuffing himself with some deep fried supper. He looked like a man who didn't miss any meals.

As fate would have it, the deputy was reviewing McAllister's file at that very moment. He was seated behind a desk, his eyes pasted on something they weren't supposed to see. It was a file labeled "McAllister Case," and Joey had seen the sheriff put it in a personal file box that he always treated with top-secret importance. Only the sheriff owned a key to the box, but Joey knew he kept a spare key underneath a small pile of bricks left over from the station's construction.

Tonight, after the sheriff left for supper, Joey sneaked the spare key from its hiding place. He wasn't trying to cause trouble, wanted to prove himself a good man, but he couldn't stand the mystery surrounding this McAllister thing. The sheriff had told him nothing about the person he was going to let Joey arrest in exchange for dropping his accusations against the woman. He only promised that it would happen soon, but Joey's curiosity had soared past the point of patience. He had to know, and he suspected that file might hold the answer.

Guilt hit him the minute he lifted the lid of the box. Inside were a lot of the sheriff's personal items—his will, house deed, a gold pocket watch. Buried beneath them, though, was the file Joey was dying to peek at. No harm, he told himself, trying to push away the guilt. I'll just look and put it back. No harm done.

He sat at the desk and studied the contents of the thin file. There were three loose sheets of paper inside, and nothing looked official. It was a file of notes written in the sheriff's hand. Some were scripted neatly and written in complete sentences as though the sheriff had taken great pains to make sure everything was precise; other notes were choppy and scrawled, and looked like they had been jotted as the sheriff spoke on the phone.

Joey had barely begun to read when a shadow fell over his light. Startled, he looked up to see Leyton Drakeworth standing over the desk, the smirk on his face indicating that he enjoyed catching Joey off guard.

Joey slammed the folder shut and shoved it beneath a stack of papers, not stopping to think that his abrupt actions might arouse Leyton's curiosity.

"Good evening, Deputy."

"I—I know why you came," he stammered, "but I don't know why the sheriff let her off."

"He gave no indication at all?"

"Nope. Just said there wasn't any case." He stood from his chair and nodded toward a tray of food sitting atop a file cabinet. "I've got to feed my inmates."

"You have prisoners?" Leyton glanced toward a door that led to the jail cells.

"Two of them," Joey said. Two restless rich boys who had decided to stuff their pockets with trinkets from a souvenir shop on the boardwalk. It was a thrill crime, the act of fellows with too much time on their hands.

"Well, I won't keep you from your work," Leyton said, his earlier smirk now replaced with a friendly smile. "I just thought you might have an idea as to why the case was dropped."

"Sorry." Joey scooted around the desk and toward the food tray, anxious to get away from Drakeworth. The man had lured him into his schemes once, and Joey didn't want any more trouble.

"If you hear anything—" Leyton started.

"Sure, I'll let you know," Joey called as he hurried through the door.

Leyton's smile dropped away and he turned to the file Joey had hidden beneath the paperwork on the desk. His heart thundered when he read McAllister Case, and he eagerly flipped open the cover, hoping to see that he had struck gold. Inside he found the same papers Joey had seen, the ones that did not strike the eye as being all that terribly important.

But my oh my, Julianna, love, Leyton thought as he scanned the words. The story these pages tell . . .

Leyton often wondered how he would feel when the People's Bandit was revealed. His identity had been a huge source of curiosity over the past several years, but now . . . at last, Leyton knew his face.

And he couldn't be more thrilled.

This is perfect, he thought as he let himself into his suite at the Ambrose Shores.

He especially liked the way Tommy Lipton fit into the picture.

Sitting on his bed, he picked up the phone on the nightstand and called a restaurant back home. It was ritzy, a business owned by Lipton that was actually legitimate, though it once covered for a speakeasy. The man who operated the place was someone Leyton knew from the bootlegging era, a crook in a suit who was keeping his nose clean for now.

When he came on the line, it was Leyton's great pleasure to say, "I know who tipped off the Feds."

CHAPTER

EIGHTEEN

Leyton was a happy man and not modest about congratulating himself on clever thinking and impeccable timing. Once again, he outwitted the plans of his runaway fiancée. And the fact that she was now another man's wife gave him little reason to pause.

After tomorrow, the vows would hardly matter.

He was on the balcony of his suite, comfortable in a lounge chair as he puffed on a cigar. It was one of his more expensive smokes, taken from the reserve he saved for celebratory moments. He fully intended to dip into the reserve a lot over the next several days. Tonight, he predicted, was only the beginning.

"Score one for me," he said to the wind. "No, make that three. Score three for me."

It had proven to be a productive night. First, the brilliant discovery in the sheriff's office. Second, the phone call to Lightfoot's crony. And third, the conversation with Richard.

He had decided to call Richard and fill him in on the recent doings of his wayward daughter. "I thought you should hear it from me," he gently told the older man. "In case things blow up and Julianna's name makes it into the papers. I believe they're taking precautions to keep her from being connected to the bandit, but you know how things can leak."

That was the guise Leyton had used, anyway. The truth, of course, was much more self-serving. "In spite of everything, I still want

Julianna," he had said, believing the profession must have relieved Richard as well as amazed him beyond words. Leyton was certain that Richard held him in higher regard than ever.

Basking in that belief, Leyton continued to lounge on the balcony with his cigar, watching the moon play hide-and-seek with a canvas of clouds. In a way, it reminded him of the game he seemed to be playing with Julianna. She had vanished only to be found, and each time she tried to slide past him, he managed to uncover her plans. He laughed out loud, thinking how foolish she had been to tangle with him, to try to alter what was meant to be.

The phone rang from inside the suite and Leyton rose to answer it, though he was in no rush to. He knew it was one of Lightfoot's people getting back to him, but he didn't want to seem desperate to have their help.

On the sixth ring, he picked up. "Drakeworth."

It was the call he had been expecting, and the news was pleasing. Lightfoot's brother was now running the fun and games, and he was willing to forget Leyton's debt in exchange for the name of the man who ratted on his kin.

Leyton had no qualms about giving up Jace's name. He did it with a broad smile and booming voice. Revenge was sweet.

"And where is this guy?" the caller asked.

"Ambrose Point," Leyton said. "It's a six-hour drive, and the Feds are taking him away in the morning."

"What route are they're planning to use?"

Leyton laughed. "There's only one road out of this puny town."

"Good," the caller said.

The line went dead.

Moonlight fell through the window of the parlor, mixing romantically with the music floating from the radio. The coffee table had been pushed off the rug where Julianna lay on her side, propped on one elbow as she gazed down at Jace.

Never had he looked so beautiful, his face flawless in the midnight moon. Gently, she traced his eyebrows with her finger then drew soft lines through the hollows of his cheekbones and across his lips.

He pulled her face to his, kissing her as one song faded into the beginning of another. As the moon's silver mist embraced them, they left the world around them, aware only of one another. They became like the waves outside the window, rising and falling again and again, their passion the current that drove them until they broke and crashed, a thunderous rhapsody upon the shore.

As she cuddled beside him, a glowing flash shot rapidly through her body, lasting only a second. Was it an aftershock to their passion? She imagined so and likened it to a shooting star, one she tried to grasp before it soared away.

Later, she eased herself from the light hold of his arms, careful not to wake him as he dozed. She wrapped herself in his shirt, liking the way it draped her in loose comfort, the way it smelled of him. Quietly, she made her way onto the front porch and sat on the steps, hugging herself as she looked toward the water.

It was a matter of hours before the night sky would move aside for the dawn. And then . . . her heart would be in two pieces. It had been ripping all night, tearing a little more each time the clock chimed. Oh, she was trying to be strong . . . she was strong . . . but strength did not ease the depth of the pain, just the way she faced it.

If only they could have had a child, a part of him to hold onto. The fact that they never would suddenly crushed her like a weight too heavy to carry. She stared at the water, feeling as hopeless as Meredith must have.

Jace came out to join her, dressed in a new shirt, easing the screen door shut so that it didn't slam. He sat beside her and followed her gaze to the waves.

"You're watching the water," he said quietly.

"Like your mother."

A few minutes passed before he said anything else. Like her, he was lost in the realm of personal thoughts.

"You're not like my mother," he finally said. "All her hopes were buried at sea with a man who couldn't come home." He pulled her head to his shoulder. "She could have watched forever, Julianna, and nothing would have changed."

A tear trickled down Julianna's cheek as she thought of Meredith and the pain she had known in her short life. How hard it must have been for the woman who watched the ceaseless waves. To know that her great love would never return in life, to know that death was the only bridge that could take her to a reunion.

"She wouldn't want anyone crying for her," Jace said. "She believed she would see him again—that's what sustained her all those years. Now that she's with him, those lost years don't matter." He wiped the tear from Julianna's cheek.

"It's just such a sad love story." Julianna sniffed.

"It was then," Jace agreed. "But now it knows a happy ending.

"I suppose." Julianna brightened. "And I know that we'll have a happy ending, too."

"In life," he assured her. "In life, Julianna, we'll be together again."

Hours later, the sun rose as always, but never had Ambrose Point seen the dawning of such a day. As promised, Jace turned himself in to the sheriff, who let Joey make the arrest. Two FBI agents arrived during the ten o'clock hour and took Jace into custody without incident. Soon after, the press was notified that the People's Bandit had been taken away, the face behind the mask revealed.

Julianna was spared having to witness the arrest. She didn't see the cameras flashing or hear reporters hurling questions at Sheriff Moll. Her last memory of Jace would not be branded by the sight of him in handcuffs, led to a waiting car that belonged to the FBI.

Instead, Jean escorted her to a quiet room at the South Sun Hotel. There, the older woman entered first and checked the room, including the closet, behind the shower curtain, and beneath the bed. "Can't be too careful, you know?"

"Yes, I know," Julianna said sadly. Having come under Leyton's sharp sword these last few days, she knew better than anyone that nothing could be assumed.

"An Agent Siebert will come for you tomorrow," Jean said. "It'll be sometime in the evening. Until then, don't open the curtains and don't open the door for a soul, except Sheriff Tucker if he comes by. Don't even let the maids in."

Julianna nodded that she understood.

"I left some non-perishables here in the room," Jean continued. "Some magazines, too. You don't need to be going out for anything."

"Thank you for everything."

"Hope things work out," Jean said, giving Julianna's hand a quick squeeze. "I really do. Now remember, the agent's name is Sam Siebert."

She left then, locking the door behind her. Julianna shivered and looked around the room. It was the first day of her new life. And she was sharing it with nothing but a bag of non-perishables.

The FBI agents couldn't help themselves. They liked this McAllister guy, they really did. Before crossing the county line, he thanked them a dozen times for making a deal and spoke so fondly of this Julianna woman that they felt a new appreciation for their own wives.

As Ambrose Point faded in the distance, he told them about the robberies, fascinating them with the details of how he pulled the jobs as a one-man show. Early on, they decided that he was smart. Too bad they were on opposite sides of the law. This guy would have been great in undercover.

It was Jace and two agents in the car as it traveled Route 3. Agents Mays and Smythe. An agent named Siebert would arrive tomorrow to help Julianna make a quiet departure. Everything seemed to be moving along as planned.

They had just cleared the Romahatchie Bridge when gunfire racked the air. The bullet penetrated the back window of the car, shimmying hairs away from Jace's head before exiting through the windshield, leaving a spiderweb crack. It took Jace a minute to realize what had happened, but Mays and Smythe were trained to act. Mays brought the car to a swerving halt, and both men leapt from the front seat with their own weapons drawn.

"There's the sniper!" Mays shouted as he pointed to a man in camouflage clothing, hurrying up a hillside toward a dense forest.

"Halt!" Smythe shouted. The gunman kept running, and when he ignored Smythe's second command to stop, the agent lifted his gun and fired.

"He's dead," Mays said as they watched the man fall to the ground and roll toward the water gushing beneath the bridge. Briefly, his shirt snagged on a rock, giving the agents a chance to venture in for a look at his face.

"Know him?" Smythe asked.

"Like I know every snake that crawls through the south," Mays answered. "That's one of Tommy's thugs. I've got pictures of him and Lightfoot together."

The man's shirt gave way, and he rolled the rest of the way down the hill, falling off the riverbank and plunging into his watery grave.

The agents returned to the car where Jace sat cuffed and shackled, but with his neck craning to see out the back window.

"That shot was for you," Mays said. "One of Lightfoot's boys pulled the trigger."

"Lightfoot wasn't supposed to know anything about this," Jace said through gritted teeth.

"No, he wasn't, but somehow he's found out." Smythe's forehead burrowed. "And when he finds out that his boy missed—"

A cold sweat drenched Jace's face. When the ole boy band of gangsters discovered he was still living and breathing, they were certain to try again. And if they couldn't reach him, Julianna . . .

"He won't find out," Mays said.

"How will he not find out?" Jace asked.

Mays jerked his head toward the front seat. "Get in, Smythe, before a car comes along and sees us. We'll talk on the road." He made a smooth entrance back onto Route 3, driving as though they had merely stopped to switch drivers.

"How will he not find out?" Jace repeated from the backseat.

"Easy," Mays said over his shoulder. "We'll just say that he got you."

Jace considered the idea. It wasn't a bad one. If the world thought him dead, it would be a safer life for both him and Julianna. And when he was released from prison in five years, a new name would have to accompany him, making it a lot easier to start life over.

"What would you say?" Jace asked.

"That somebody took a shot from the Romahatchie Bridge," Mays said. "Only, this version would say that he got you."

Smythe turned around in the front seat. "Hoover will probably approve the plan," he said. "Since you helped us bring Lightfoot down."

"But don't think this gets you off the hook," Mays said. "You'll still do five, McAllister. Only difference is that you'll come out with a different name."

Jace shrugged. "I wasn't looking forward to starting over as a former bank robber anyway."

The agents laughed. "So that's it McAllister?" Mays asked. "You're a dead man?"

"Only to the world," Jace said. "My wife has to know the facts.

Tucker Moll does, too."

"Agent Siebert will handle that," Mays assured him. "If the boss approves this, nothing else will change, see? We'll relocate your wife as planned."

"Truth is, McAllister," Smythe added, "if you want to protect her—protect yourself—this is really your only choice."

Jace nodded then looked down at his hands, noticing that they were shaking like tree limbs caught up in the November gales. A delayed reaction to the bullet's near miss?

Maybe . . . or was he getting the feeling that things were starting to go wrong?

Terribly wrong.

CHAPTER

NINETEEN

Tucker Moll got word early the next morning.

The People's Bandit, dead.

No, he thought, head lowered as he rubbed his temples and squinted to hold back the tears. It can't be true.

But it must be true. The radio was blaring it, the newspapers were rushing out special editions, and the FBI was confirming all reports.

Tucker knew he had to give Julianna the news himself, had to lay it on her as gently as possible, had to be there to steady her when she wilted against his chest.

At first she didn't believe him. At first she actually laughed before her eyes turned stormy as she demanded to know how he could invent such horrible lies. She shoved past him and went to the drawn window where she stared at the drapes, her arms folded across her heaving chest.

He went and stood behind her, placing his hands on her trembling shoulders.

"Julianna, I wish I was lying."

She turned then and he could see that her disbelief was cracking. The truth, awful and excruciating, was worming its way inside to destroy every trace of happiness this woman had known.

The sobs came. Deep, wrenching cries that emerged from the core of her being, that reached from her and touched Tucker, breaking his heart and bringing more tears to his own eyes. Holding her, he could feel the sobs shaking her frame from head to toe.

"Go on and cry," he said. "Nobody here but you and me."

How long it went on, he couldn't say, nor did he care. After a while, though, she lifted her head from his chest and turned her face toward him. It was swollen and flushed, but her cheeks were dry. For now. He felt sure she had only been through the first round of tears.

"I'm . . . I'm okay now." Her voice was hoarse.

"No, you're not," Tucker said. "I'll stay with you as long as you need me to."

"Thank you, but no." She shivered and looked around the dark, shaded room. "I . . . my head is pounding. I need to be alone—to sleep, to think."

"I understand, but . . ." Tucker gave her a concerned look. "Are you sure you want to be alone? If you want to sleep, I'll sit with you."

"I need to be alone."

He nodded and patted her arm then turned to leave her as she wished. He paused in the doorway to say, "Julianna, to the best of my knowledge, Lightfoot still has men on the loose, and Agent Siebert will still be coming for you this evening. If I hear differently, I'll let you know." Hating what he needed to say next, he smacked the doorframe with his fist. "Uh, I'll let you know about the details." He cleared his throat. "I figured you'd want to bury him next to his mother and grandfather, up in that little cemetery that overlooks the breakers."

"Yes . . . yes, I think that's best," she said, her voice weary as she sat down on the bed. Tucker took a last look at the woman as he turned to leave. She leaned back on the pillows and closed her eyes, already forgetting his presence.

Leyton left Ambrose Point that morning, but planned to go back.

Thanks to that sheriff's good note taking, he, too, knew the FBI's plans for Julianna. He certainly intended to thwart them, but right now he was scouring the roads outside of the town.

He was looking for a drifter. The roads were full of them, downtrodden and dirty, their jalopies piled high with junk, or their shoes worn thin as they trudged from town to town looking for jobs.

Ah, there she is. His eyes fell upon a woman who appeared to be in her late teens. Dusty, dirty, a tad plain—but she would probably clean up nicely.

He wheeled the Duesenberg up beside her and rolled down the window, prepared to make an offer that would change her life.

Julianna was lost, remembering the first time she had ever seen the man she now found herself mourning. For a second, she smiled, but the truth quickly returned, an unwelcome guest barging in on a private party for two.

He's dead. No . . .

And so it went for a while. She would remember him and smile then shake her head in stubborn disbelief as reality crashed in.

I remember when he . . .

Now he's gone . . .

No, no, NO . . .

She burrowed beneath the covers and curled her long legs to her chest.

Sleep. That's what I need. Just sleep, and when I wake up none of this will be real . . .

She fell into a dreamless state, one that might as well have been timeless. When she first awoke, it seemed as though a year had passed. Or maybe it had only been a minute. Time seemed to have no meaning now, and the only thing she was aware of was how she felt inside.

Sad. So incredibly, indescribably sad.

She crawled from the bed and went to the window. Jean had told her not to open the curtains, but she did now because she could see the ocean and watch the water.

She wasn't sure how long she stared upon the rolling waves, but they lulled her into a transe-like state that was only broken by a rapping on the door, so loud and fast that it implied the person on the other side had been trying to get her attention for more than a few minutes. Disoriented, she stumbled from the window and to the door. "Who is it?"

"Agent Siebert," came an authortive but muffled reply. "FBI."

She quickly undid the chain lock and opened the door.

When the sound of the sliding chain hit his ears, Leyton couldn't help smiling. Everything was falling into place so nicely.

"Sorry about your loss, love."

Julianna's eyes flew wide open, and she tried to slam the door, but Leyton was quick to push his way inside. She was aware of the danger, but so foggy headed and shocked by the sudden intrusion that she could barely even put up a fight.

"I have to do this, love" was all he said before he knocked her over the head.

He caught her as her knees buckled, then carried her into the bathroom where he placed her in the tub. Yanking the towels from the rack on the wall, he made a pillow for her head.

"This is for the best," he said to her unconscious face. "You'll see that you and I are a better match than you and McAllister. He was beneath you, love."

He hurried from the room and down the corridor to a sitting area. The woman he brought with him sat alone, fidgeting nervously with the hem of her dress.

Exasperated, Leyton sighed. "You're not projecting a ladylike image, Gretchen."

Gretchen jumped to her feet and smiled at Leyton, her eyes begging for his approval. That was better. After all, he'd plucked her off the road that morning and offered her a handsome fee for a short stint of acting—he was sure she didn't get an offer like that every day. He then took her to his room at the Ambrose Shores where he instructed her on making herself over.

He had to admit that he'd made a good choice, that she had responded nicely to the shampoo and cosmetics he'd allowed her to buy at the drug store. The new dress and shoes had been sent over from Lucinda's Boutque, as Leyton doubted the girl would know what to do in a store such as that. Lucinda had welcomed his phone call, happy to oblige his wish to choose and deliver an outfit to his room. He was very convincing in his lie that it was a surprise for his wife who would be arriving that night.

For the umpteenth time today, he gave Gretchen a long once-over, making sure that she looked just right. Of course, trash is trash, he reminded himself. No matter how much money he gave her to play Cinderella, or how presentable she looked in new clothes, she was still the drifter he found on the road, not far from the gutter. Trash.

"We've gone over this a hundred times," he said. "Every response, scenario, and safe answer you can give if this agent catches you off guard."

"I'm ready," she insisted. "Don't worry."

He glanced down the corridor. It was almost evening, which meant Siebert was certain to arrive shortly to collect Julianna.

Only . . . Julianna would refuse to go.

"It's almost showtime," Leyton said to Gretchen. "Let's go, Julianna."

》《

It was just after six o'clock when Agent Siebert stopped by the sheriff's office. He needed to inquire about Julianna's whereabouts, as well as give Tucker the good news about Jace.

"You've done me a world of good," Tucker said, his relief obvious on his face. "I just wish me and his wife had been let in on the secret earlier, you know? Would have saved us the grief."

Siebert's look fell somewhere between sympathetic and matter-of-fact. "I wish it could have been that way, too, but we didn't know how many of Lightfoot's men might have been in the area. We still don't know who the informant was." He jammed his hands in his pants pockets. "McAllister and his wife are dealing with some dangerous lowlifes, so we had to make the death look real—if that includes your grieving, well, I'm sorry it had to be that way."

"Oh yeah, I know," Tucker said. "I'm not about to make a ruckus over it. I mean, a short spell of heartache versus great news like this? I'd say the good news wins hands down."

"I'm serious about things looking real," Siebert told him. "I'll need you and the wife to do your part—empty casket in a grave, headstone, the works."

Tucker was rapidly nodding his intentions to comply and waving Siebert toward the door. "Hurry and tell Julianna," he said. "She needs to hear it even more than I did."

"Wrinkle your dress," Leyton ordered Gretchen as they waited in Julianna's room. "Splash water on your face and smear your makeup. Your husband just died—look distraught."

She did as told then sat on the edge of the bed, thinking of all the things she'd buy with the money she'd earn by giving her great performance.

A knock on the door was Leyton's cue to hide in the bathroom, out of the agent's sight and in close watch over Julianna. She had stirred a couple of times, uttering low moans as though she might be starting to come around.

"Thank you for coming," Gretchen told the agent after ushering him into the room. "But in light of Jace's death, I don't see the need for me carry on with our plan."

"I have great news, though," Siebert smiled. "Things aren't as they appear."

"I . . . I beg your pardon?" she asked, trying to stay calm. Now was not the time for her sweat glands to go nuts, or for her voice to go nervous. Too much money was riding on this.

"You've had a lot of shocks today, but here's a good one," Siebert said. "Your husband is alive."

Okay, things were not going as smoothly as Leyton had told her to expect. He'd said nothing about this bandit guy still being alive. What was she supposed to say to that?

"Well . . . uh, I'd like to believe that, but—well, it doesn't matter."

Siebert's eyebrows sprang into an arch. "It doesn't matter?"

She was winging it now. "No, you see, this whole thing is just . . . I don't know, crazy. I've had a change of heart about all of it."

"You might still be in need of protection," Siebert warned.

"I'll be fine. Jace and I, you see, we should've never gotten married. I just want my life to go back to the way it was before we met."

Gretchen could see she'd said the wrong thing. The agent looked dumbfounded.

"I can't force you to go with me, ma'am, and I guess I'd understand your reluctance if you thought your husband was dead. But—" Siebert's arms fell to his sides, "he's not."

"My feelings for him are," she insisted. "I don't want any part of this mess anymore."

"You want a divorce?"

"Yeah."

"You won't know how to get in touch with him."

"I'll—I'll figure it out," she stammered

"I . . . suppose you could talk to the sheriff." The agent shrugged, but he sounded angry. "Listen, lady, we made some big exceptions to ensure your safety, went the extra mile to give you a chance at happily ever after."

He took a step closer and stared firmly into her face. "And here's something else, missy—not a word leaves this room. I find out you've said anything about your husband being alive—anything that might get him killed and mess up the Feds' plans—I'll hunt you down like the lowest form of life. Got it?"

She swallowed hard then squeaked, "Yeah."

"Have a good life, then," he growled as he turned and slammed out the door, jarring the room as he left.

It brought Leyton from the bathroom. "How'd it go? I barely heard a word."

"He's gone, isn't he?" Gretchen gestured about. "But I need to ask you something about this bandit."

"What?" Leyton said. "He's dead, that's all you need to know."

It hit her that he knew nothing about the bandit being alive. He must not have been able to hear much from the bathroom. She started to tell him, but something stopped her. I'll hunt you down like the lowest form of life. "Oh, nothing," she said. "When do I get paid?"

"Now," Leyton said as he counted out a stack of bills. "Give the agent ten minutes to get out of here then you leave, too. And forget you ever saw me."

》 《

Julianna awoke lying on the bed, a throb pulsating in the top of her head.

Jace, she thought as the day's memories attacked. She covered her face with her hands, shoulders shaking as she cried softly.

"Crying won't bring him back," Leyton said from a chair across the room. "It's best you put this behind you and go on with our life as husband and wife."

"No . . ." she said through the parched dryness of her throat.

"Can't you see the foolishness of your actions, Julianna?" He was now walking toward her. "You should never have interfered with your father's plans. Had you stayed out of McAllister's life, he'd be alive."

"Don't say that to me!" she screamed as she shot up to a sitting position. Her head retaliated with blinding pain, forcing her to lie back down and close her eyes. A few minutes passed before the pain relented. When she opened her eyes again, Leyton was standing above her, his expression triumphant.

To her surprise as much as his, she spat at him.

A scowl crossed his face as he retrieved his handkerchief from his pocket. Wiping vigorously at the spittle on his sleeve, he said. "See what happens when you run with garbage? You begin to act like garbage."

"Everything was fine before you came here," she seethed.

"That's absurd, Julianna." He extended his hand. "The man was a bank robber and bound to get taken down eventually. Now, get up. It's time we went home and married."

"I'll never—"

She stopped. What was the point anymore?

Like Meredith, she would never be able to love again, so what did it matter where she ended up? What did anything matter?

She took his hand and let him slowly pull her to her feet. It was then that she noticed the diamond-and-ruby ring had disappeared from her finger, replaced by the glaring stone that had signified her and Leyton's engagement. She couldn't keep the horror from her face.

But Leyton just laughed. "While you were resting, love, I took the liberty of returning the proper ring to your finger." He studied her hand, lifting it to the light. "I must say, my selection is more beautiful than the gaudy bauble McAllister gave you. It was from McAllister, wasn't it? I mean, judging from its inexpensive quality—

"Where is it?"

"Gone." He shrugged and gestured toward the window that faced the Atlantic. "Tragic what a person can lose in the ocean."

She stared at him and shook her head slowly, jaw tensed with rage. She looked towards her hand again, and that's when she realized that her watch had been returned to her wrist.

"You left that at home the night you disappeared," he said, "and perhaps that's why you lost track of yourself." He smiled and wrapped his fingers around her wrist, pressing so hard that the watch band was sure to leave an imprint on her flesh. "But now it's back, as a reminder of where you're always supposed to be."

Now she looked away, from him, the ring, the watch. Instead she looked to the window and to the ocean that filled its view.

He thinks he's won . . .

But hadn't he? No, she resolved, I won't let him. With that thought, something new flared to life inside her. A plan took its first breath. She would marry Leyton. Oh yes, she would be his wife, but not for better. Only for worse. He would pay dearly for the life he'd stolen from her, and she would do nothing to stop it from happening.

Someday the man will fall . . .

She planned to be there.

END OF BOOK 1

ABOUT THE AUTHOR

Donna Gentry Morton lives in the foothills of the North Georgia Mountains, a proud resident of the rural community of "Ducktown," which is close enough to Atlanta to enjoy it, and far enough away to ignore it. Widowed from the love of her life, John, she strives to carry on as he would want her to, which includes enjoying time with their two sons and other close-knit family, her supportive circle of gal pals, and her menagerie of pets. She often writes with two parrots sitting on her shoulders.

She holds a B.S. degree in Journalism from East Tennessee State University and has been a professional writer for more than twenty-five years, writing for radio, television, newspaper, websites, and retail and industrial marketing. She is the recipient of ten Excellence in Advertising awards for creative writing and has had her work appear in numerous publications.